MEATBALL
BIRDS AND SEVEN
OTHER STORIES

Books by Kenneth C. Gardner, Jr.

Novels
> *The Song Is Ended* (2011)
> *The Dark Between The Stars* (2012)

Non-Fiction
> *Echoes of Distant School Bells: A History of the Drayton Public School, 1879-1998*, Volume 1 (1994); Volume 2 (1999)

MEATBALL
BIRDS AND SEVEN
OTHER STORIES

KENNETH C. GARDNER, JR.

iUniverse, Inc.
Bloomington

Meatball Birds and Seven Other Stories

This is a work of fiction. All of the characters, names, incidents, organizations, and dialogue in this novel are either the products of the author's imagination or are used fictitiously.

iUniverse books may be ordered through booksellers or by contacting:

iUniverse
1663 Liberty Drive
Bloomington, IN 47403
www.iuniverse.com
1-800-Authors (1-800-288-4677)

ISBN: 978-1-4759-9441-4 (sc)
ISBN: 978-1-4759-9442-1 (ebk)

Printed in the United States of America

iUniverse rev. date: 06/17/2013

CONTENTS

DEDICATED TO

my three sisters:
Lois, Kay, and Mary

THE CANADIAN

One summer I got pleurisy. It was the same summer that The Canadian froze to death.

Several weeks after my fifth birthday I was in our backyard, leaning against the cottonwood "table." It had been cut from an old cottonwood toppled by a storm into the Jacques River on the north side of our town. Boss and Bear, my father and grandfather, had hitched a team to it and dragged it on shore. They'd spent most of an afternoon with a cross cut sawing a section out and getting it home. Then they'd skinned off the bark, let the wood dry, and painted it white. The "table" was almost five feet in diameter and about three feet high.

I had a summer cold and was sort of dozing on the north side of the table when Boss and Bear came out and pulled up chairs on the opposite side. I heard ice clinking in their glasses. They settled in.

Bear said, "Margaret makes good lemonade, not too sweet."

"Yes, she does." I heard ice clink again.

"I like this old stump. There ain't too many ancient things in this here country, but this is one of 'em."

"Yeah, but it was a chore gettin' it up here."

"You're right. I thought Monkey Ward would be gettin' a truss order for certain." They laughed.

More clinking.

"What're ya gonna do about it?"

"What d'ya mean?"

"You're the mayor of the town."

"D'ya want the job back, Bear?"

"Nosiree. What I'm sayin' is it's illegal."

1

"And, in the eyes of some, immoral, too, but I figure they're two grown men—free, white, and twenty-one—and I do like a good bareknuckle scrap."

"Ya mean like Wednesday night's?"

"That wasn't nothin'. The gandy wasn't up to it."

"Ya never did finish tellin' me."

"Well, with Margaret comin' in and all, how could I?"

"Ya can now."

"And I will." Boss paused and then I heard him plunk his glass on the table, the ice skittering. "This Canadian hops off the freight from Kingston and carries his leather satchel across St. Paul to the Woodson Hotel."

"Cheap enough."

"Lemme finish. He registers as William Smith of Winnipeg, Manitoba. Harold, the day clerk, noticed his knuckles; they were big, but kinda splayed out and leathery. After he cleans up, he comes down and asks Harold real casual who's the toughest man in town. Harold tells him Boss Cockburn is."

"Modesty, modesty."

"Now that's what Harold said, and I'm gonna tell this true, if ya'll let me. Anyway, The Canadian heads for the door, like a cat Harold said, askin' where he can find this 'Boss'. Harold tells him either at the Bank 'cause he's the president or the City Hall 'cause he's the mayor. Then The Canadian grins and asks who's the second toughest. Harold says he doesn't know."

"Very diplomatic."

"The Canadian strolls around 'til he sees the section gang north of the elevators by the mill. He walks the tracks and stands there watchin' for awhile. Finally, he asks the straw boss who his strongest boy is. When the straw boss asks why, The Canadian says he's got a hundred dollars that says he's stronger. By this time the gang is all handle-leanin', so the boss looks 'em over and motions to Tom Gilbertson."

"He's big enough."

"Yeah, about six inches taller and sixty pounds heavier than The Canadian. They jaw awhile, and The Canadian says he's worked the CP, which was a lot tougher than what any Americans had ever done. That got the boys dander up, so the gang gets a hundred dollars together, and the match is on, providing they can find a spot. They don't want a barn in somebody's backyard where a busybody can stick her nose in. The Canadian points to the old Covered Bridge. Tom agrees and . . ."

"And that's where you come in."

"Correct. The boss comes to me and we work it out."

"You, an elected official, guilty of aiding and abetting."

"They're grown men. Now d'ya want to hear the end of it or not?"

"Go on."

"I had Clyde from the brickyard dump some clean sand inside the bridge and at seven that evening close to a hundred of us showed up there, the news having made the rounds. We smoothed out the sand, put up some ropes, and blocked off Glen Haven Street with 'Bridge Under Repair' signs. Tom was already there with us, and about quarter after we saw The Canadian comin' down the hill. When he came into the bridge, he looked around the crowd before he put his satchel down near a corner of the ring. The straw boss introduced us, but all The Canadian said was 'Mayor, you hold the purse.' He dropped five double eagles into my hand, and the boss handed me a hundred dollar gold certificate because he'd changed all the small bills in for one at the Bank. The Canadian stripped off his shirt and stepped through the ropes. He showed knotty muscles and no fat. He tested the ropes, but they were too slack for a real ring. Tom climbed through the ropes. His belly had run to fat, though his arms and chest were bigger than The Canadian's."

"Just like his old man."

"They squared off and we let out a cheer, but as it was dyin', Billy Wilson, the young one—Bill, Jr.—shouted, 'Look out there!' and we see a horse comin' in the north end of the bridge. Young Wilson grabs it and it's pullin' old Widow Harris in her buggy. She's late for her prayer meeting and won't go around to the West Bridge, so we get the fighters out of sight and take down the ropes. She touches up that lathered bay with the whip, glarin' at everyone. We get everything back in order, but some of the men are spooked because their wives will be at the same prayer meeting with Widow Harris, and they'll probably call the cops. I tell 'em that the Widow doesn't know what's goin'on, and even if she did, that I'd told Chester that his evening's duty consisted of one thing—to see that the fight comes off without interruption. That calmed 'em down."

"Mayor of the town? You should be President of the whole U.S. of A."

"All right, all right. Anyway, they squared off again with Bill Byars keepin' the time on that Jeweled Special Railway Watch with the Alaska Silver case he's so proud of. Tom opened with a roundhouse right that he telegraphed all the way across the ring. The Canadian was quick; he moved his head back, Tom's fist missin' by three inches; then he tattooed Tom's ribs and face. For the rest of the round, he hit Tom upstairs, downstairs, anytime he wanted, really workin' the gut. He nailed Tom five times for every one of Tom's, and most of Tom's were on the forearms or shoulders. He couldn't get The Canadian's head 'cause of the bobbin' and weavin'. We didn't have a real bell, so Chet Donovan rang a cowbell to end the rounds."

"That's original."

"Tom hung in for three rounds real well, even though he was takin' punishment, but in the Fourth The Canadian forgot the gut and opened up on his face. Pretty soon Tom's cut around both eyes, his lip's split, and his nose looks broke. But he wouldn't quit."

"All fair-skinned fighters cut easy."

"After Round Six Tom's face looked like a plateful of spaghetti. The straw boss threw in the towel, but Tom snatched it out of the air, wiped his face, and stepped on it. He made it to Round Eight when The Canadian haymakered him on the jaw, and Tom spit out a tooth. Before it even hit the sand, The Canadian roundhoused a right into his ear and blood shot out. Two rails jumped into the ring and grabbed Tom. He'd have never gone down; he'da let that Canuck kill him first."

"Just like his old man."

"The Canadian picked up his satchel and waited up against a wall. Finally, some rails helped Tom out and we took the ropes down. The Canadian got a bottle out of his satchel and washed up. He put on his shirt and came over to me. I paid him the purse, and he nodded at Tom wincing up the hill under a ton of iodine. 'Tough kid.' Nobody said anything, but it wasn't a dangerous kind of quiet; it was more a respectful one. Remember when we were huntin' deer near Big Sam—when was it? '87? '88?"

"I remember. It was '87, the big blizzard year."

"Remember watchin' that pack of prairie wolves chase the big whitetail down. We were on the shoulder of the hill, and we could have shot at those wolves in the valley any time, but we just sat there in silence, overwhelmed by the precision and the smooth-death of the pursuit and kill. Our silence in the bridge was like that."

Bear was quiet for awhile and I was trying to keep from sneezing. Finally, he said, "O.K., so now I know. It was rough, but it was clean, and Tom'll be all right, minus a tooth, and I've lost a few of those myself, which only counts if you're fond of corn on the cob. What I want to know is why in Sam Hill you're gonna let Muley fight tomorrow night."

Boss kind of grunted, then he said, "Right now I couldn't tell ya. When Muley came in and said he wanted to take up where his brother left off, I thought it was for the family honor or revenge or somethin' like that. But Muley and Tom ain't never been that close; Muley wasn't even at the fight as a second. Now I don't know; I just don't know."

Bear, who had retired as bank president, but who still knew all the Bank's business, said, "He drew out almost all his money—two hundred dollars—leavin' a balance of two dollars in his account."

"That'll be the purse."

"I'm surprised the dimwit had that much. It must have taken him years to get it."

"Maybe he sees the fight as a way to get out of here. He puts up two hundred dollars and wins it back plus another two hundred. That would get him some place."

"So what? He's nice enough and a good worker, strong—he must be two inches taller than Tom and weighs as much without the flab—but he was born to follow a plow, and he can do that here. He ain't never gonna be nothin' that don't have dirt under its nails."

"Still and all maybe he wants to try."

"Maybe. When is it again?"

"Tomorrow night. Eight o'clock. Plutowsky's icehouse."

"Away from the Widow Harris, huh?"

They laughed.

"More lemonade?"

"No, thank you, Boss. I'll just say goodbye to Margaret and be goin'."

"How've you been doin'?"

Bear stood up. "Fine, fine. Don't worry about me." They walked into the house.

I wiped my nose on my sleeve and sat there electrified. A prizefight at Plutowsky's! And I knew about it—my older brother Josh didn't, Ma didn't, just me. I got up on the table and stretched out. My legs were asleep. While I waited for the needles to flash through them and disappear, I plotted my way into Plutowsky's.

Saturday morning went as slowly as the day before Christmas. The afternoon went faster because I saw a Broncho Billy two-reeler at the Blackstone Theater. After an early supper I told Ma I was tired and wanted to go to bed.

"Lige, are you feeling worse?"

"No, I'm just tired, that's all."

She felt my forehead with the smoothness of her wrist. "Well, you're not feverish." She carried me upstairs and saw to it that I brushed my teeth. I threw my clothes over the back of a chair; she folded the knee pants and the shirt and placed them on the chair. She tucked me in, helped me with my prayers, and kissed me good night.

"I'll check on you later, Lige."

"Ma?"

"Yes."

"I'm really tired. Maybe you shouldn't disturb me until Boss gets home; maybe you both can check on me together."

"All right, my little lamb. If that's what you want." She kissed my forehead and went out the door and down the stairs, carrying my stockings.

As soon as I heard her finish the dishes and leave the kitchen, I got dressed and crept down the stairs and out the east door. Boss had left right after supper, and Josh had eaten at the Pike boys' house, so he would be there until at least ten. Ma had gone into the living room with her Bible, preparing for the Sabbath.

I walked the alleys west to the lumberyard, then north to Stimson, turned west and crossed the NP tracks. I took Chicago north, paralleling the railroad, but where Chicago met Park Avenue, I went across the ditch, rolled under a barbed wire fence, and walked Martin's pasture to the river. The water was already low; it had been a dry spring, so I walked the dried mud west, knowing the reeds shielded me from the south, and hoping that none of the "river rats" to the north would notice me.

A couple of chained dogs began barking, and I scared a blue-winged hen and her brood out of some reeds, but I was pretty sure I made it to the ice house pond undetected.

Plutowsky's ice house was a big, faded-red barn on the south side of a stretch of the river which widened out into an almost circular pond. I moved through the reeds, made a dash for the door, and looked inside. I couldn't see much at first, but after I closed the door and waited a minute, I saw a wide path surrounded by blocks of ice stacked up on the east, south, and west sides. In the middle of the path, four posts squared three saggy ropes around an elevated ring.

I picked out a spot above the ring, but well back in the darker shadows. I climbed the natural stairway of the stacked ice blocks, stepping on the sawdust and straw that insulated each layer of ice.

The air wasn't as cold up on my perch as it had been near the floor, but the ice block I was on chilled me, and then my pants and stockings started getting wet. I listened, but didn't hear anything, so I got down and scooped up some sawdust. I climbed back to my hiding place and put the sawdust on the ice block. I repeated the process until I had a pile which I spread out a little, then I put my cap on it and sat down. I wished I had brought my jacket.

I waited. It was dimmer than when I had first entered the ice house. And it was quiet inside. I could hear the occasional creaking of the door, the waves against the rocks on the south shore of the pond, and every couple minutes or so a "river rat" dog.

After thirteen dogs I heard hoofs and wheels and then boots and shoes on gravel. The door came open and a light came in, followed by more lights and dark men.

"Gad, it's cold."

"Yeah, but it's gonna warm up."

A couple men laughed. The dark figures crowded around the ring. A couple dozen kerosene lanterns were placed on ice blocks, and the gray dimness brightened. The figures had faces: I saw Boss, Bear, and dozens of our town's important and not-so-important men, including most of the town officials—the councilmen, the auditor, the treasurer, the assessor, and one of the justices of the peace. The only ones missing were the on-duty police officer, the off-duty one who had gone to

Fargo, and the other j.p. whose wife never let him out of the house alone at night.

Muley and Tom came in. Tom looked like Halloween with scabs, bandages, and two blackened eyes. A cheer went up, and Tom lifted a rope and Muley climbed a couple steps and ducked into the ring. Tom went around to the southwest and stared across the ring at the door.

Most of the men were talking and laughing when off to the left I heard "Sh-sh-sh-sh," and The Canadian walked into dead silence. He held his satchel and looked around. It was so quiet I could hear some water dripping. The Canadian climbed into the northeast corner, took out ten coins, and clinked them one at a time into Boss's hand. Muley walked over and carefully handed two bills to Boss, while The Canadian put his shirt in his satchel and then pushed on the ropes.

Muley took off his shirt. He had a massive chest and shoulders built out on the farm where he'd fill in any slack time by lifting an old anvil. Boss said he could do that for hours without getting bored because his brain was as dense as the anvil. When he turned around, the flickering light played little waves in the thick hair on his back.

The Canadian spoke to Boss, who looked up, then walked to a wall and released a rope on a pulley. There was a hook on the end and Boss told Bear to hang a lantern from it. Then Boss raised it ten feet over the floor. It gave better light to the edges of the ring, but didn't give any more light to the center.

Boss talked to the fighters in the center of the ring, and then they went back to their corners.

Mr. Donovan rang the cowbell, and Muley came bull-charging across the ring and caught three shots in the face while missing wildly himself. The Canadian moved to his left, and Muley backhanded his shoulder for which The Canadian hit him on the ear; it began to crimson. Muley stalked the shorter man and sledgehammered some blows off his shoulders and chest, but The Canadian made him pay for it in blood. The crowd was yelling so loud it was hard to hear the cowbell.

In Round Two it was The Canadian dishing and Muley taking until just before the bell a wild right from Muley caught The Canadian on the temple and snapped his head around to the yells of the men.

Muley's face opened up in the next round, and every punch The Canadian landed sent blood flying. Toward the end of the round,

Muley was trying to grab a hold on The Canadian and punch him in the face or on the back of the head, so Boss went to his corner and talked to him between rounds.

Halfway into Round Four Muley was rubbing blood out of both eyes. He could hardly see to punch. He grabbed The Canadian's arm and began slugging him in the head, so Boss jumped in and pulled his hand away. Muley backed off and tried the bull rush again, but The Canadian sidestepped and drilled him hard in the kidney.

Muley stood near the ropes and started to cry. I could see the tears, and when his shoulders heaved, he made a snorting sound. He turned and made another rush, grabbing The Canadian by both arms. The Canadian must have seen Boss running in because he was just standing there when suddenly Muley had him higher than his head and then threw him over the top rope onto the ice blocks.

A couple men yelled "Foul!" and "Disqualification!" Most of the others were cheering and yelling for Muley. Boss grabbed Muley and dragged him back to his corner.

The Canadian was down between two stacks of ice. I could see one of his feet sticking up. It wasn't moving. Bear climbed up the ice, then turned around. "Quiet! Quiet down!" He kneeled beside The Canadian and reached down. Boss stood by the ropes. Bear looked at him. "He's dead."

There was a moment of silence. I heard a trickle of water, then it was drowned by the sudden jabbering of the men. A couple of them headed for the door. Boss went through the ropes and grabbed them before they could get out. "Chet, guard the door." He walked back and got up by Bear.

Muley was sitting in his corner, his face leaking blood through his fingers.

"Men," Boss began, "there's been an accident. A man's dead and nothin's gonna bring him back, but if someone here wants to report this to the police, I told Chester I'd check with him after this thing was finished, so we can get it done then if anyone's a mind to."

It was quiet, except for Muley's sobs.

"All right. Then does anyone object to Bear and me handlin' this as we see fit?"

No one spoke.

"Good. First off, everyone here is sworn to secrecy. I want this night a closed subject. Agreed?"

A few men mumbled "Agreed." Most of the others were looking at the floor.

"Agreed?" Boss's voice echoed.

This time it was answered by a baritone and bass chorus of "Yes" and "Agreed." The men looked up at Boss.

"O.K., then. This is the way it's gonna be. Most of you can go home and forget about it. Leave here one at a time or in groups of two or three, but go home. The less you know, the better. I want Chet, Ed, Elmer, Bill, Jim, and Perc to stay here."

Richard Flowers, the feed and seed man who had been pretty worked up during the fight, looked subdued as he reached up and shook Boss's hand. He left quickly. Each of the other men shook hands with Boss, too, but none of them spoke, at least not that I could hear.

When the last man had pushed the door shut, Boss gave orders and everyone worked taking down the ropes and posts and carrying them and the wood and canvas that made up the ring outside. While the other men were rubbing out any signs of what had happened, Perc West went two blocks to his barn, returned with a wagon, and the stuff was loaded. As soon as it was done, the six men left after a word with Boss.

Muley and Tom had been off in a corner the whole time. Boss and Bear went over to them.

"Muley?"

Muley wasn't crying anymore. He looked at Boss.

"Muley, get up."

The big man stood and looked around. He saw the foot sticking up and turned his back on it. His shoulders started heaving and he sat down. Boss said to Tom, "The way I figure it, we made a mistake, a bad mistake, but that's not the question. The thing is what are we gonna do about it. I don't see implicatin' everyone that was here."

"Neither do I," Bear said.

Tom put his hands on Muley's shoulders.

"And I don't want Muley to do any time. What good would that do?"

Tom looked at Boss, but didn't speak.

"The Canadian was a fighting man and as good as they come. I guess he wouldn't want another fighting man punished for what anyone could see was a pure accident."

Bear was staring at Boss. Boss turned and looked at Bear. Finally, Bear dropped his eyes to Muley and said, "Right. An accident. That's all it was."

Boss said, "Yes, an accident—no one meant it to happen. And somethin' else. I figure that Muley won the fight on account of The Canadian's inability to continue."

Bear started to say something, but Boss put his hand on his shoulder and nodded at Muley, so Bear stopped. Boss reached in his pocket, took out the four hundred dollars in twenty dollar gold pieces and bills, and handed it to Tom. "You got some place he can go to for a spell, some place far away?"

"Yeah, we can go to . . ."

"I don't want to know where. You take Muley back home, and after his face heals, bring him into town and put him on a train to wherever. Stop in at the Bank on Monday and I'll change these hundreds for you."

"All right, Boss. Thanks."

"Take Muley home now. And don't worry."

Tom went out with a lantern in one hand and Muley's hand in the other. When the door closed, I noticed it was pretty dark with only two lanterns left.

After the Gilbertsons' buggy was gone, Boss said, "I'll have to talk to Chester and to Doc Lee. We'll have to call a coroner's jury, but between Doc and me we'll come up with somethin'."

"Maybe you should let Plutowsky discover the body on Monday. He's got a strong heart. It won't hurt him none."

"Yeah, I think you're right. That way there's no direct public connection with any of us, and with that leg up Plutowsky can't miss it."

Boss opened The Canadian's satchel and went through it. "Well, will you look at this?" He pulled out a revolver. "An Iver Johnson Hammerless .38. I don't think it would be a good idea to let this be found."

"No, just pocket it."

"Towels, water bottle, tape, coin purse, but no identification—no name, no address, no letters, no telegrams. Here's a money clip. He's got . . . he had money. There's at least five hundred dollars here. Let's hope Plutowsky doesn't keep it as a finder's fee."

"You'd better take it, just in case. We can figure what to do with it later."

Boss checked The Canadian's shirt and cap, but found nothing. Bear climbed up and felt in his pockets. "His pants are as empty as the poor box in a Scottish church. By jiminy he's gettin' cold."

"He might have left somethin' in his room at the Woodson. We'll have a look-see after the big 'discovery' on Monday. Let's go."

They picked up their lanterns, looked around once more, and left.

I sat high up in the darkness and shivered. Soon I could see shapes and stepped on the blocks up to a door on the south side from which Plutowsky lowered ice to his wagon. I swung it open and gray light spilled onto the ice, the straw, and the sawdust. And the foot.

I stepped down to The Canadian. His body was wedged between two rows of ice blocks. It was hard to see his face. I kneeled close to him. I'd never seen anyone dead before; he looked asleep. I'd never touched anyone dead before; he was cold.

Outside, I heard the cry of a nighthawk against the sky, so I climbed up to the door and saw it flitting for bugs. I closed the door and walked down in a wide circle because I didn't want to step on anything softer than ice.

Just at the door I coughed and it echoed lightly.

It felt warm outside, and the further I walked uphill toward home—first on Guilford, then Gregory, and finally on Salem (I didn't want to walk any strange alleys at night)—the warmer I got. I turned in at our alley, walked past the gravel pit Boss swore was going to get filled in or he'd know the reason why, opened the back yard gate, and headed up to the house.

I wondered if Ma had checked on me, but she said she would wait, and since I didn't have a fever, I knew I could trust her.

Only one stair creaked, and I knew which one.

I undressed and got into bed. I thought I should pray for The Canadian and for Muley, but I fell asleep trying to figure out what to say.

I woke up coughing and hot. When I called Ma, my voice was strange. She turned on the light with Boss behind her. Her wrist was cool on my forehead. "Why, the poor child is burning up. Quickly, Boss, fetch an ice bag and a glass of water." Boss left.

She held me close, sort of rocking back and forth, until he got back. After she had everything arranged, she kissed me and told me not to worry, she'd check on me in a little while. She got up and Boss tosseled my hair and winked. He headed for the door, while Ma picked up my clothes.

"I thought I folded these clothes once before tonight, and these stockings shouldn't be here. And they're damp." She shook my pants and looked at the floor. "What's this? It looks like . . . it is. Boss, look at this sawdust. Lige, were you out in the barn tonight?"

I held my gaze as steady as I could. "No, Ma'am."

"Oh, well, I'll clean up here in the morning. Good night again, Lige." I heard her on the stairs.

Boss straightened up and dusted his fingers. He came over and stood above me.

I looked up into his eyes, brown just like mine, then I pulled my right arm out from under the covers and slowly shook his hand. His hand tightened, but his face said nothing. He left.

The day I recovered from my pleurisy well enough to go out, Ma took me uptown. It was a sunny day, so we sat in the Railroad Park just west of the tracks. Ma walked across Chicago Street to the bakery and brought back some cookies, two oranges, and two lemonades.

We ate and drank and watched the horses, buggies, and wagons on Chicago. The passenger train came in from the north, and I covered my ears from the noise of the locomotive. I followed the black engine as it passed and saw Tom and Muley come out of the waiting room onto the platform, then the train blocked them out.

Tom was back in a few days, but he didn't work for the railroad anymore. He was one of Bear's hired men on a farm in the hills far off to the east of our town.

Muley was gone for two years and when he came back, I only saw him once. His father died, and they had the funeral service in the Gilbertsons' farm house south of town, then the hearse came through our town, followed by a long procession of buggies with the family and the mourners, heading north to Eternal Rest Cemetery.

The Potman twins, Merle and Pearl, and I were fishing from the old covered bridge, except it wasn't covered anymore. It was just the steel skeleton that was left after the rotten wood had been removed.

The procession wheeled by and I saw a huge man riding with Tom. His belly and thighs jiggled as the buggy crossed the bridge. He looked squishy, without an ounce of muscle in his body. He stared at me as they went past, and I recognized Muley's face behind the mask of flesh.

Muley died of influenza in 1919. They had to build a special coffin for him.

As for The Canadian, a day or two after Muley left on the NP for parts unknown, I was in our living room looking through *A Trip Around the World*, a book of photographs. One of the two big front windows was slightly raised when Boss and Bear came and sat on the porch.

Boss said, "The Canadian's stuff came back today. I mailed it to the Winnipeg address he wrote in the Woodson's register, but it came back, not at that address."

"What'd you do with it?"

"The clothes he'd left at the Woodson I gave to Captain Iverson of the Salvation Army. The shaving gear, toothbrush, and other personal stuff I threw away."

"What about the five hundred dollars?"

"Captain Iverson was the recipient of an anonymous gift of four hundred dollars."

"Good. And the other hundred dollars?"

"Anonymously to Plutowsky."

"Good, good. I thought maybe you used it to bribe Doc Lee."

"No, Doc was very understanding after I explained things, and with every member of the coroner's jury having been present at Plutowsky's, the verdict was short and simple."

"I still can't credit it. 'Death due to freezing' and in June. I hope it's buried deep in the files."

"It is."

And after all these years, it still is. If you don't believe me, you can come to our town and look it up yourself.

I have.

ROYCE HARE

oyce Hare was a good friend, devoted as they come. Maybe too devoted.

Roy, as his friends called him, lived in a shack with his mother and little brother Jackie. He didn't have a father, that I knew of. His mother made candy and clerked in the fruit and confectionary store on Villard Avenue. With her reputation she wouldn't have been there, except that her candy was the best in town. To our older ladies melt-in-your mouth fudge, toffee, and divinity seemed to be unmistakable signs of moral regeneration.

The Hares' shack was on Gorringe Avenue, shielded from the Great Northern tracks just to the north by a growth of poplars and willows.

Roy and I were in the same grade in school, but he was smaller. He wasn't my best friend, but we liked each other well enough to play ball, swim, fish, hunt, and skate together. Eventually, I began to see myself as a somewhat distant, but still nice, bigger brother to Roy.

The fact was he didn't have anyone who was really close to him until Frank Cooper came home from the Great War.

Back in September 1917, when I was twelve years old, the young men and old boys of our town began to leave for the War as Company B of the North Dakota 2nd Regiment.

Two guys left in early September for Camp Dodge, Iowa, from the Northern Pacific depot, sent off by a cheering crowd, the band, and a speech by a lawyer.

In the middle of the month, a second group left for Dodge. They formed up at the court house. The band played, the Congregational minister said a prayer, a different lawyer spoke, and so did the county judge. Then we all marched to the NP depot—the band, the draft board, the men of Company B, the townspeople, and then all of us school kids, each holding an American flag.

On the platform the Company B men gave a yell:

"Riff! Raff! Ruff!
Riff! Raff! Ruff!
Company B!
Pretty hot stuff!
We won't quarrel!
We will fight!
We're all right!
Hitting-Crashing-Punching-Smashing!
Company B!"

The final quota men were honored on the last Saturday of September by over three thousand people. Again we met at the court house and then marched down Villard—Company B, the school kids again (with both American flags and patriotic red, white, and blue streamers), the Red Cross workers in decorated automobiles, then more marchers, and then more decorated autos.

At Guilford we made a right and spilled out onto the grounds of the defunct Congregational Academy. The Catholic priest gave the invocation, and the judge addressed us on the virtues of patriotism. A lieutenant responded and then another lawyer made a speech. The Company Captain responded with a word of thanks to all of us.

The next day the boys formed up at the Railroad Park and marched down Villard, turned left onto Dakota, and were cheered on their way to the Great Northern depot by a thousand voices, including mine.

When the train pulled in, hardly anyone said a word, and a lot of girls and women were crying. My brother Josh was already a soldier and stationed at the Presidio in San Francisco, but when the train pulled out, it was almost like he was aboard and I just about started crying. Ma already was.

Company B went to Camp Greene, North Carolina, where they became part of the 164th Infantry of the 41st Division, and were shipped over to France in December.

At least twenty-four of them never made it home alive. Two of them were killed just shy of the eleventh hour of the eleventh day of the eleventh month of 1918.

Later that month our first wounded man came home on crutches. It was on a Sunday and we all met him at the depot. The next Friday the community gave him a hero's reception at the Masonic Temple.

In April 1919 the students were let out of school to see a demonstration by a tank that had actually fought in France.

Most of our boys came home in early August of that year to a tumultuous welcome. My grandfather Bear said there were ten thousand people cheering as Company B stepped off the train. He claimed it was the largest crowd in the history of our town.

Our band played and so did the bands from two other towns. There were speeches, singing, ball games, free movies, picnics, a trick aviator, two dances, and a fireworks display that was better than the one we'd had on the Fourth of July. Our American Legion Post was organized that day, too.

Frank Cooper didn't come home in August. He'd been gassed and his lungs were shot, but even worse, while he was struggling to breathe, a shell from a trench mortar exploded near him. The trench walls caved in and he was buried at the bottom of four feet of earth. His buddies dug him free, but he was never free from the suffocating nightmares of being buried alive.

When Frank did come home after a series of unsuccessful stays in hospitals in France and on the East Coast, it was snowing, and there was no one to greet him on the GN platform.

While in France a letter had informed him that his parents were dead of the Spanish Flu, and that their farm house had been severely damaged by a lightning strike, not that he could have lived by himself anyway.

He checked into the Oleson House and phoned my father, who was known as Boss and who was the Bank president, and told him to sell the farm. Frank was an only child.

He never left the Oleson, which had a dining room, until the day he had to sign papers at the Bank dealing with the sale of the farm.

That day was a bitter one, with a sleety wind cutting into Frank's lungs and the temperature below zero. The walk down a flight of stairs in the Oleson and bucking the wind to the Bank left him exhausted, so the frozen trip from the Bank back across Villard and into the wind just about did him in. Coming out of the Eat Shop, Roy saw Frank fall. He ran over to him, helped him to his feet, and guided him to the Oleson.

After they got back to Frank's room, Doc Blanchard checked Frank over, saying he had to take it easy. What else could he tell a dying man? Doc then went back up to his third floor room to lose himself in one of his morphine dreams, while Roy and Frank talked.

The rest of the winter it was Roy and Frank, Frank and Roy. Maybe Roy was looking for a father and Frank for a son, or maybe they thought of themselves as brothers. Maybe they just liked each other, I don't know. After while I got a little jealous that maybe Roy had really found a new "big brother."

In the spring they'd walk together to the Railroad Park just east of Chicago Street and only a block from the Oleson and feed the pigeons that lived in the elevators. They'd sit on a bench and watch the trains and talk, or sometimes just sit and be together. Whatever they did, Roy told me it was nice. He always went home feeling good, which wasn't the way his life had been before.

One night in July Frank died. Hiram, the town drunk, told me that at first Frank sounded like a banshee, screaming about dirt and 'get it off' and 'lemme breathe'. Then he was coughing his lungs out. Then it was quiet. Hiram and Doc Blanchard went into the room, but Frank was dead, the bed covers all twisted around him, with blood on his lips and nose. Doc just looked at Frank, never even touched him, shook his head, and walked out.

The next day I was fishing the river north of Winslow's pasture and east of the old swimming "beach" when Roy ran up.

"Lige, Frank's dead."

"Yeah, I heard. I'm sorry."

"He knew it was comin'. He told me. But the important thing is he wanted to be cremated, none of that bein' buried in the earth. I told you how he was in France."

"Yeah."

"He didn't want to be buried. He told me. He made me promise he wouldn't be."

"But what can you do? Old R.I. is gonna bury him sure. It's money in his pocket and it won't be if he ships him somewhere to be cremated."

R.I. Walaker was our town's undertaker, as well as a furniture dealer, and he loved money. One time Bear and R.I. were coming back from the cemetery north of our town when they met old Mrs. Appleyard and her son. R.I. had buried Mr. Appleyard the week before, and he began to sympathize so much with the widow that pretty soon tears ran down his cheeks. Then, not thirty seconds after the Appleyards had driven away, Bear said R.I. was rubbing his hands together and giggling about how much money he'd made off that funeral. So I knew that Frank was going to be buried.

Roy said, "Help me, Lige. Can't you think of anything?"

But I couldn't. Besides, Frank was Roy's friend, not mine, and Roy had done the promising.

The fish weren't biting, but I stayed put. Roy sat over by a log and stared at the water. I lay back and let time pass, but Roy was sitting bolt upright.

About half an hour later, Roy got up and said he was leaving. Then, kind of casual-like, he asked if I would play War with him that afternoon. I said I would and we set a time.

Playing War was something we did behind the buildings forming an "L" on the corner of Chicago Street and Lamborn Avenue. Directly on the corner was the brick Farmers & Merchants Bank. Going west on Lamborn you came to an empty building, a barbershop, a bakery, the alley, the big three-story brick hotel they'd put up the year the boys marched off to war, and a small empty building. Running north down Chicago were a restaurant, a small empty wood frame building, an empty lot, Walaker's Furniture Store and mortuary, another empty lot, and the Hayes house on the corner.

On spring or summer days when baseball, swimming, and fishing failed, the boys of our town could be found fighting the "air war" by turning the landings on the hotel into Sopwith Camels or Snipes, or by bombing London (using water-filled cans) from our Zeppelins, which was the rear balcony for the apartments above the F&M Bank. The back lots became the Western Front and hundreds died on patrols probing through the barbed wire of no-man's land to determine enemy strength. Sometimes a patrol that went too near the barrels behind the hotel's café or the Chicago Café, barrels filled with grease, rotting meat, and maggot-infested garbage, had to throw on masks to ward off the inhuman mustard gas attack launched by the Huns, the rapers of poor little Belgium. But usually War was a series of ambushes between the doughboys and the Jerries, which caused countless arguments about who got who first.

It didn't dawn on me until later that Roy rarely played War, and that for him to suggest playing it was unheard of. We liked it when he did play, however, because he wore one of those spiked German helmets that Frank had given him. It made everything seem more authentic. Roy said he wouldn't part with it for a million dollars.

That afternoon we were the only two soldiers. We couldn't play Zeppelin because old lady Kennedy had her wash strung across the balcony and to touch it meant an instant attack on your undefended rear.

That was all right with Roy. All he wanted to play was Scout and Ambush. The only trouble was all his ambushes were right around Walaker's.

Walaker's was really two buildings. Originally, it had been a two-story wooden frame structure, housing the furniture store Walaker had bought in 1892. He'd built a one-story wooden addition after he'd become an undertaker. A few years before the War and apparently frightened by an elevator fire just east of his business, Walaker had torn down the furniture store part and put up a two-story brick building separated by a firewall and fire door from the older, wooden addition. He and his wife lived upstairs.

After five straight ambushes by Roy in the doorways or around the corners of Walaker's, I told him to ambush me somewhere else. His next ambush was in the weeds of the lot just north of the mortuary. When I saw the spike on his helmet, I told him I was quitting.

"Aw, c'mon, Lige. Once more."

"No, you always hide in the same places. What's so special about Walaker's?"

Roy blinked. I forgot Frank was inside. Neither of us spoke, and I could hear old lady Kennedy giving her kids what for.

Finally, Roy said, "Let's go to Donovan's; I'll buy ya a double-decker."

I didn't know Roy had so much money. "Chocolate?"

"If ya want."

We walked over to Villard and his mother put two scoops of rich, homemade ice cream into a cone and handed it to me. Roy had the same. He paid with the most money I ever saw him carry.

While I was licking, Roy said, "Lige, do me a favor?"

"What?"

"Find out . . . ask old man Walaker how much insurance he's got on his building."

That was one of the dumbest things Roy had ever asked me. "What for?"

"Oh, I don't know. Just curious, a big building like that and all. Remember how that old elevator went up. It must take a lot of insurance."

"I s'ppose. Ask him yourself."

"Aw, he don't know me from Adam. And everybody knows you. You're Boss's boy. He'll tell you."

"Well, maybe he will. What d'ya want to know for? Ya studyin' to be an insurance agent?"

"Yeah, that's it. Maybe I'll give it a whirl sometime."

He smiled that gap-toothed Roy-smile, and the ice cream flowed down my throat, and I said I'd do it.

It wasn't too hard. I went over to Walaker's and started looking around. When he saw who I was, Walaker started talking and once he got going no one could stop him unless they walked away, and some people claimed that even so he probably kept right on talking.

Anyway, I found out that Mr. Walaker was a great believer in insurance, would never be without it, and was more than adequately covered. I declined his invitation to see Frank Cooper and went back to the confectionary.

As soon as I told Roy, he said he was going over to see Frank one last time before the funeral, which was set for the next day. I decided not to go and headed home instead.

"Lige?"

It was dark.

"Lige?"

It was Ma.

"What?"

"There's a big fire downtown. I thought maybe you'd like to see it. Boss is already gone."

"Yeah, wait'll I get dressed. What time is it?"

"A little past three."

We walked down Lamborn toward the bright red-orange-yellow glow. We crossed Glen Haven and I thought I knew where the fire was. When we crossed St. Paul, I knew exactly where it was. We turned right on Chicago and the back of Walaker's was burning right down to the ground despite the efforts of the volunteer fire department.

Ma and I edged and squeezed our way as close as we dared, and I could see Boss standing big and black against the flames.

Ma went over to comfort Mrs. Walaker, who was sobbing inside a circle of women.

Something collapsed inside the building and sparks spiraled and eddied against the black sky. As I watched the sparks, I felt hands grab me and a shrill voice squealed, "I've got him! I've got him! This is the one! This is the boy that set fire to my store!"

The fingernails of old man Walaker were digging into my shoulders. Then he let go with his right hand and began slapping me across the top of my head. Suddenly, he grunted and stopped. My grandfather Bear had his big paws around Walaker's wrist and squeezed until he let go of my shoulder.

"Lige, what's the trouble here?"

"Old ma . . . Mr. Walaker thinks I fired his store, but I didn't. Honest."

"Oh, ho, then why did you come into my store not twelve hours ago and ask me about my insurance? I will have you arrested. I will . . . ."

Bear cut him off. Ma had come over. "Margaret, take Lige home. Mr. Walaker is a little excited and we're going to have a talk in my office."

As I walked away with Ma, I turned to Bear. "I didn't do it, Bear. I didn't burn his store." He nodded at me and then he and Walaker started moving through the crowd.

Neither Bear nor Boss ever spoke to me about Walaker's accusation, and I never did find out what Bear told Walaker in his office, but from then on Walaker was very quiet and respectful toward me.

Neither the insurance company investigator nor the official from the state could find any evidence of arson, and it went down as another "fire of unknown origin." The insurance company paid off Walaker, who put up a real fine brick mortuary on the lot just north of his furniture store.

Some long bones, teeth, and parts of the skull were all that was left of Frank Cooper.

I didn't sleep much from the time I got home until eight o'clock when I ate breakfast and headed for Royce Hare's house. They didn't have a phone.

Jackie answered the door and then his mother came out of the tiny lean-to kitchen. "Oh, it's you, Lige. I thought maybe it was Royce. Have you seen him? He ain't been home."

"No, but if I do, I'll send him along home right away."

I walked the GN rails northwest to the depot platform and turned north up Dakota. Crossing Dunnell, I met Hiram and his big-headed black Lab, Jack Johnson.

"Hiram, have you seen Royce Hare today?"

"Nope."

"O.K. Thanks." I walked past.

"But I seed 'im last night."

I turned. "Where?"

"Ya got anythin' fer me, Lige?"

"You know I haven't."

"I knowed it. Just astin' to be perlite. I seed Royce over there." He pointed to a clump of willows and weeds. "JJ and me was sleepin' and alla sudden JJ lets out a howl ta wake me up and there's Royce. He'da stumbled right over me if it warn't for JJ." He reached down and patted JJ's head. "He took off and went acrost the tracks just ahead of a drag freight . . . Say, Lige, did somebody paint the town orange last night? It looked orange ta me."

"No. No, it was just a fire."

"Do tell. C'mon, Jack Johnson. Be seein' ya, Lige."

I didn't see Roy for about a month. Then I heard he was back, and a couple days later when I was fishing near the wooden wagon wheels stuck on the north side of the river, I saw him.

I stood up and socked the end of the pole into the mud. Roy stopped in the little trail he'd been following. I walked over and jumped on him. He grunted and struggled, but I was bigger and he went down. I sat on his stomach while he kicked and wrenched and shook. The trail dust started covering us.

I held his wrists down and sat on him for a long time. He couldn't move me, though he never quit trying. Pretty soon tears were rolling through the dust on his cheeks. He was trying to stop them, but they kept coming.

Finally, I wasn't mad anymore, and I rolled off careful-like so he wouldn't get in a kick, but he just lay there in the dust.

I whacked the dust off my clothes and went back to my pole.

After awhile I heard Roy stand up. "I wanted to tell you I had to open the coffin. It was metal." He said it to my back.

When I finally turned around, Roy was a little light and dark dot heading west on the trail.

A few days later at the supper table, Boss, who had been named administrator of Frank Cooper's will, said, "I had the Hare family into the Bank this morning."

"About the Cooper estate?" Ma asked.

"Yes. I gave Mrs. Hare a check in the full amount and suggested she open an account with us, but she cashed the check and she and the boys left. Oh, yes, Lige, (he reached over to the counter and opened a bag) Royce wanted me to give this to you."

He handed me the spiked German helmet.

I put in on the table and Ma said, "Oh, how nice of him."

"I gotta go." I ran out without Ma's usual fifteen minute waiting period after a meal.

Before I left the yard, I had to tell my dog Ted to "Stay." Then I ran all the way down Salem Street, past the school, across the tracks, turned on Gorringe, and, with lungs slamming, stopped at the Hares' door.

It stood wide open and the shack was empty, except for a few boxes of junk.

I never saw Royce Hare again, but I envy anyone who has him as a friend.

"HOME"

When the *Empire Builder* rumbled over the Jacques River bridge, Boy woke up with an apprehensive look. I squeezed his hand and he closed his eyes. Another five minutes and we'd be home—Menninger, North Dakota—which I'd left four years before. It was a little past three in the morning so I'd have to wait to surprise Ma, who always smelled like white lilacs.

I remembered coming into Menninger from the other direction on a freight the summer of '23 after the Potman twins, named Merle and Pearl, and I had been to San Francisco, where we saw my older brother Josh.

I was sweet on Emily Livingstone, but our little romance faded during our senior year, and then Bessie Stark transferred in from Fishtown when her Dad became the new station agent for the Northern Pacific.

We had a couple girls in town who had been called "Bessie" when they were young, but as soon as they got into high school, it became "Elizabeth." Bessie Stark was also named "Elizabeth," but she preferred "Bessie" because Queen Elizabeth I of England had been known as "Good Queen Bess."

She was a tiny girl: when we slow danced she would put her head on my chest. Her skin was soft and she kept it covered from the sun. It was so pale that it reminded me of a porcelain figure in Ma's china closet. It was a lady in a pink dress curtsying to a man dressed in blue who was slightly bowing as though they were going to dance.

The lady had black hair while Bessie's was like spun sugar, but I still thought of Bessie as being as fragile as the lady whom Ma forbade us kids to touch.

After we graduated from Menninger High, I went to Fargo and entered Dakota Business College, while Bessie moved to Kingston and began studying nursing at the hospital there. Because her Dad worked for the NP, she could get passes and visit me in Fargo.

We went to movies and dances and walked up and down Broadway and in the parks in nice weather and made plans for our future. Sometimes in the movies or in the shadows we'd kiss, and I'd always want more than she was prepared to give. She wasn't as shy as Emily, but she wasn't as wild as Annie, a girl I had met in Spokane on my way to San Francisco, so when she boarded the train to go back to Kingston, I always felt frustrated.

That feeling faded one spring evening. Bessie and I had gone to the Garrick Theater on Broadway, where we saw *The Enchanted Cottage* with Richard Barthelmess and May McAvoy. I had liked Barthelmess as the lead in *Tol'able David* and as the Chinese man in D.W. Griffith's *Broken Blossoms*. I could recall seeing May McAvoy as one of the children in *Mrs. Wiggs of the Cabbage Patch*, but she was older now, and I thought she did a good job as the woman who helps Barthelmess deal with his war wounds by revealing the house he has retreated to is an old honeymoon cottage where many couples began their married lives.

We were sitting toward the rear and off to the side, and our kisses became more passionate as the movie progressed. Bessie even let me put my hand on her leg, but when I ducked my fingers under her skirt and they began caressing their way along her smooth skin, she grabbed my wrist and whispered, "No."

During the rest of the movie, I was wondering what it would be like to have Bessie with me in a honeymoon cottage, and that maybe she was thinking the same thing. The lights came up and we walked onto Broadway holding hands. We stopped by the statue of the Indian just north of the NP tracks and crossed over. I took it as a good sign when she began leaning against me, so I guided her into the shadows and kissed her. Her arms went around my neck and she kissed me back, harder.

I pushed her against a building and my body flowed against hers. Our kisses streamed from open mouths. My hand went to her breast and her body tightened against mine. Our tongues went exploring.

Then she took my hand and kissed it. "No, not yet. Wait 'til we're married like in the movie and I'll give myself to you. We can do everything and we'll have lots of babies."

My breath was rushing in and out in little torrents. I held it a few seconds and then whispered, "Yes." Then "I love you." I had never said that to any other girl.

"Oh, Lige, I love you, too." She hugged me and then gave me a kiss, close-mouthed, but with such warmth it meant that much more to me. We left the shadows, and I walked her up Broadway to the YWCA, which was on the upper two floors of a building.

Another kiss.

"I love you."

"I love you."

A second kiss, but that was all because if the matron saw us, Bessie would have been written up and maybe tossed out.

"Good night."

"Good night."

The door closed, and I walked to my room feeling like the only man on earth and Bessie the only girl. That night I dreamed of warm golden days and sweet silvery nights with Bessie as my wife.

When we walked to the NP station the next day, that feeling was still there, and deep in a fragment of my heart it has never left.

After I got out of DBC, I had to find a job. My Dad, nicknamed Boss, said he wouldn't make an opening just for me at the Bank, but if I made good at something else, he would consider my application.

Blind Anton was a well driller who couldn't see. He wasn't born blind, but an accident with dynamite cost him his sight and a scarred face which he partially hid behind dark goggles. He could still "smell" water better than anyone around and could help a little bit with the drilling and the preparation and setting off the dynamite, but he needed someone to drive his team and do most of the physical labor because his son who had helped him for a couple years was going to graduate and head for the West Coast. I applied; he accepted.

Being together from morning to night for several months, Blind Anton and I became good friends. Magdelena, his wife, would have me over for a meal at least once a week.

Such delicious Bohemian food: roast pork with onions and caraway seeds and served with bread or potato dumplings, gravy, and red cabbage; Vomachka—rolled-up bacon and round steak flavored with garlic, carrots, marjoram, and sour cream; Bohemian goulash with paprika, garlic, onion, caraway and dill seeds; chicken roasted with onions, tomatoes, green peppers, pepper-corns, and spices and served with fried potatoes; a sweet, braided bread called Houska; a Bohemian cake called Babovka made with lemon rind and ground nuts and sprinkled with powdered sugar; prune, apricot, or cherry Kolaches for dessert; coffee called Kava, which could float a nail and left dark sludge in the cup.

The only things I wouldn't eat were Sulc or headcheese made from pig's feet, hearts, and tongues, all in a meat jelly; Jelita, which was a blood sausage, very dark in color; and pig brains scrambled with eggs and onions.

With all the good things Magdelena made, I was surprised Anton stayed as thin as he did.

Of course, I knew that loading, driving, and unloading the wagon; setting up and dismantling the drilling equipment; lighting the dynamite fuses; even occasionally feeding and watering the horses would only be temporary, but it kept me busy while Bessie continued her nursing studies in Kingston.

We wrote to each other and she would come up the branch every other weekend. We'd go to barn dances, movies, walk the town holding hands, and make plans for our wedding.

It was understood that we were engaged, although I'd never formally proposed. Even so, Bessie was eager to get our picture in the local paper, so she had me make an appointment with Mr. Baylor, the photographer, and came up on the train on July 3 for our picture.

She wanted to go on a picnic on the Fourth and talk about our wedding. She was upset when I told her I had signed up to play baseball in a game against Fishtown, and half-jokingly she said I cared more for baseball than I did for her.

When the team took the field, I saw Bessie, all in white with a large white hat to protect her face from the sun, sitting in the stands beside a man dressed in a gray suit and dark hat. It was Red Lewis. In high school he had been sweet on Bessie until I beat his time. I guessed she was trying to make me jealous, but I figured I'd show her.

I singled my first time up, stole second, and came home on Merle Potman's double. I dusted off my uniform and looked at Bessie; she was busy talking with Red.

When I ran back to right field to start the second, Bessie and Red got up and started to leave, but not before she gave me a smile. Red was smiling, too.

I went hitless the rest of the day, striking out twice and fouling out once.

Just as we were shaking hands with the Fishtown team, the fire siren went off and firemen in the crowd and on the team headed for town. Soon people were talking about a drowning. Then they were saying Bessie's name.

The fire engine went clanging by, pulling a trailer and boat, and Merle and I jumped into his car and followed its dust, along with dozens of other vehicles.

There was a lake three miles southwest of town. The family that owned the land on the north side of the lake called it Lake Alma, while the owners of the land on the south side named it Lake Catherine, both after sainted grandmothers. By the time we got to the lake, the firemen had the boat out on the water and were probing with grappling hooks.

I saw Red Lewis, wet, muddy, and staring, sitting on the north shore. I started for him when a cry went up from the boat and something white surfaced. It was pulled aboard and the boat slowly turned toward me.

I walked into the water to help take her out of the boat, the mud sending up a sucking sound and a rotten-earth smell. Bessie looked asleep, but she wasn't. Her hat was gone and the water had curled her hair around her face like a halo and I started to cry.

With Bessie lying on the ground, I took off after Lewis. We were grappling in the mud when friends pulled us apart. Merle threw a blanket on the seat and we drove back to town.

My life blurred out. There was a wake, a funeral, and a burial; I went, but I was numb.

After the interment, I went to bed and didn't get up for twenty-four hours. For a week I darkened my room and got out of bed only for necessities.

Ma tried to soothe my feelings with soft words and my favorite foods. Boss tried the man-to-man talk, saying how we have to bear up under life's adversities. Rev. Micah sat by the bed, trying to read the Bible in the dark and giving up, finally ending with how Bessie was in a better place.

I scarcely heard them. I burrowed deeper into the blackness.

Dr. Lee was called. He left muttering that there was nothing he could do.

I'd lie in bed and try to remember the plots of the novels and short stories I had read, or I'd recite the poetry I had memorized, but I'd fall asleep, my mind going as dark as my room.

"Lijah! Lijah!"

It was morning and someone was calling me from outside. Maybe they would go away.

"Lijah! Get up; I need you!"

It was Blind Anton.

I went to the window. In July I slept with it open. I looked out and there was Anton in his wagon pulled by a team of blacks. "I can't help."

"Yah, you can. Jorgenson wants his well. I need your help."

"I can't."

"If I can, you can."

I went back to bed. The explosion had almost killed Anton, took his sight, and tore up his face. I got out of bed and walked back to the window. He hadn't moved. One of the blacks snorted and stamped. Anton would wait all day if he had to. "I'll be down."

"Good."

Jorgenson, then Mattson, Hines, Corning, all on the Flats, and Wheat up near Divide wanted wells, so Anton and I were busy morning to night, and I was thankful for Ma's supper and the oblivion of my bed. However, in September the demand for wells dried up.

Then Merle and Cecilia Livingstone broke up. She said she was concerned he had no ambition.

The black demons were fringing my thoughts, so when Merle came by with a couple bottles of booze he'd gotten from Doc Carlson, a blind pig on St. Paul that we'd helped get out of a scrape in the summer of '22, I accompanied him on a moonlight walk east of town.

We stuck to the high south bank of the Jacques, crossing some fences, and ended up looking down on the river from the top of a small cliff. Merle, his twin brother Pearl, and I had done a lot of hunting there, so we each cracked a bottle and drank to Pearl, who was working at radio station WDAY in Fargo.

We toasted each other, drank to the trip we had made to the West Coast in the summer of '23, and then he proposed a drink and good luck to Cecilia. I kept Bessie locked away.

After it rose, we drank to the moon, which had gone past full a few nights before, and then drank in silence. I watched the thin black ghosts stretching out from the bases of the fence posts, but they didn't move. Soon, neither did I.

I woke up with a coyote or a wolf calling to the southeast, until I figured out it was a dog on the Johnson place: coyotes and wolves had become victims of progress.

"C'mon, Merle, we gotta get home."

Merle snored on.

I pushed him in the side with my foot until he sat up. "We gotta go."

We swayed over the prairie toward the dim lights of town. I heard a raspy gushing sound and Merle was down on his knees, puking. I walked over to him. He said, "I gotta rest."

I led him to a little hill. There was a depression in the center with thousands of buffalo bones which had been overlooked by the bone hunters. Merle never made it. When I looked back, he was at the base of the hill, all curled up. Just as I crested the hill and saw the bones in the moonlight, I passed out.

The sound of cows woke me up. They were leaving the Pound farm after the morning milking and were walking single-file in a cowpath.

I got Merle up and we moved toward town. Walking down Lamborn, we heard the bells of the Norwegian Lutheran Church. Halfway down our block we met members of the congregation hurrying to avoid being late, but not in such a hurry they couldn't give us the once over.

Rather than pass the church, Merle headed for the alley, and I climbed the stairs to my room and fell into bed.

When Ma and Boss came home from church, she came into my bedroom and talked to me. She never mentioned drinking, but I could tell she knew and was terribly disappointed.

After she left, Boss came in and told me I smelled like a distillery and he wasn't going to put up with drinking by anyone living in his home. I wanted to argue, but my brain was hammering on my skull, trying to get out, so I just stayed on the pillow and took it.

That afternoon Bear came over and lectured me on the evils of drinking. As a younger man he had been a real carouser. He was a big man and it took a lot of alcohol to get him drunk, but he managed it.

One rainy Fourth of July in southern Minnesota, the saloon ran short of beer, but word came that a wagon filled with barrels of beer had bogged down on the trail just outside of town. The men rushed to the rescue, but those who stepped into the mud and grabbed a barrel got stuck.

Just when it seemed Independence Day was going to be a dry one, Bear mucked through the mud, wedged himself under the wagon, lifted it and the barrels, and set them down a couple feet closer to dry ground. He continued to lift and move until after fifteen minutes a cheer went up: the beer was safe.

Back in the saloon so many men bought Bear drinks that he passed out and was unconscious for three days. When he woke up in a pile of saw dust near the mill, he swore off liquor and hadn't touched it since.

Even though I knew the story, he repeated it, and I nodded at the parts that showed the evils of liquor, but I realized that if I needed to blot things out of my mind, I would go back to drinking.

I had a friend, an older man who lived just off the Great Northern right-of-way on the west side of town. Twig had lost a leg, so I knew since he had gone through that he could help me, but he had gotten sick and was in St. Paul. He had worked on the Northern Pacific, as well as the GN, so he was in the NP Hospital and a long way from being able to help me.

After enduring lectures from Rev. Micah and Miss Sargent, the local head of the WCTU, I got hold of Merle and we spent a night at Doc Carlson's. The next day Boss confronted me and repeated he wouldn't have a boozer living in his house. Ma cried and that was worse than anything Boss said.

I moved out.

For a year I worked at an elevator and flour mill in Caseyville by day and by night became a regular at a blind pig known as Lona's Place on the south edge of town. I didn't get drunk that often, and as long as I showed up and did my job, the mill owner didn't care.

On July Fourth (actually it was July 3 because the Fourth was a Sunday), Merle came down and we tied one on. The next morning as church bells clanged their way into our brains, we began to discuss our plight—work, drink, sleep; work, drink, sleep. That was no way to live.

We decided we had to leave North Dakota. One of his cousins had gone to work for Henry Ford at his massive River Rouge Complex in south Detroit. Maybe that was the place for us. We shook hands on it just before he drove away.

I packed my two suitcases, bought a ticket to Menninger, and walked to Lona's. Even though it was still morning, there were a few farm hands and a couple of men from the Encampment enjoying Lona's wares. The Encampment was a bunch of buildings snaggled over the glacial hills southwest of Caseyville, and the inhabitants were notably unfriendly to outsiders.

Regardless, I bought a round for the six men who made up the house. The "Campers" accepted with a glower, but never said a word or offered a return of the favor. However, each of the farm hands bought a round and raised their glasses to me. Soon I was feeling pretty good, and then I wasn't because I heard the train whistle.

I grabbed my suitcases and stumbled against a table. Horselaughs from the "Campers" accompanied me out the door.

Lona's was on a curve of the tracks, and the train was already around the curve and heading north. I chased the train, the suitcases banging my legs. The conductor came out onto the rear platform and yelled something. I couldn't hear him and kept running.

Slowly I caught up. The conductor took my suitcases and gave me a hand up. "Son, you didn't have to run so much. We're stopping at the station."

I went into the coach and collapsed into a seat. It was next to the spittoon, and I smelled old stogies and chew all the way to Menninger.

I had time to clean up at home and get presentable before train-time.

Merle's family and Bear, Boss, and Ma saw us off at the Great Northern station. Bear paid for both of our tickets on the *Oriental Limited*, and both Bear and Boss slipped me some extra money. Ma cried and kept hugging me even after the conductor called for passengers to board. Long after I was settled in, I could smell her perfume.

Merle and I talked about the train trip we had made to the West Coast three years before, but Pearl had been with us then, we were kids, and it had turned into an adventure of hitching freights and meeting people. This time we were riding inside on the GN's premier passenger train, we weren't kids, and our reward at the end would be hard work.

The prairies drifted by and then the woodlands of Minnesota. The geographical sameness blurred as Merle and I found compliant conductors and porters who could produce bottles of liquid forgetfulness for the right price.

At St. Paul the *Oriental Limited* was transferred to the tracks of the Burlington Route, which took us to Chicago and the new Union Station. Merle and I sat in the Great Hall until we could get our bearings. After we felt better, we walked Jackson, crossed the river, and turned south on Michigan. Grant Park was on our left as we made our way through the noise to Roosevelt Road and the Central Station.

After we took care of our tickets and baggage, we had time to kill, so we went over to State Street ("that great street") and walked it north to Madison. State and Madison, "the busiest corner in the world" or so we were told, and I could believe it. We'd never seen so many people as we had in San Francisco in 1923 on Market Street, but Chicago was a "toddlin' town." It was swarming—looking like a beehive with thousands of large, multi-colored, wingless bees going in all directions. Automobiles inching along; streetcars grumbling their way on the two sets of tracks, with their electric cables stretched up to the overhead wires like dark umbilical cords; even horse-drawn wagons overloaded and in the way. All boxed-in by cliffs of buildings a dozen stories high.

We drifted down State, caught sight of the Dearborn Station off to the west with its red brick twelve-story clock tower, and on 23rd Street cut east. At Michigan, we came to the seven-story Metropole Hotel with its four corners looking like rounded towers of a castle.

By that time Merle and I were thirsty, but not for water. We stopped a likely looking prospect, but he winked and told us to try the hotel and ask for the "Big Fella." I heard him laughing as we went up a couple steps and entered the hotel lobby.

The desk clerk gave us the "stink-eye," so we knew we'd get nothing from him. We got away from the lobby and ducked into a service elevator. There was nobody on the second or third floors, but when we stepped out on the fourth floor, four big gorillas in suits and ties grabbed us.

When they found out we were looking for a drink, they laughed, put us in arm locks, and shoved us into the elevator. On the ground floor they "bum-rushed" us to the door, stopped short, and hit each of us in the gut. They tossed us onto the sidewalk.

I rolled onto my back just as a large man stepped out of a black limousine. He was wearing a dark green suit, vest, and tie, and a bright yellow shirt. On one of his pinkies, there was a huge ring which glittered like a piece of ice nailed to his hand. He was surrounded by more gorillas.

He pinched his fedora down closer to his eyes so he could get a better look at us in the sunlight. "Who are these bums? Chi sono questi barboni?"

One of the gorillas whispered something and the big man laughed. They walked inside.

Just as I was able to stand up, a swarthy guy came out of the hotel and handed me a card. The printing on it read "Room 21 2110 S. Wabash" and in ink "One free drink. Al."

The dark guy pointed north and said, "Two up and one over." Room 21 looked more like a warehouse than a business. The card got us in and a drink of whiskey; we also bought two pints for the trip to Detroit.

We walked Michigan Avenue north and made it to the Central Station with a half hour to spare.

Chicago to Detroit was lubricated with the contents of a bottle hidden in a paper bag. I was feeling pretty good when Merle's cousin Ike met us at the Michigan Central Station. He was not too happy with us as we drove to his apartment, but he didn't say much as he showed us the cots where we'd sleep until we found our own place.

That changed the next morning. Ike was upset about our drinking. "If you show up for an interview smelling of liquor or acting like you've been drinking, forget it. Ford doesn't like drinking, or smoking, for that matter. Get yourselves cleaned up and splash on a little Bay Rum. If you get a job, make sure you hide any liquor you have in your apartment.

Ford sometimes sends guys over to check on you unexpectedly, and if they find booze, you're out.

"It isn't as bad as it was in the old days because Ford is busy fighting the Jews who he thinks cause most of the problems in the world.

"Look presentable, be as honest as you can be about things they can check up on, and you shouldn't have any problem getting hired.

"Once you're in, never show up drunk or you'll be out. Do your boozing at home or a 'speak'. Oh, yeah, don't let the foreman hear you cuss; Ford hates profanity."

Ike was right; we did what he said and were hired on the spot.

In 1917 Henry Ford had begun construction on the Rouge Complex beside the Rouge River in Dearborn. President Wilson and Secretary of the Navy Josephus Daniels urged him to build the anti-submarine patrol vessels known as Eagle boats.

After the war, production switched over to the Fordson lightweight tractors. The coke ovens and foundry produced the castings for the Model T. They were then shipped over to Highland Park where the "T's" were assembled. However, Ford was preparing to put assembly lines for the new Model A in the Rouge Complex in the Dearborn Assembly Plant.

The massive River Rouge Complex sprawled over a square mile right in the middle of Detroit and smelled like new tires and old smoke. Merle and I worked on the assembly line for Fordsons and in 1927 moved over to the Model A assembly line.

Ike's warning had an effect and we swore off booze. At first working on the new auto line was enough, but after a year even moving to different jobs on the line—installing the radiator, over to brake drums, and then to the carburetor—became a drag.

We continued to toil for Ford by day and fell into a bad crowd at night.

I was lonely and Blanche Walker helped fill up my loneliness. She was a dishwater blonde hash slinger near our apartment house. I went back to filling the void in my life with booze, and Blanche and I spent a lot of time in the speakeasies or drinking on Belle Isle in the middle of the Detroit River and enjoying the Conservatory and the botanical garden there. An aquarium was open to the public, and I liked watching the fish, although usually through an alcoholic haze.

Blanche had her own small apartment above the hash house, and I began to spend time there, safe from Ford's agents.

One thing led to another and one evening she announced she was pregnant. We were married in front of a J.P. that weekend. Merle stood up for me; I didn't even know her attendant. Merle moved out of our apartment and Blanche moved in.

As she grew larger, Blanche gave up drinking. After the birth she cuddled and took care of our son as though she were born for it, but when Roger was a month old (she named him after her father, an alcoholic mechanic fired from every job he ever held), she changed. She didn't want to do much of anything and cried a lot for no reason.

We had to leave Roger in the care of an elderly French-Canadian woman named Marie, who lived on our floor. Blanche spent most of her time in bed, sleeping or listening to the radio, especially music or light drama programs.

Sometimes after I ate breakfast and got Roger ready to go to Marie's, I'd hear the radio go on in the bedroom and a voice would say, "Good morning, this is Cheerio," followed by organ music or maybe a poem.

In the evening after we ate supper, I'd do the dishes and get Roger ready for bed, and Blanche would go into the bedroom and click on the radio. She'd listen to music from the *A&P Gypsies*, the *Cliquot Club Eskimos*, the *Smith Brothers*, the *Happy Wonder Bakers* quartette, and *Jones & Hare*. Sometimes she'd listen to variety programs like the *Eveready Hour* or dramas like the *Physical Culture Hour*, *Real Folks*, and *Empire Builders*.

Eventually she gave up the radio and took up Solitaire. She'd sit for hours at the kitchen table with a cup of coffee and a deck of cards, go to bed, get up, and deal out the cards again.

As bad as it was when Blanche was absorbed by the radio and then by the cards, it got worse: she took up drinking again. At first, just a beer or two or perhaps a little wine, but soon her consumption increased, as did her capacity for holding her liquor. It seemed like she wanted to make up for lost time.

She started going out for a "snort" during the day, which was easy because Roger was almost always with Marie. When I wanted to stay home with him at night, she'd run off with a new crowd she'd met. I didn't like that so I'd call Marie and tag after Blanche.

When they weren't in the "speaks," Blanche's crowd liked to rent a boat and drink in the middle of the Detroit River or cross the boundary and drink legally in Windsor. I never did get over the fact that the Canadian city was actually south of Detroit.

The more Blanche drank, the more we fought. Finally, I couldn't take it and told her she had a son and had to take better care of him. She dared me to go out with her that night, so I did, intending to make it the last time for either of us.

We met four guys at the Woodbridge Tavern. After a few drinks Blanche told them I didn't want her hanging out with them anymore. I told her it was time to leave and took her arm. One of the guys said, "Hold on, Buddy," and held up his hand. He spread his forefinger and middle finger and there was a purple tattoo. The other three did the same. If they were part of the Purple Gang, I didn't want to have anything to do with them. I left.

Blanche didn't come home for three days.

Things got worse. Blanche had gone back to work, but her drinking got her canned, and I had to take a second job "pearl diving" on the weekends in the same hash house. That made her sore and she got mean. Her language was filthy and she threw things. She also took up smoking.

Without a job she had more time to watch Roger, so for a few months Marie faded into the background.

One night I climbed the stairs surrounded by the smell of cabbage and cheap meat. I went into the apartment and Roger was crying. I walked to the bathroom where Blanche had been changing him, and the "full-diaper" smell overwhelmed the room.

When she saw me, she picked him up and snarled, "Who wants this boy? Do you want this boy?"

I just had time to say yes, when she threw him at me. I caught him and she pushed by me, smelling of Chesterfields and perspiration. Ten seconds later the door slammed. Roger was screaming.

His little bottom was a rash of pink-red sores.

I remembered something Ma had told me. I got Marie and when she saw Roger, all she could say was "Mon Dieu! Mon Dieu!" I bought some Argo Cornstarch and Vaseline at the corner store, made a paste, and put it on Roger. It took awhile, but he began to settle down.

He fell asleep in my arms and I kept him there all night.

Blanche wasn't back the next morning. I didn't care. During the night I had decided two things. I had only met Roger Walker three times: once in a "speak" and once just after Blanche and I were married when he stopped drinking with his Polish friends long enough to come down from Hantramck. I also saw him in the hospital when he was dying and cursing. I didn't like him. And I wasn't going to call my boy after him.

And we were going home.

I packed what I could and caught Merle before he left the apartment house next door. I told him what I was going to do and asked if I could borrow some money. He was my best friend and he gave me almost all the cash he had saved. I told him it was a loan. We smiled, hugged, and he went to work.

I took half the cash Blanche and I had put in a large envelope and hidden behind the bedroom mirror. I was surprised it was still there. I left the apartment with my Boy, a suitcase, and a backpack. I was ashamed we had no pictures of him. As we passed Marie's room, she came out, smoothed Boy's hair, said, "Adieu, mon petit ange," and retreated behind her door.

We had a second-hand "flivver," but Blanche could have it. We took a streetcar to the Michigan Central Station over in Corktown. As we approached, Boy pointed at the eighteen-story tower. He had a habit of pointing with his pinky finger. After I bought tickets, Boy and I walked around in the crowd, looking at the marble walls and the huge paired columns; it was like being in a temple.

"What's his name?"

A young girl sitting with an older woman spoke from a nearby bench. "I call him 'Boy'."

"I'm Jeanne. We're going to Spokane. My grandmother doesn't speak English. She's French. I think Boy needs to be changed." I was embarrassed I hadn't noticed. "We can do it, if you want."

The older woman was dressed in a white and purple dress with a lavender hat. She and Jeanne took Boy to the women's restroom. I handed them the corn starch and Vaseline paste, explained why, and told them to toss the diaper; I had plenty.

"Purple Grandma" insisted on buying supper for us. She and Jeanne mashed up some carrots and peas and cut up a hamburger into small pieces for Boy and helped him drink milk from a glass.

As I looked at the three, I realized I didn't know my Boy at all. He understood French as easily as English and always looked serious, never smiling. Three years old already; where had I been? I thought back: working and drinking. I cursed my stupidity.

All of us walked down the platform and boarded the night train. As we started to move, I could see a dozen sets of tracks spread out like a flat forest of steel inhabited by black locomotives breathing smoke and steam. Soon, Boy was sleeping beside me in the coach, while Jeanne and Purple Grandma went back to a sleeper.

We pushed west across Michigan, went south along Lake Michigan, switched over to the Illinois Central tracks at Kensington, and pulled into the Central Station south of Grant Park. Boy "pinky-pointed" up at the clock tower and said something like "horloge," which sounded French.

I wanted to stretch my legs so I carried him through Grant Park. The breeze was off the lake and it smelled fresh. We walked Jackson to Canal and entered the Union Station with its huge Great Hall. Boy seemed tense as the city woke up and the noise and traffic increased. Suddenly, I realized that although he had lived in downtown Detroit, he had rarely been outside our building. Hugging him to my shoulder, I silently vowed he would spend a lot of time outdoors in North Dakota. I bought tickets on the Burlington and we sat down to wait. Boy pinky-pointed at the large skylight.

Having taken a taxi, Jeanne and Purple Grandma were already there. We sat with them. Boy played with Jeanne and whispered with the grandmother. They were working on something.

Late in the morning we headed for the tracks and boarded the *Empire Builder* with motive power from a 4-8-4 locomotive which had the air pumps mounted in front of the smoke box and with a green and silver paint scheme.

After a late breakfast, we settled in and the *Builder* ate up the miles of Illinois and Wisconsin. We shared Boy. Sometimes Jeanne and he would go for a walk.

After we crossed into Minnesota, we stopped at the Union Depot in St. Paul, chugged high over the Mississippi on the Stone Arch Bridge, picked up more passengers in Minneapolis, and headed for home on the Great Northern.

We went to the dining car and wrote out our orders for supper. The special was turkey and all the trimmings which made our little table smell just like Ma's dining room on Thanksgiving. I insisted on paying.

I mentioned that I was worried Boy hadn't needed to be changed, but Jeanne said, "Just wait," and smiled. A half hour later Boy tugged on my arm. "Allez, papa, allez."

"He wants you to take him to the . . . restroom."

"What?"

"Grandmother and I have trained him." She looked at Purple Grandma. "Grand-mère, il est prêt."

The older woman smiled and gestured towards the rear of the car. "Aller."

When Boy and I returned, I shook Purple Grandma's hand and gave Jeanne a kiss on the forehead. "Merci, merci," but if I had said it a thousand times, it wouldn't have been enough.

We pulled into Menninger in the dark. We hugged our quick goodbyes. Jeanne cried. I asked the agent if we could spend the night in the station. I didn't want to wake the folks.

"You're Boss's boy."

"Yessir."

"I guess it'll be all right."

I pushed two benches together and made a bed for Boy with my coat.

After we woke up, we waited for the morning to warm, washed, and left the station.

I walked up Dakota Street, carrying Boy. I didn't turn on Villard because I didn't want to pass the Bank and take the chance of running into Grandpa Bear or Boss. That could come later. I turned east on Lamborn and headed up the hill, Boy enthusiastic about the red fire engines they were washing in front of the City Hall and me about the smells coming from the Golden Crust Bakery.

When we passed the Norwegian Lutheran Church, I looked over the hedge at our house. The coast was clear. I carried Boy onto the porch and told him to stand by the door. "Now, don't move no matter what, O.K.?" He nodded, but looked apprehensive.

I opened the screen and knocked on the oak door. I ran to the edge of the porch, jumped off, and hid behind the corner of the house.

When I looked at Boy, he appeared so solemn, but he stood straight and tall.

Suddenly, he looked up and the door opened. Ma looked around and then down. She had a wisp of hair that had worked out of her baking kerchief and a smudge of flour on her cheek. "Well, what do you want, little boy? Are you lost?"

Boy stared up at her and then looked over at me. Ma's eyes followed and her mouth dropped. I stepped up onto the porch. "Hi, Ma. His name is Roger, but I call him Boy. He's your grandson."

We moved together in an embrace. The apple pie smell from the house mixed with the White Lilac Perfume of Ma.

I looked over Ma's shoulder. Boy pinky-pointed at Ma and smiled.

MEATBALL BIRDS

always liked red-winged blackbirds. Most black birds I didn't care for and I hated one kind, but red wings were special.

Brewer's blackbirds were all right; they just hunted through the grass, looking for something to eat, never saying a word.

If I could get a shot off at a crow, I'd take it. Even if I was out looking for gophers, and I heard that mocking "caw-caw," I'd keep an eye peeled just in case that black devil would come within range.

Grackles had a nice purply sheen in the sunlight, but the way they "graaaked" and croaked at me from my own trees, like they were mad at me for walking in my own yard, made me dislike them, and so did the way they stuck their bills straight up when another grackle got too close, not even friendly.

Brown-headed cowbirds were the ones I hated because they laid their eggs in the nests of another species. When the cowbird chicks hatched, they would force the young of the other mother bird out of the nest, and that mother would become the unsuspecting adoptive parent.

Yellow-headed blackbirds were more colorful, but their "craaack" and "screeack" were ugly sounds. One spring I'd been down by some trees just off the GN mainline, and I heard this loud ratchety screech that began low and went high. I thought it was an eagle or maybe a hawk, when a yellow head appeared out of the foliage and off it went, carried away by chevroned white and black wings. That piercing cry scared me, so maybe that's why I didn't like the yellow heads.

Red wings were different. The males trilling whistle was almost like water running over pebbles. I liked their red shoulder patches and yellow wing bars. When I was out gopher hunting near a marsh, sometimes I'd take some time off and sit and listen to the red wings, trilling in the cattails and showing off their red patches.

I liked red wings and that made it so strange when I joined Bobby Swain in his campaign.

Bobby's Dad was Francis, who was called "Frank" or sometimes "Cowboy" because he had a bow-legged walk. He ran the airport north of town, Carroll Field. Bobby's older brother Phillip helped his Dad. Bobby was like an afterthought, ten years younger than Phil, whom he idolized.

I was only five, so I didn't know anything about Frank Swain or his work, but Grandpa Boss was the bank president, so he spent a lot of time checking up on the money the bank had put into the airport. Grandpa seemed to know just about everything that went on in town, and I learned about the Swains from him.

Somehow Frank Swain got hold of a Stearman Model 75. It was a biplane and had been used as a military trainer by the U.S. Army Air Corps. The rumor was that it had crashed and Frank got it at a bargain price, but when it showed up on an NP flatcar and was unloaded, none of the parts that showed from under the canvas covering looked damaged.

It was loaded on a wagon, pulled north by a team of horses to the airport, and rolled into a hanger. Phil was almost sixteen and got right to work on the Stearman. He and his Dad had done a lot of work on airplanes and their engines, so he knew what he was doing.

They worked on the seven-cylinder, air-cooled, uncowled radial engine that could generate 220 horsepower and hit 135 miles per hour. Grandpa was there the day they fired it up, and he enjoyed telling how it started coughing its way to life and then burst into a loud, smooth roar that shattered the peace of the hanger and endangered uncovered eardrums.

The Swains replaced some of the wood ribs and spars in the wings and in the center section with lumber from a local yard and some aluminum panels with the help of "Tinner" Trent. They did have to send to Wichita for a new tail-wheel shock strut and support assembly.

The Stearman had tandem cockpits, and after it was airworthy, Frank would take the front one, Phil would sit in the rear, and up they'd go, with Frank teaching his son how to fly.

Frank was a natural flier. After Woodrow Wilson got Congress to declare war on Germany in 1917, Frank joined the 94th Aero Squadron at Kelly Field, Texas. The fliers were transferred to Hazlehurst Field in New York in October and to France a month later.

At first he flew a French-built Nieuport 28, a bi-plane with twin synchronized machine guns, and then piloted a SPAD S.XIII with two Vickers .303 machine guns when that plane became available. Although he didn't shoot down any enemy planes, he was credited with one observation balloon, which was considered a more dangerous target because the Jerries defended them with anti-aircraft guns, fighter planes, and barrage balloons.

Frank told Grandpa he thought he was just ready to hit his stride as a pilot when he was shot down by a Fokker D.VII and spent the rest of the war in a French hospital.

After his two broken legs healed, he returned to the States. On board the same ship was John Hawthorne, a fellow pilot who was also recovering from war wounds. After they rammed around New York City, working odd jobs, they hitched a freight to Buffalo, where they bought a surplus Curtiss JN-4 biplane that had been used as a trainer for the Army.

The "Jenny," as the model was known, was powered by a Curtiss OX-5 V8 engine with ninety horsepower and was capable of seventy-five miles per hour. They worked their way along the southern shore of Lake Erie, giving joy rides in the Jenny, sometimes using a farmer's field as a runway. When they were close enough, they would fly out over the lake, thrilling the passenger, especially if she were female, with a view of the lake water as it changed from green to blue, or if there was a lot of sand along the shore, from green to brown to blue.

At Sandusky, Ohio, they began flying further out over the lake to Kelley's Island or even to Pelee Island. One of their joy riders was a young woman named Norma. Both men fell for her.

She paid for her first ride, sitting in the rear cockpit, with John in the forward pit. To impress her, he flew over the Cedar Point Resort and buzzed the Hotel Breakers, continued out over Lake Erie, and on the return flight buzzed the steamer *G.A. Boeckling*.

After hearing Norma say how thrilling the ride had been, Frank was determined not to be outdone by his rival, so he gave her a free ride. He headed for Cedar Point and buzzed a roller coaster called the Leap Frog

Scenic Railway, gained altitude, and pretended to strafe the Leap the Dips roller coaster, coming so close he almost clipped the cars.

Norma was even more thrilled, and John was preparing to give her a third flight when the sheriff and his deputies showed up and put them all under arrest. Norma's father was an attorney and real estate mogul and bailed them out after the local magistrate imposed a heavy bond because his grandson had been riding the Leap the Dips.

After they pled guilty and paid their fines, the men left Sandusky and Norma went with them. She was one of the new liberated post-war women with bobbed hair, rolled stockings, and short skirts, and did whatever she felt like doing.

The men had always flown in the Jenny from town to town, but there was no room for three, so Norma's father bought her a 1920 REO Roadster, and she drove through Indiana and Illinois and into Iowa, stopping wherever the men decided to try and make some money.

Outside Mason City another Jenny was dropping leaflets. Norma picked one up and showed the men when they met. The next day they, along with hundreds of others, followed the directions on the leaflet. They paid five dollars and ended up in a field. The pilot of the Jenny took off and went through a series of maneuvers, such as loop-the-loops, barrel rolls, and buzzing the crowd. The showstopper was the female wing-walker whose antics on top of the speeding Jenny took the crowd's collective breath away.

It also gave Norma an idea which the men reluctantly accepted.

She had a local seamstress make her a red, white, and blue costume, bought a pair of goggles, and began practicing wing-walking.

As the Jenny and the REO made their way into Minnesota, Norma, Frank, and John had become official barnstormers, maneuvering the Jenny into loops, barrel rolls, half rolls, half loops, turns, and dives, as well as buzzing the paying customers.

However, as the show moved along, Norma became more daring and was soon the acknowledged star, with her own billing as "Ariadne, the Daring Queen of the Wing." To begin her performance she would just stand on the wing, strapped to a couple vertical braces, but later would slide from one side of the plane to the other, holding a guy-wire. By the time they shut down for the winter, she had added something else: a headstand.

The trio spent the winter in Minneapolis. The men got jobs at the airport, Wold-Chamberlain Field, the new name for Speedway Field, and Norma worked as a salesclerk in Dayton's Department Store on the corner of Nicollet and Seventh.

She also spent some time working out some new wing-walking routines, and since one of them involved two planes, they bought a second Jenny and were ready to roll in the spring.

They decided to follow the Great Northern Railway tracks northwest of the Twin Cities. At first they didn't try any of the new routines, so the people of Maple Grove, Rogers, Albertville, and Monticello saw the old Ariadne, but at Enfield, Norma was transformed. She still had her red, white, and blue costume and did her old tricks. The changes came when she crossed over from Frank's Jenny to John's plane while their wing tips were almost touching, then she transferred back again. The planes roared apart and Norma parachuted, trailing long red, white, and blue streamers. Almost the entire village of Enfield had turned out, and they were the first to see Ariadne turn into "Miss Liberty."

After their performances outside Hastys, Clearwater, and St. Augusta, they pulled into St. Cloud and had their planes repainted red, white, and blue. They also had new leaflets printed, headlining "Miss Liberty and her Amazing American Air Aces," although neither pilot had made a kill during the war.

They rented a field outside Waite Park, buzzed the town, and dropped their leaflets. A crowd headed for the field, including a bunch of men from the Great Northern shops. Norma added a new opening for her act. She was strapped onto a metal brace, unfurled an American flag, and waved it as the Jenny flew ten feet off the ground in front of the cheering spectators. She also added another stunt before she did her wing-walking: as the Jenny thundered past the crowd, she used a .22 rifle to break a large balloon centered as the bull's eye in a target.

Miss Liberty was a huge hit, and the crowds grew as they put on their air show near St. Joseph, Collegeville, Avon, Albany, Freeport, and Melrose.

In the lakes country northwest of Sauk Center, they branched off, flying between the towns on the Soo Line to the southwest and the Northern Pacific to the northeast, making money until they ran across towns where a twelve-plane barnstorming "flying circus" had performed a week earlier and dried up local enthusiasm for aerobatic stunts and joy rides.

They moved south to the Soo Line and worked their way to the North Dakota border, where they followed the Milwaukee Road tracks south to Ortonville. A couple months earlier a blast of wind had flipped a plane that had just landed at McNiff Field onto its back, so hundreds of people turned out to see them, many of the patrons probably hoping for a similar incident. If so, they were disappointed, but they did contribute to the largest gate receipts yet.

They gave hundreds of rides over Big Stone Lake, flying low over islands named Skeleton, Mud, Kite, Frying Pan, Pancake, Manhattan, and Goose. With plenty of money in their pockets, they flew to Milbank and put on shows along the Milwaukee tracks up to Sisseton. Then they hopped up to the Soo Line and did performances at Rosholt, went east to White Rock, and followed the Milwaukee north to Brixton.

From there they went along the Great Northern northwest to Swan Creek, moved east along the Northern Pacific to Fargo, south with the Milwaukee back to Brixton, then north following the GN on the Minnesota side to Fargo, where they put on a show, taking off and landing at the Fairgrounds, and stayed the winter.

John got a job as a charman in the Norgaard Hospital on Fifth, while Frank worked as an usher in the Liberty Theater on Broadway, and Norma clerked in Jones Candies, also on Broadway.

They took two rooms on the third floor of the Donaldson Hotel above the Odd Fellows Lodge on the northeast corner of Broadway and First Avenue.

Throughout the winter the men competed for the affection of Norma. On Christmas Eve John proposed and was rejected. Frank proposed on New Year's Eve with the same result.

As spring approached, they began discussing plans for the upcoming season.

John wanted to repaint the Jennies. One would be the plane of the ace Georges Guynemer, who had fifty-three kills, complete with the blue, white, and red bull's eye roundel of the French Air Service on the wings and tail and "Vieux Charles" on the fuselage. If they decided to go into Canada, they could redo it to be the plane Canadian ace Billy Bishop flew with his seventy-two kills in the British Royal Flying

Corps, changing the French roundel into the British one with a red, white, and blue bull's eye.

The other plane would be painted to resemble the Fokker D.VII of the German flyer Ernst Udet, including the German Iron Cross identification insignia, the name of Udet's childhood sweetheart, Eleanor "Lo" Zink, and the message "Du doch nicht" on the fuselage. Udet had sixty-two kills with the German Imperial Army Air Service, far fewer than the "Red Baron," Manfred von Richtofen, with his eighty kills. When Frank questioned him about it, John replied that Richtofen flew a Fokker Dr.1 tri-plane, and the Jenny only had two wings.

Frank argued they could still use the Jenny as the Baron's plane because earlier in the war Richtofen was in the cockpit of biplanes, such as the Albatros D.II and D.III.

John countered that he wanted to recreate the famous dogfight between Guynemer in his SPAD S.VII and Udet in his Fokker. After the two had ripped through various aerobatic maneuvers and exchanged bursts of machine gun fire, Udet's gun jammed, and he couldn't clear it. Seeing his opponent was defenseless, Guynemer flew by, waved, and headed back to his base.

While John and Frank played the roles of the two aces in the sky, Norma would be on the ground and describe the action for the crowd.

Frank had come up with his own idea for Norma. They would fix a trapeze which could be lowered below the wheels of the Jenny. Norma would work her way down the side of the plane and onto the trapeze. She would hang upside down by her knees, Frank would fly low to the ground, and Miss Liberty would snatch an American flag waving from a ten-foot pole.

John argued it was too dangerous. Norma didn't take sides, so the dogfight and the trapeze were both discarded as they prepared for their new season.

However, another conflict arose. Frank wanted to follow the Northern Pacific tracks west out of Fargo and attract crowds in Worthington and Kingston; John wanted to work the Great Northern towns north to Grand Forks and then either swing west to Sacred Water or continue on into Canada.

Norma finally stepped in with a compromise: they would follow the Carver Cut-off northwest. After twenty-four performances, they reached Menninger.

The town fathers were preparing to put an airfield north of the Jacques River on land donated by Charlie Carroll, and they thought that allowing the barnstormers to use the site would promote public support.

A large and enthusiastic crowd crossed the river for the show, but just as he touched down, Frank's foot bar that controlled his rudder broke, and they had to lay over while it was repaired. They drove the REO to the Oleson House and checked in.

That evening in the dining room Frank unveiled a new stunt: John would drive the Roadster with Norma standing in it. Frank would fly a Jenny just overhead with a rope ladder dangling from the plane. Norma would climb onto the ladder; the plane and the vehicle would turn around; and Norma would descend and end up in the car in front of the crowd.

John seemed to think it was possible, but Norma made an announcement that broke up the act. She said she was tired—tired of sleeping on the lower wing on nice nights or in flea-bag hotels in wet weather, tired of trying to pick her way across the countryside on dirt roads while the men flew, tired of not seeing her Dad, and tired of putting her life on the line just about every day. She wanted to go home.

The men were stunned. They started to argue her out of it, but she ended that when she added a kicker—she was going to have a baby.

She realized the baby could be either man's, but after careful consideration, she was convinced it had to be John's. Besides, he always seemed more concerned about her than Frank did.

She turned to John and said she was ready to accept his Christmas Eve proposal, if he was willing to return to Sandusky with her.

The men were silent, but John recovered first and quickly became Norma's fiancée.

They decided to do one more show, so the next afternoon they drove across the Jacques and up the hill. Before they took off, Norma and John kissed for good luck and it worked for them. Frank didn't have the luck. Maybe it was because he had tossed and turned all night, thinking of what had happened in the dining room; maybe it was a wind gust; perhaps it was just one of those things that happen to flyers. Whatever it was, he came in too hot, hit the ground, and flipped the Jenny on her back.

Frank was rushed to the three-story, white frame hospital on Tilden Avenue, where the doctor set his broken leg. Norma and John visited him in one of the six private rooms on the first floor. After paying the doctor and the hospital administrator enough for Frank's care, they told him they were leaving in the REO. They signed the good Jenny and the wrecked one over to him. John shook his hand, Norma hugged him, and they were gone.

After he was released, the town officials signed him to be the manager of the new airport, although there was some dissension: one city commissioner complained instead of hiring the pilot who crashed, they should employ the one who hadn't.

Regardless, Frank bought a 1920 Ford Model T pickup and went to work at the airport.

That wasn't all he was working on. He had met a young nurse, Marjorie Fowler, while he was in the hospital. After Marjorie graduated from Menninger High School, she had gone to Kingston, obtained a nursing degree from the hospital there, and returned to her home town.

She was a shy girl, but when Frank winked at her from his bed, she appeared flattered. After he got out, she began to see him on a regular basis.

Suddenly, they were standing in front of a justice of the peace, and soon it was noticeable that Marjorie was gaining weight. She quit her job and spent most of the winter in the couple's room in the Oleson. The baby came so fast that the doctor had to deliver him right in the room.

It took quite awhile for Marjorie to get over her shame, which increased when the local newspaper, *The Messenger*, carried an announcement with a typo: "On Monday an 8 lb. sin was born to Mr. and Mrs. Frank Swain."

The quickie wedding never bothered Frank, and neither did the "too-soon" birth of the son they named Phillip after her father. When Frank would take advantage of the nice spring weather and push Phillip around in a perambulator, he would introduce him to passers-by as his "seven-month wonder."

The Swain family moved into a house down Glen Haven Hill, so Frank had an easy drive of about a mile to the airport.

A year later a daughter they named Polly was born, but she was a puny thing and was dead within two weeks. After the burial no one ever heard Frank or Marjorie mention her. Frank concentrated on building up the airport, Marjorie devoted herself to being a good homemaker, and both of them doted on little Phil.

The three of them seemed such a complete unit that it was a surprise that Bobby came along. Ten years younger than Phillip, it was as if he were the family postscript. As soon as he was old enough to walk, he began to follow Phil around like a puppy. When Phil began going to the airport to help his Dad with a new hanger or to patch and level a runway or mow the grass, Bobby was lost until his big brother returned home.

When Bobby was five, Frank began taking him along, and the two brothers worked together at the airport, at least on the jobs where Bobby could help. He washed the Stearman so many times it was a wonder he didn't scrub off the paint, which was green, instead of the original blue and yellow. Phil had repainted it to honor his new radio hero, the Green Hornet, although his favorite radio programs were *The Air Adventures of Jimmie Allen* and later *Captain Midnight*, the story of a former World War I pilot and his fight against evil. Sometimes we'd listen to the Captain with Phil, while we drank our chocolaty Ovaltine. It would start with a church bell tolling midnight, the breakneck dive of an airplane, and an echo chamber voice: "Cappp—taaiinn Midnight!"

Phil's first solo flight was delayed because as he began taxiing, he clipped the wings on a building due to the fact that the Stearman had somewhat limited forward visibility.

Repairs took a couple weeks, and then Phil put a leather flying cap and goggles over his black hair, snugged a red silk scarf around his neck, hitched up his pants, climbed onto the waist-high lower wing, and settled into the rear cockpit. Frank stood near the left gear leg, cranked away until the flywheel on the inertia starter screamed, pulled out the engagement lever, and the big radial roared into life.

Frank backed off and moved to the concrete apron, nervously standing on one foot and then the other. I was there that day, next to Frank, while Bobby was in his pedal-push airplane. You pedaled it like a tricycle, but it had a metal fuselage, wings, and tail, so it looked like a plane. It had two fake wheels in front and in between them you could see the big wheel. Instead of having one wheel in back, it had two small ones, so I didn't think it looked that much like a plane. Maybe I was jealous.

After Phil got comfortable, he moved the plane out slowly and was careful to avoid any obstacles. He used the steerable tail wheel to maneuver onto the runway, waved to us, and moved away. He gunned the engine and the *Green Hornet* lifted off long before I thought it would.

As Phil took off, Bobby pedaled his "plane" to the end of the concrete and cheered, just as Frank and I did.

Phil had agreed with Frank to circle the field and then land, but that wasn't Phil once he got airborne. He buzzed over the town, making certain that his Mom saw him, then banked and made a long, leisurely turn, sweeping around to the southwest, west, northwest, and headed back over the railroad tracks.

At first it seemed he was coming in too fast, but he put the nose up and the *Green Hornet* lost speed, hit on the main gear, bounced once, and settled onto the grass. Phil taxied back to the hanger, jumped out with a grin, and was surrounded. All of us were hugging him and he was telling Frank that he had seen his Mom waving. Frank was so happy, he didn't say anything about their broken agreement.

Not that it would have made a whole lot of difference to Phil, who did what he wanted to do as soon as he left the earth.

The Swains bought another Stearman, but it had the larger Lycoming R-680 engine which generated 225 horsepower. They replaced some of the fabric with a metal skin, attached a hopper below the fuselage, and took up crop dusting.

Despite growing legal restrictions on pilots, Phil flew when and how he wanted to.

After the Gold Star Highway was constructed, an overpass was built over the Great Northern tracks southeast of town. The overhead roadbed was held up by two large concrete supports. One morning Phil loaded Bobby and me into the airport's 1934 International panel truck and drove south on the Gold Star. He pulled off on a gravel road and parked. We got out and walked to the GN tracks. When we got to the overpass, Phil produced a large tape measure. He had Bobby and me hold the tape on one support while he crossed the tracks and read the tape against the other one. When he yelled across, "Seventy feet," he seemed pleased.

We drove back into town and he asked us if we wanted something. Of course we did. He bought us a pop and candy bar apiece and we went back to the overpass. He tucked us up on the north side under the road bed, told us to stay put, and left.

We ate and drank and watched a couple freights chug by, covering our ears from the locomotive noise and breathing their smoke.

Just when we were getting worried that Phil had left us on a "snipe hunt," we heard an airplane. Off to the west the *Green Hornet* dropped out of the sky and leveled off above the tracks. Suddenly, it dove and swooped under the overpass, its motor roaring ten times louder than the locomotives, with Phil grinning and waving as he thundered by.

Bobby and I charged down to the tracks and stood waving at him. As he banked, he came around and waggled his wings after he saw us. We were jumping and yelling at our hero. Bobby was screaming, "That's my brother! That's my brother!" and I felt Phil was like my brother, too.

When he came to get us in the International, we hugged him and he hugged us back. His brown leather flight jacket felt warm in the sun.

That wasn't his only air exploit. In downtown Menninger there were two ancient grain elevators that had been condemned and were going to be demolished. They stood in tandem along the NP tracks with probably sixty feet of space between them. One July Fourth just as the parade was winding down Chicago, the *Green Hornet* buzzed in low over the store roofs and flashed between the two elevators. Phil then banked over the courthouse and came back, ripping holes in the air. He zoomed even lower between the elevators and cut a quick climb over the store fronts.

The parade halted while people stared. Our family was there, and as the *Hornet* banked south over the post office and then roared over Chicago, heading for the airport, the crowd seemed suspended in disbelief and then broke into cheers and applause. The town loved Phil as much as Bobby and I did.

Stevens County had put a bounty on varmints, so wolves, coyotes, and fox were fair game. Of course, there were no wolves left, and the coyotes were confined to some of the wilder regions of glacial hills in the eastern and northern parts of the county, but fox were everywhere.

Frank and Phil bought a Piper J-3 Cub. Although its wing span was slightly longer than the *Green Hornet's*, it was a smaller plane, and its flat-four power plant only generated sixty-five horsepower for a top speed of around eighty-seven miles per hour.

They replaced the wheels with a pair of skis and after the first snowfall took the Cub up. They'd find tracks and follow them. When they found the fox, Frank would swoop low and slow and Phil would blast it. They had a retriever named Gold Dust, and after they landed, she'd jump out and bring back the fox. If the terrain was rough, and they had to land a distance away, Goldie was especially valuable.

If the snow was deep enough, the hunting was easier because they'd run the fox until it was exhausted, land, and shoot it.

At county fair time, they would fly down to Caseyville or over to Fishtown and charge the fairgoers for rides.

When Phil wasn't flying or working on planes or the airport, he liked to shoot gophers. Sometimes he'd take Bobby and me north to Eternal Rest Cemetery and kill gophers with his .22. We'd cut off their tails because the county paid three cents apiece.

Before he got his .22, Phil had a Daisy b-b gun. He would target shoot with it, and he also used it on sparrows and gophers, but he'd have to be close and it would take a lucky head shot to kill one of the striped rodents.

There were some gophers that would burrow alongside the runways. Phil would let Bobby have the Daisy and he'd walk a runway until he saw one. Phil made him a blind out of an apple crate. He'd poke the Daisy through a hole and wait for the gopher to come out of its burrow, even if it took a half hour.

Sometimes I would sit with Bobby, but you had to wait and wait for the striper to appear. Even then you couldn't shoot because it would just fall down the hole, so we'd sit some more until it moved away and then Bobby'd aim for an eye.

Most of the time it became so tedious for me, that I'd wander back to the hanger or the office and try to help Phil or Frank.

That is, until I got a Daisy of my own. Then hunting was more fun.

At one of his birthday parties, Phil invited every member of his class and some other friends, and they all brought him packages of b-b's. His mother couldn't figure it out until Susan Tracy informed her that Phil had told each of the guests he wanted b-b's. The next year, as a joke, everyone brought b-b's again.

That was the birthday Frank bought him a .22, so the joke was on the guests, sort of. The b-b's went up on a shelf in the basement, along with the Daisy.

One summer day in 1941, Phil became an even bigger hero to Bobby and me. Out of the clear blue sky he asked us if we'd like to go up. He put cotton batting in our ears, Bobby and I put on oversize flight jackets in the hanger, and Phil boosted us into the front cockpit, which was so big both of us had plenty of room. He gave each of us a huge pair of goggles, belted us in, and told us to stay put. I was gawking at all the castings, the large control stick, and the cast aluminum rudder pedals, when suddenly the Stearman began to move. Phil had grabbed a prop blade and jerked down, firing up the motor.

He dodged around the wings, jumped onto the waist-high lower wing, and vaulted into the rear cockpit. Quickly he adjusted the seat and checked the rudder pedals. He took hold of that big control stick and we were taxiing.

As Phil powered up the motor, the tail lifted, and then we were off the ground and climbing easily, but slowly, leaving the runway behind.

We headed for town, but Bobby and I were stuck so far down in the cockpit, we couldn't see, so we unbuckled and peered over the side. I looked back at Phil, but he didn't seem too concerned.

The river flashed below, the sun glinting off the water, and Bobby pointed at his home. Phil headed over my house, and I ducked down after seeing Mom in the backyard. I knew she wouldn't be too pleased at seeing me with "Crazy Phil," and I never told her about my aerial exploit.

Bobby and I were fascinated by the mosaic of roofs and yards and the green and black checkerboard of the growing and summer-fallowed fields. At least I know I was.

We followed the GN tracks southeast to the river and then traced that blue, twisting ribbon back to town. We passed over the three bridges, the railroad bridge, and the dark water of the reservoir and, too soon for me, banked right and came into the airport from the northwest. Phil signaled us to buckle in and then put the nose over.

I had been hoping for a dive or a roll or a loop, but I was more than satisfied when Phil put her down on the main gear, hopped once, and settled on the grass.

On the ground Bobby and I waited until Phil hangered the plane, then when we were all out, we ran over and hugged his legs and tried to tell him everything we saw, but since we were shouting out our excitement at the same time, he put his hands over our mouths until we quieted down.

He said I could keep the goggles, but I told him no because if Mom saw them, she might ask questions, and if I lied, she'd know it, and everything would come out. Maybe I'd never be allowed to go to the airport again.

Of course, I was hoping to go up with Bobby and Phil, or maybe just Phil, again, but the chance never came.

Phil had graduated from Menninger High that May. In the fall he headed for the State School of Science in Brixton. He was home once in October and for Thanksgiving.

The first time, Bobby called me on the phone and told me Phil was back. It was a cool fall day, but I felt warm when I ran down the Glen Haven Hill. When I got to the Swain's place, Phil and Frank were raking leaves, and Bobby was loading them in a wagon and dumping them on a growing brown and yellow pile near the alley.

The week before, my brother Boy had wanted me to do some raking with him, but it was too much work, and I sneaked off with half the yard to go. With Phil raking it was different and I pitched right in.

We stopped once for a couple of cookies and a drink, but mostly just kept at it until all the leaves were heaped in a giant pile. Frank went inside and Phil walked into the garage. He came out with a gasoline can and sprinkled some over the pile. He made us stand back, struck a match, and woosh! the leaves flamed up.

Phil loved fire, and I loved standing by him and feeling his hand on my shoulder and the warmth and smell of the burning leaves. I looked up at him and the flames were reflecting off his face.

I didn't see him at Thanksgiving, but I hoped I would at Christmas. Then came December 7.

The day after Pearl Harbor saw a flood of college boys heading for Fargo to enlist, but Phil caught the *Empire Builder* and headed for Menninger. He had telegrammed his folks and they met the train at the station. He gave them one of his bags, hugged and kissed Bobby and his mother, shook hands with his Dad, and told them he had to get to California because the Japs might try to invade there. He boarded the train and the *Builder* chugged away to the west.

When Bobby told me that Phil had been in town, I was hurt that he hadn't gotten me up, so I could have said goodbye, too, but the *Builder* arrived in the early hours of the morning, so Mom wouldn't have let me go anyway. Still I was cool to Bobby for a couple of weeks until he showed me a letter from Phil in which he said to say hello to me. Then we were friends again.

The GN High Line took Phil to Tacoma and then south. After he transferred to the Southern Pacific, he got off at San Francisco and enlisted in the Army Air Corps.

He ended up at Gardner Field, a newly activated training base nine miles southeast of Taft in the foothills of Kern County. He trained with PT-17's which were Model 75 Stearman Kaydets, so he was right at home, and then with the more advanced single-wing Vultee BT-13 Valiants that had two-way radio communication with the base, something new to Phil.

Many of the pilot trainees had participated in the Civilian Pilot Training Program or had been involved in the Army Air Corps Aviation Cadet Program, so they got their wings, commissions as Second Lieutenant, and assignments ahead of Phil. When he was commissioned, he was transferred to Luke Field near Phoenix, which was the AAF Flying Training Command.

He trained in an AT-6, sometimes known as the T-6 Texas, a single-wing, single engine plane manufactured by North American.

After his commission he was transferred to Alaska, where he flew a Bell P-39 Aircobra armed with one 37 mm cannon and two .50 caliber machine guns out of Nome. When he came home on leave, he told his folks he was so bored he was going to ask for a transfer where there was some action.

He got his wish and was assigned to Hamilton Field north of San Francisco, where he trained in a Lockheed P-38 Lightning. The P-38 had twin engines, two .50 caliber machine guns, two .30 caliber

Browning machine guns, and a 37 mm cannon, all in the nose. The Lightning had twin booms with the pilot sitting in a central cockpit. The Germans called it the "fork-tailed devil," while the Japs said it was "two planes, one pilot."

In the spring of 1942, he was temporarily grounded for flying under the Golden Gate Bridge.

The Far East Air Force had been driven out of the Philippines by the Japanese and moved to Australia, where it was reorganized and renamed the Fifth Air Force. Phil joined a Fighter Group there. After that we didn't hear from him; it was like he'd dropped off the face of the earth.

That didn't stop Bobby, however. He got a large map of the South Pacific and Eastern Asia with Japan and the territory under its control colored red and with the war flag of the Imperial Japanese Army and its big red meatball in the center with its sixteen red rays and tacked it to a piece of plywood and kept it in his room. It was scary when I would see Japan, Manchukuo, parts of China, French Indo-China, Thailand, Burma, the Philippines, British Malaya, the Dutch East Indies, most of New Guinea, Formosa, and many smaller islands showing up red. Would anyone be able to stop the Japs?

Bobby'd get information on the war from newspapers, magazines, the Sunday supplements, radio, and the movie newsreels at the Blackstone—Movietone News, Universal Newsreel, Paramount News, Pathé News, and the March of Time. Then he'd move little paper ships, soldiers, and one airplane he'd made to new locations on the map. The pilot of the plane had black hair, so I knew who it represented, but its location on the map was always a guess. In the fall of 1942, he was able to take a blue crayon and begin to color over some small areas of red as the Allies counterattacked.

When Mr. Pomeroy, the Menninger High School science teacher, organized a series of scrap drives, Bobby became a dedicated volunteer.

In May 1942 students rallied to a call by FDR to collect rubber for the war effort. The president suggested collecting everything from old tires to garden hoses to raincoats. Bobby and I collected a bunch of old rubber heels from Hans Vogler at his shoe shop over on Dunnell. Mr. Vogler was only too happy to show he was a patriotic German-American. We brought the heels to the Standard Station.

There were some old tires people had tossed into a little marsh near the GN-NP crossover. Bobby and I waded in and pulled the tires out, with the red wings scolding us from the cattails. After we scraped off the mud with a stick, we rolled them one at a time to the Standard.

Hans Skaar was a farmer who'd worked at the Goodyear Tire plant in Akron, Ohio, before his Dad retired and he took over the farm. One Saturday night he got to talking in Gimpy's Holiday Spot and informed his listeners that collecting rubber was a waste of time: rubber's chemistry was so complex and making recycled rubber into a finished product was so expensive, and recycled rubber was so inferior to natural rubber that the stuff collected would end up discarded. Gimpy kicked him out and the next Saturday he apologized and never spoke about rubber again.

When I heard what Skaar had said, my enthusiasm for collecting rubber dropped, but Bobby only renewed his efforts. He made a sign for the back of his wagon, "Save Some Rubber and Help My Brother Slap A Jap," and continued his search.

He also went all over town, collecting old newspapers, hauling them in his wagon to the office of the *Menninger Messenger*. The owner/publisher/editor H.H. Hemmingsen told Bobby and me that the papers would be used to make paperboard as packing material for shells, and that he would get the papers to a salvage station. That made me eager to get my hands on any old copies of the *Fargo Forum*, the *Minneapolis Star*, the *Minneapolis Tribune*, or the *Messenger*.

When Bobby heard that glycerin from fat and grease was used in making gunpowder, he was off on a new crusade, with me in tow.

We cleaned out some large cans and left them with the housewives in our neighborhoods. When the cans were filled with cooking grease, we'd pick them up and take them to the Menninger Meat Market, where we got four cents a pound. We used the money to buy savings stamps for ten cents each, trying to save enough to purchase an $18.75 defense bond.

Bobby and I went to Fatty's Eat Shop, the Burger Baron . . . and Fries, and the Menninger Café, as well as the kitchens of the Oleson House and the Hotel Logan, and persuaded their owners to save us their cooking grease. Bobby's Dad tipped a large barrel on its side, welded on some wheels and a steering handle, cut an opening and put a cover on it, and we were in business. We quickly learned to wear old clothes on collecting day because no matter how careful we were, we ended up greasy.

The Nakamura family owned the Menninger Café. A few months after FDR's infamous Executive Order 9066 interning Japanese in camps, Yoshiro Nakamura was arrested and taken to the Ft. Lincoln internment camp south of Bismarck. He and his wife Sumiko were Issei, Japanese who had emigrated from the old country. Their two children, Taro and Katsumi, were Nisei or second-generation Japanese-Americans.

They mounted a campaign to get Yoshiro released, and with the support of the Menninger business community, he returned home after two months. The only opposition came from a farmer northeast of town whose son had been badly wounded at Pearl Harbor.

After the internment the Nakamuras were even more anxious than Mr. Vogler to show their patriotism. They urged their customers to save grease and put a sign by the cash register which stated that three pounds of fat contained enough glycerin for a pound of gunpowder.

Our most successful campaign, however, was the scrap metal drive.

We had just started collecting old aluminum pots and pans when we read that only aluminum with no other metals or alloys could be used in the manufacture of airplanes, so we dropped that idea.

Tin was another matter. The government informed the public about the importance of tin: in instrument panels, bearings, and as solder in airplanes; for syrettes for hypodermics; and for shipping food across the ocean since salt water didn't corrode a tin can. Bobby and I talked to "Tinner" Trent and he gave us permission to haul off his discard pile. We also collected tin cans from the city dump one mile east of town.

Iron and steel proved to be the pinnacle of our efforts. Everyone knew those metals could be melted down and used in the war effort, so junked cars, abandoned farm implements, old tools, defunct iceboxes, galvanized washtubs, stainless steel cutlery, even some non-working revolvers ended up in a junk pile just west of the NP tracks, where every once in awhile a gondola would be loaded with the scrap metal, which was quickly replaced by more patriotic donations.

Bobby even convinced the county commission to donate the sixty feet of black wrought iron fence in front of the court house to the war effort.

Bobby and I were good customers of the Blackstone Theater, so we spoke with the owner Silas Warner, and when Buck Jones, Tim McCoy, and our favorite movie villain Roy Barcroft appeared in the Western *Below the Border* one Saturday afternoon, any kid that brought at least two pounds of iron or steel got in free.

All this work tired me out that summer of '42, and sometimes I'd head off for a swim or to fish in the Jacques River or bum around the two railroads we had, but Bobby never seemed to take any time off.

On June 4 our Navy won a great victory over the Japanese at the Battle of Midway, but the pilots involved flew off the carriers *Enterprise*, *Hornet*, and *Yorktown*, so while Bobby got to put an American flag on his map for the victory, we had to wait for any of Phil's exploits. We anticipated they wouldn't be long in coming once American forces invaded Guadalcanal in August.

As the smell of burning leaves escorted autumn into the Upper Midwest, the Allies were still reeling from the Japanese onslaught in the Southwest Pacific. However, during the winter General MacArthur and Admirals Nimitz and Halsey developed a plan for a parallel attack: McArthur to move north on New Guinea and Halsey to advance on the Solomon Islands. While Bobby and I toiled away in the fourth grade, American power was being prepared to hammer the Japs.

The Fifth Air Force was busy flying patrols, escorting transports and bombers, pounding Japanese airfield and supply lines, and covering landings as Buna and Gona became Allied targets on the New Guinea coast. Bobby and I kept busy with our grease patrols through the winter.

They came to an end, as did our other patriotic drives, one day in March.

I had gone to Bobby's house after school. We were in his bedroom reading some of Phil's old comic books. I had a copy of *Famous Funnies*, which reprinted color comic strips, including *Scorchy Smith*, who had adventures all over the world as a pilot-for-hire, and *Tailspin Tommy*, a young pilot who had air adventures with his pals Betty Lou Barnes and Skeeter Milligan. Bobby was reading *Tailspin Tommy and the Sky Bandits*, a Big Little Book from Phil's collection.

There was a knock at the front door.

We heard the voice of Oscar Wolfe, the telegrapher at the GN depot. The door closed. Ten seconds later Bobby's mother began screaming. I heard his Dad running from the kitchen, and then I was alone because Bobby had shot out of the bedroom.

Their living room became a three-person Bedlam of crying and shrieking. I waited until Bobby and his Dad took Mrs. Swain into the big bedroom, then I crept out and headed for the door.

On the floor lay a piece of paper. Across the top it read "WESTERN UNION." There were some letters, numbers, "WASHINGTON DC" and a date, followed by "Mr and Mrs Franklin Harrison Swain" and then their address.

I began reading. "THE WAR DEPARTMENT DEEPLY REGRETS TO INFORM YOU THAT YOUR SON LT PHILLIP FRANKLIN SWAIN USAAF WAS KILLED IN ACTION IN THE PERFORMANCE OF HIS DUTY AND IN THE SERVICE OF HIS COUNTRY. THE DEPARTMENT EXTENDS . . ." I threw the telegram down, grabbed my coat, and ran out the door.

I could hardly see, but I made my way to the river and got under the bridge where I bawled until my eyeballs burned.

It was cold and dark when I got home and tears had frozen to my cheeks. When I told Ma why, she began to cry, too.

Bobby missed school the next few days and he was changed after he came back. When I asked him if he wanted to collect grease on Saturday, he said no, so I did it myself, but without him, it wasn't the same, so that was my last time.

He didn't want to do much of anything, keeping to himself and heading for home as soon as the final bell rang.

The snow melted, the mud came and went, rain fell, and grass and trees greened up.

When I walked by the Swain house on my way to go fishing, I noticed that the Blue Star Service Flag in the living room window had a gold star sewn over the blue star in the middle. It wouldn't be the last house in town with that emblem.

When Joey Winchester was killed in France, his mother Alice sewed a gold star on her flag and became a recluse. The Winchesters lived a block west of us, so I saw the flag every time I went downtown.

Whenever Joey's Dad Ralph was in the yard, he'd say hello and ask how I was doing, but no one ever saw Alice, except the priest.

What happened to Alice Winchester was bad, but that didn't occur until 1944. What happened to Frank Swain happened a lot sooner.

A rumor started that rather than a hero's death, Phil had actually been flying away from a fight when he was shot down. No one knew how the rumor got started, but since it floated around the community like an infectious ghost, it was impossible to stop. I don't think most people believed it: Phil was anything but a coward, yet the contagion hung in the air.

After Phil's death and the persistent rumor, Frank just kind of wasted away. I didn't want to go to Bobby's house anymore, but I'd see Frank uptown, puffing on a cigarette and shuffling on his bow-legs to the post office or to a store. Sometimes he'd lean on a building to catch his breath.

One June day Frank drove out to the airport and climbed into the Stearman. When he didn't come home, his wife called the sheriff, who went out to check on him. Frank was slumped over in the cockpit, dead of a heart attack. His cigarette had scorched a small hole in his pants.

I saw Bobby at the funeral, but I didn't know what to say.

It was shortly after that when people began noticing Bobby leaving town with Phil's b-b gun and a sack. It wasn't every day, but when he did go, he rarely got home until dark.

I found new friends and when school began, I would hang around with them. The few times I asked Bobby to join in one of our games, he'd just shrug and walk away.

His grades dropped and he barely passed the fifth grade, in part because that spring he picked up the b-b gun and sack again.

One morning after school got out for the summer, I was fishing off the Steel Bridge when Bobby came trudging by with his gun on his shoulder.

"Hi, Bobby."

"Tommy."

"How about some fishin'?"

"I'd like to, but I have important things to do."

"How about a grease run?"

"Naw."

"Wanna see *The Spoilers* at the Blackstone on Saturday? John Wayne and Randolph Scott are in it."

"Naw."

"The *Spy Smasher* serial is playin'; I think the chapter is 'Secret Weapon'."

"Naw, I gotta go."

He kept walking up the airport road.

He had never smiled once and it bothered me, seeing my friend so down in the dumps. He was wearing Phil's old hunting coat which hung on him like a bag. I thought it was strange he would be playing soldier.

After I left the Blackstone that weekend, instead of thinking about John Wayne or Spy Smasher, I was worrying about Bobby because I'd heard the usher and the lady who sold tickets talking and she said she thought the Swain boy was "touched." The usher called him the "Bag Boy."

I decided I'd follow Bobby. It took me awhile, but eventually I saw him on Glen Haven, heading south with his gun and bag. I grabbed my bike, peddled downhill, and turned onto Glen Haven. I was in a fix. He was a block-and-a-half ahead, but if I stayed on my bike, I'd soon catch up to him, and then what would I say.

If I left my bike, someone might steal it, so I got off and walked the bike after Bobby. He turned on Oakes Avenue and went east to Salem Street and south to the Great Northern tracks. I hung back on Oakes until he was well down the tracks because that portion of Salem had no sidewalks and no trees to hide behind if Bobby turned and looked behind him.

When I did get to the tracks, he was almost to the overpass and showed no signs of stopping.

I peddled home and told Ma I was going on a little picnic. I packed two bologna sandwiches, an apple, and a couple of Ma's chocolate chip cookies. I filled my canteen with water and peddled back to the GN.

I looked down the tracks, but Bobby wasn't coming, so I wheeled my bike into a copse of willows and sat down to wait. A freight with a Lima-built locomotive with a 2-10-2 wheel arrangement chugged by. I counted the cars.

The sun spangled the willow leaves. Two more freights whipped by. Each one was composed of flat cars, and whatever was being shipped was covered with canvas, indicating it was military stuff. As the war continued, the Carver Cut-off saw a big increase in freight traffic.

I ate my lunch, letting the cookies melt in my mouth. I drank some cool water and adjusted my cap. Another freight with forty-four cars went by.

I walked onto the tracks and looked. No Bobby.

Back in the willows the sun sprinkled itself on the leaves. I lay against a tree. There was marshy ground all along the right-of-way with plenty of cattails, but I never heard a single red wing. I thought that was strange . . .

I woke up with a start. A red caboose flashed by, heading west. I thought I'd missed Bobby, so I ran onto the grade and stared down the tracks. At first I didn't see anything, but then there was a dark something. I scrunched down and waited. The dark thing was getting larger and then I could see it was human.

I scooted into the willows and waited. Soon Bobby passed me, carrying his gun on his shoulder and a sack full of something in his hand. He kept walking the tracks.

If I got onto the tracks and he looked behind him, there was no cover, so I kept him in view from my hiding place. When he passed the GN-NP crossover, I hurried over to the ditch and watched as he left the right-of-way, looked around, and disappeared into a tangle of willows and weeds north of the tracks.

I peddled as fast as I could down Salem, took Dunnell west, crossed the NP tracks, and rolled down the small hill south on Chicago. I put my bike in the ditch and hoped Bobby hadn't left.

When our town of Menninger was started, it was bordered on the south by a long narrow slough, which some people called a creek during high water. When the GN built the Carver Cut-off, they filled in a lot of the slough and ran their mainline right over it, but the marshy ground squished out on both sides of the right-of-way and in some spots willows sprang up. Some thirty years later many of them were pretty good size and formed a "tree island" almost a block long

The ground on the north side of the "island" was all marshy and too wet, and the east side stopped right at the ditch, so I went around to the railroad side and walked slowly to the west until I saw a little patch of hard soil with no grass which ended at an old rusted barrel.

I pushed the barrel aside and there was a well-worn path winding off to the west. With the overgrowth it was like a tunnel, so I got down and started crawling.

It zigged and zagged, went up over little rises and down little drops, and there was even a board that bridged a small trickle of water.

I kept moving and a freight rattled westward. When it was gone, I heard someone crying. I crawled into a small clearing and Bobby was sitting in front of a little shrine. It was an apple crate and inside were a school picture of Phil, another photo of him in uniform, and a home-made model plane that looked like a P-38, but the shocking thing was a pile of dead red-winged blackbirds just north of the shrine.

There must have been a couple hundred, the ones on the bottom nearly unrecognizable, but those on top must have just come out of Bobby's sack.

I gasped and Bobby whirled around, going for his gun. I don't know what he would have done with it anyway, but he put it down and snarled, "What're you doin' here?"

"Bobby, what're you doin'?"

His face melted into tears. I sat there helpless and waited. He turned away from me; I suppose because he didn't want me to see him cry. Finally, he wiped his face with a handkerchief. "It's so hard."

"I know."

He looked at me. "I miss Phil so much."

"Me, too."

He wiped some more.

I pointed at the dead birds. "Why this?"

"For Phil. I had a nightmare. Phil's plane was on fire and it was crashing with Jap planes chasing it. I could see the big red meatballs on their sides. You and I were there, and we were shooting to save Phil, but when I looked, it was a bunch of red wings dive bombing us with their meatballs showing on their shoulders. I woke up sweating. After that I started killing the meatball birds 'cause they were Japs."

At first it didn't make sense to me.

"I feel a whole lot better. Every time I kill a meatball bird, it's like I'm killing a Jap."

At least Bobby was doing something that helped. Phil's death was still a cold rock in my heart.

A train whistle sounded at the Fifth Street crossing. Bobby drew a cloth across the front of the apple crate and Phil's face disappeared. We crawled out of the willows with the train rumbling by.

"I suppose you're gonna tell on me."

"You know I wouldn't do that."

We walked in silence up the hill and through downtown Menninger. At Glen Haven Bobby turned off. "Thanks for not tellin'."

"That's O.K. Bye."

"Bye."

I watched him a minute heading for home, just a boy and his gun. Then I headed up the hill, carrying my thoughts.

I tossed around in bed that night and couldn't get comfortable. An idea kept cropping up and finally I knew what I had to do. The next morning I walked down Glen Haven and knocked on Bobby's door. His mother answered. "Tommy, how nice to see you. I'll get Bobby."

Bobby came out onto the porch and I explained that I wanted to help him shoot meatball birds. He was hesitant. "Why?"

"Phil was like my older brother, too. Besides, you said yourself I was in your dream. It's like an omen or something."

He thought awhile and then agreed I could help him.

So while U.S. Marines were assaulting Tinian, Guam, and Peleliu; MacArthur was clearing New Guinea; and American planes were attacking Japanese bases on Mindanao, Bobby and I were ridding the marshes around Menninger of the meatball birds.

We had quite a feathered pyramid by the time migration saved the few remaining red wings.

In October the Battle of Leyte Gulf removed any Japanese ability to fight a major naval battle and opened the way for MacArthur's return to the Philippines. In early 1945 a month of hard fighting by the Marines gained control of Iwo Jima; in April, May, and June American blood freed Okinawa from Japanese control.

Bobby and I were spilling the blood of the meatball birds, believing each downed bird brought the war closer to a conclusion.

In May Germany, pounded and crushed by the Allies, surrendered. Hitler had already blown his brains out in Berlin.

In June the *Western Star* pulled into Menninger. Among the passengers was a young man in a USAAF uniform—coat, shirt, tie, pants, and cap all khaki. He had silver wings above his heart and a blue shoulder patch with gold wings and a red and silver star. As he limped up the hill on his bow-legs, several men offered to carry his bag, but he politely declined.

Bobby and I were on Villard when we saw the young airman enter the Oleson House. After he checked in, he came out and started walking east. We followed. At Glen Haven he turned north and two blocks later was starting down the hill. When he came to Bobby's house, he turned in. We couldn't believe it.

We went around the house and came in the back door. Just to the west was a little sign that said "Goldie." I'd helped bury her there. Voices came from the living room. Bobby walked in.

"Bobby, I'm so glad you're here. And Tommy, too. Come in, Tommy. This is Captain Hawthorne. He knew Phil, didn't you, Captain."

"Yes, Ma'am. He saved my life."

Mrs. Swain had us sit down while she got some coffee for the Captain and herself and some milk for us boys. He sat very upright in his chair, and we didn't dare say anything to someone who had actually been in a war.

After a few sips he explained that he was fulfilling a vow he'd made. He asked if Mr. Swain would be home and became flustered when he found out about Frank. He said he was sorry at least four times before he went on about meeting Phil and how they became good friends.

He told us how they'd always sleep near their planes. "We could be sound asleep and an American plane would come over and we might open one eye or maybe not, but if a Jap plane was anywhere near, we'd be wide awake and heading for the nearest shelter. Our senses got to know the sound of their motors."

He didn't go into detail about the missions they flew, just that as good friends they watched out for each other.

He started out sitting in his chair, but then asked if he could move around; it made the telling easier. Mrs. Swain said, "Certainly."

"I want you to know that Phil saved my life. The only reason I'm here today is because he gave himself up for me, and that's something I can never repay."

Mrs. Swain was wiping tears off the picture of Phil she had placed on her lap. I heard her whisper, "I knew it wasn't true. Oh, Phil, I knew it wasn't true." She got up and hugged Captain Hawthorne, with Phil's picture looking down at Bobby and me crying on the sofa.

When she asked if he could stay for supper, he said it would be a privilege. She had me call Ma so I could stay, too. It was just hamburgers, baked potatoes, and some early garden peas, but the food was good. I was disappointed there was no more talk of combat.

After supper Bobby showed the captain the map in his room. He hadn't worked on it for a long time, so the captain showed him what to color blue. When he finished, there wasn't much red left.

Bobby and I got to walk the captain to the Oleson. When he asked if there was a weekly paper, we showed him the *Messenger* office.

The next week's edition carried a lengthy story about Phil and his heroic death. Most residents puffed up their chests about our hometown hero, and those who had been whispering the dirty rumor of cowardice either retired from chin-wagging or pretended they were innocent.

When the City Council met, they voted to change the name of the airport from Carroll Field to Carroll-Swain Field and put up a sign to that effect. Mrs. Swain was invited to the dedication.

After Bobby and I showed the captain the *Messenger* office, we begged him to tell us more about Phil. For about an hour he described the air war as he knew it.

Some of it was just routine, flying cover for transports and scouting. Some stories were about attacking enemy bases, killing Japanese troops, and strafing supply lines which got my blood pumping; but I was electrified by his tales of aerial combat.

Actually, Phil and he had been involved in only three dogfights as partners.

"We were green as grass and on our first patrol when a couple Zekes—we didn't call 'em that yet—jumped us out of the sun. Both of us took hits. My tail got shot up, and Phil's wings were peppered, but after one pass the Japs scrammed—we didn't get off a shot. They must have been low on fuel, and it was a good thing for us, or we would probably have ended up in the drink.

"Our second time we saw a flight of Jap bombers 10 o'clock low. Phil yelled, 'C'mon' and went into a dive, and I was right behind. Later we called that kind of bomber a Betty, but because with the right hits they would burst into flames, we called 'em 'flying Zippos.' We were warned to watch their tail because there was a cannon there, so we hit 'em from the side.

"I got one pass in, but Phil went back for another, then we split for base, hitting a cloud bank to escape the Zeros. Just before I lost sight of her, I saw Phil's bomber trailing smoke, so we put in for a 'probable' kill, but nothing came of it.

"The last time with Phil we took off over a sky-blue ocean and flew over a string of green islands fringed with palm trees and white combers beating the shore. We strafed a Japanese supply depot south of Lae and headed for home. A couple Zeros caught us and put some holes in our Lightnings, but we holed one of them and he began to lose speed. The other one got on my tail and I couldn't shake him. My tail assembly was looking like Swiss cheese when Phil came out of nowhere, pulled up beside me, and motioned for me to dive. When I did, the Zero stayed with him and put some shots into Phil's plane.

"We began maneuvering—Phil to shake him and me to get in back of him. When Phil's plane began to smoke, he dove for the deck and skimmed across the waves, maybe six feet above the sea with the Zero right behind.

"I went down after them when Phil headed for an island. There were two palm trees almost together. He flew right at them, tried to angle his plane through, but a wing caught, and he exploded. The Zero was so close he crashed right into a palm in a ball of fire.

"He saved my life."

Bobby was crying and I put my arm around him. The captain came over. "Bobby, your brother was the best man I ever knew." He hugged Bobby, too.

The next day he took Bobby and me out to dinner at the Eat Shop, but we didn't talk about the war. We did talk about Phil, and after we left the café, Bobby and I showed him where the two elevators had stood and about Phil's Fourth of July stunt. The captain stood near the tracks for a long time; I thought he was imagining Phil's flight.

We walked down the Glen Haven Hill and he said goodbye to Mrs. Swain. He told her he would be heading home to Ohio. Just before train time Bobby and I walked him to the GN depot, one on each side.

We met Denny and Lenny Hoge on Dakota. They were twins six years younger than Bobby and I and were so rambunctious that their parents got them off the farm in the summer and shipped them into town with their grandparents. Unfortunately for the town Grandpa and Grandma Hoge couldn't keep up with their grandsons and soon gave up their feeble efforts.

As we got closer, the twins angled off the sidewalk and into the ditch: we'd had some run-ins with them and they didn't want to be within arms' length of us. Bobby and I glared at them as we passed.

A voice yelled at our backs: "Hey, Bow-legs! Where's your horse?"

Another voice: "Hey, you walk funny! Ya got a sore butt?"

Laughter followed.

Bobby and I turned, and the Hoges sprinted up the hill, turning once to flip us the "bird."

The captain chuckled, put his hands on our shoulders and headed us toward the station. I said, "I'm sorry," but I don't know why. I wasn't guilty.

"Let it go; there's lots worse things in this world."

The *Western Star* was on time. We shook hands, and the captain pulled out a large white cloth with a red circle in the middle, Japanese characters written in black, and a drawing of a dragon. It was a flag and it was burned along one edge.

"I traded for this. It was supposed to bring the soldier luck, but I guess it didn't." He handed it to Bobby. "Here's one Jap who didn't make it home."

He went with the crowd and was gone.

We waited until the caboose was a red dot framed by the overpass.

Bobby put the flag in his shirt and we went hunting Hoges; they had to be somewhere. We walked every downtown street and alley, but no Hoges. Maybe they were heading to their grandparents' for supper. We walked down Chicago and there they were, coming out of the Silver Dime Store. We tailed them across Lamborn and closed the distance.

Lenny (or maybe it was Denny, I couldn't tell them apart) looked back and yelled. The twins took off, but we caught them halfway down the block and pulled them behind some lilacs.

"Bow-legs, huh?" I punched one of the twins in the stomach and he started crying.

"Sore butt, huh?" Bobby did the same and the other twin bent over. Bobby shoved him down, so I pushed mine into the dirt, too.

We didn't want to hurt them too badly, so we walked away with a warning.

"Stupid ass wipes!" They hadn't learned so we went back and slapped their faces, causing more tears. We walked away again.

"Stupid ass wipes!" We turned, but the twins had a block lead on us and were only a block from home. We kept going; we had the rest of the summer to teach them a lesson.

As American bombers softened up the Japanese homeland, Bobby and I expanded our campaign against the meatball birds after we had killed all those close to town.

We eradicated all of them from the small watercourses, ponds, and little lakes south of town. We annihilated every one we located along the river east and west of town. We ranged through the marshes on either side of the railroad and destroyed every flier with a red patch.

East of the Catholic cemetery there was a marsh, one of the last refuges for our enemies. We packed lunches and filled canteens, collected our guns and ammunition, and donned our war gear, which consisted of our brothers' old hunting coats, and walked the airport road.

We passed the cemetery and went down into the marsh, where we separated. Bobby stayed on the west side, while I went east. Technically, I suppose it was more swamp than marsh because there were willows growing on some small hillocks protruding from the wetland.

The red wings were upset that we had invaded their territory and flew above us, calling out their displeasure.

I settled in on a small ridge and waited. The cattails were drifting back and forth in a slight wind. A red wing caught one with its toes and locked itself in place, riding the cattail. Slowly I poked the b-b gun through the reeds, sighted, and squeezed the trigger. The red wing released and spiraled down. I could see red splashed on black, so I knew I could find him later. I withdrew the gun and waited.

Another red wing tried to steady itself on a cattail. I got ready. It cocked its head and looked at me with its black eyes. I slowly pulled on the trigger and the bird dropped, leaving a feather floating off to the north.

A brownish bird with a dirty-white breast flecked with brown and a pale yellow throat landed on a cattail. Its head turned nervously from side-to-side, but it didn't have to worry: we never shot the drab females.

When it few off, I took off my shoes and socks and waded out to collect my trophies. Dropping them into my bag, I moved to a small rise to the east and waited.

Soon I head "chip-chip-chip" to my right. I moved my gun slowly in that direction, and there was a "meatball" angry at me. His "chip" turned into a whistle, and I pulled the trigger.

Five minutes later Bobby came through the willows. I bagged the bird and we started west on the county road.

We hunted the railroad north a couple miles, downed a few red wings, and ate at a country crossing. While we ate, we made plans to hunt a marsh half a mile west of the cemeteries.

Just as we got ready to move into the marsh, we heard the fire siren and the sound of church bells ringing in town. The last time that happened was May 8, V-E Day. School let out, and people gathered downtown greeting each other with smiles, laughter, and tears. After the celebration died down, Ma led us to our church and we spent some time thanking God for victory, baby Chris sitting on her lap.

Bobby and I hurried south on the county road, crossed the West End Bridge, and got in on the tail end of the celebration marking the end of World War II. Ma grabbed me and our family went to church again with Bobby tagging along.

Afterward Bobby and I headed for our shrine. We dumped the new birds on the pyramid and sat in silence. A great emptiness overwhelmed me and some tears dropped onto my lap. When I looked, Bobby was crying, too.

A freight with canvas-covered war equipment thundered by, uselessly heading west.

We crawled out of the willows and walked up the hill. At the corner of Lamborn and Glen Haven, we agreed to meet the next day.

I read about Hiroshima and Nagasaki in that evening's *Fargo Forum*.

The next day I carried the red can of gasoline into the willows and waited for Bobby. When he showed up, we said a prayer, and he took the pictures of Phil and the model P-38 out of the apple crate. He moved the crate next to the bird-pile and covered the front of the crate with the Japanese flag.

We gathered some dry grass, weeds, and wood and covered the pile. I poured gasoline on the wood and the pile.

Bobby and I shook hands. We had swimming, fishing, baseball, and the Hoge twins to keep us busy before school took up.

Bobby struck a match and whoosh! flames shot upward.

Soon heat and the awful smell of burning meat and feathers surrounded us. We moved back.

There was a crackling sound and we saw fire crawling through the willows and weeds to the west. It was too late to stomp it out, so we took off running.

I made it to our garage just as the fire siren sounded.

THE FALLS BRAWL

After their wedding Kentaru and Misako Takahashi went to the northern island of Hokkaido, where they marveled at the Garo Falls in May with the ever-changing rainbows at its base.

Life was good until economic hard times forced a move. During World War I the national debt of Japan increased and inflation forced consumer prices up, especially the price of rice. This led to "rice riots" from July to September 1918 which were harshly suppressed by the government. In the summer of 1918, Japanese troops were sent into Siberia in an anti-Bolshevik move. Korea was simmering close to the boiling point over Japanese rule. The Communists and Socialists were gaining support. The Takahashis sold their little restaurant and bought steamer tickets to America.

West Coast hostility to Asians drove them eastward along the railroads, and they ended up in Caseyville, North Dakota, where they cooked in the NP Hotel and Restaurant. They saved their money and awaited opportunity.

When a tract of land on the western edge of Caseyville came up for sale, residents were surprised when the quiet Japanese couple outbid the other four would-be owners. Backed by a bank loan, the Takahashis built a dozen small cabins just south of the Mid-State Highway.

They built a working replica of Garo Falls, added coy ponds with arching bridges, small vermilion torii with black lintels, and hung the grounds with colorful lanterns called chochins. Misako worked diligently on several traditional Japanese gardens with azaleas, camellias, and small evergreens, interspersed with flat rocks as steppingstones, vertical rocks symbolic of mountains and volcanoes, and white sand for purity.

The Falls, "North Dakota's First Motor Court," was a tremendous success until hard times in the farming section were intensified by drought and dust storms.

Kentaro added a dance hall and bribed the Caseyville cops and the Walters County state's attorney to blind themselves to the beer and liquor that lubricated the Friday and Saturday night dances. Although the cops did have to break up the inevitable fights—known as Falls Brawls—none of the clearly intoxicated participants were ever charged with a violation of the Volstead Act.

When the "Noble Experiment" of National Prohibition ended in 1933, North Dakota voted to legalize beer, but remained dry on liquor until 1936, when its sale was partially legalized, giving law enforcement in Walters County three extra years of illicit wealth. In 1938 dancing was prohibited wherever liquor was sold, but the Takahashis hadn't sold that much hard stuff anyway.

In the late-Thirties, the fortunes of the Falls oscillated along with the fluctuations of the economy. In 1940 and 1941 there were good profits, but then came December 7. Pearl Harbor shocked the nation, and tolerance was forgotten as the drums of war pounded out their tattoo. Japanese-Americans were rounded up under Executive Order 9066 signed by President Franklin D. Roosevelt in February 1942.

The Takahashis were arrested and hauled off to Ft. Lincoln near Bismarck to spend the rest of the war on the inside looking out.

The Falls was closed and fell into disrepair. It was doubtful it would have survived anyway, due to the rationing of gasoline and tires for the duration of the war.

When the Japanese government came to its senses after two A-bombs—Little Boy and Fat Man—killed 200,000 people in Hiroshima and Nagasaki and signed the papers of surrender on the deck of the battleship *Missouri*, the Takahashis were released and returned to the Falls.

They worked to restore their business and reopened in time for Thanksgiving. In the spring they prepared for their first dance in five years.

Southwest of Caseyville glaciers had rippled the earth into a washboard of hills. The highest one was Red-Tail Ridge, six miles from Caseyville if you were a crow. It was one of the landmarks the Indians had used as guides on the rolling prairies between Sacred Water Lake and the Missouri River, along with other buttes such as Buffalo Hump, Rainy Butte, Turtle Back Hill, Thunder Butte, and Bunch Grass Hill. The first two were located far off to the northeast of Caseyville, while the other three emerged from the prairie dozens of miles to the west and northwest, but Red-Tail beckoned to local picnickers, hikers, and teenagers. However, no one ventured beyond Red-Tail because of the Encampment.

The Encampment was an accumulation of buildings that formed a little village, with other houses scattered throughout the glacial hills. The "Campers" were descendants of the dispossessed and rejected.

After the Civil War some Southern hill-dwellers and their families moved north and used their abilities as bullwhackers and muleskinners to set up a freight line, hauling supplies from Ft. King and later the town of Kingston on the Northern Pacific to Ft. Sully a hundred miles north. In the early Eighties the railroad pushed a branch northward and put the freighters out of business. They moved into the glacial hills on land no one else wanted.

Some young Sioux men had joined them in their freighting venture, so when the company went broke, they moved into the Encampment and brought brides in from the reservations.

A couple Negroes were running a tent of ladies of easy virtue in Fargo until the authorities kicked them out. They took the NP as far as Kingston, where they heard of the Encampment. They hired a wagon to take them as far as Red-Tail, where they got out and walked into the hills.

In the 1890s a caravan of Romany people drove into the hills and never came out.

The people of the Encampment hunted when they wanted to hunt, fished when they wanted to fish, and trapped when they wanted to trap. They raised cattle, sheep, and pigs. And they made and sold moonshine.

Moonshine was the money-maker because North Dakota joined the Union in 1889 as a "dry" state. Any government agent foolish enough to enter the Encampment in search of booze or stills in the roughest part of the hill country was prone to an accident: stumbling over a cliff into a rock quarry or falling off a log bridge and drowning in the six inches of water that ran through Two Bear Valley.

When the Campers first settled the hills, buffalo bones were everywhere and would bring a good price if they could be transported to the railroad. The Campers began gathering the bones and hauling them to Caseyville or to Chester after the tracks moved west of Caseyville, where they were loaded and shipped Back East.

After most of land was picked clean of bones, a few Campers began going into the gullies and valleys, looking for strays. A couple of young Sioux made a strange discovery in a steep-sided valley. Tramping through the undergrowth, they came upon a clearing where two grizzly bears had fought to the death maybe twenty years before. The leg bones had been pulled several yards away by varmints, but other than that the skeletons were complete and even had some remnants of fur.

It must have been a bloody, slashing, biting fight, with both male bears giving and absorbing punishment. It appeared that the smaller of the two had actually bitten into the skull of the larger one above the eye socket and died on top. Maybe both had bled to death.

It didn't make any difference how they died; they were big medicine. The Sioux got a boiler, filled it with water, put it over a fire, and boiled the bones clean. It took a couple of days and then they wrapped most of the bones in blankets and put them on scaffolds they and some other Campers had made out of tree limbs and branches.

The two skulls were painted with red ochre and wedged into the crotch of a cottonwood. The place was named Two Bear Valley and became a sacred place to the Campers, even the non-Indians.

Campers went there only to listen to the Spirit World, and woe to a non-Camper who violated the peace of Two Bear Valley.

There was another place, a place that every Camper avoided—Dead Horse Draw. On Thanksgiving 1896 a large group of Sioux were making their way from the Missouri River to Ft. Sully when they were caught by a huge blizzard. The men, women, and children hunkered down beside Red-Tail Ridge and let the ponies fend for themselves.

A few of the animals drifted with the storm onto the prairies where they died, but most of them tried to shelter in a narrow valley and froze to death. All-in-all about forty ponies died.

In the spring the corpses in the valley were exposed and nature began working to reduce the skeletons. The whitening bones spooked the Campers—it was bad medicine. No Camper ventured into Dead Horse Draw, which also became a Spirit World.

Except for an occasional trip into Caseyville, the Campers insulated themselves from the outside world, sustained by their own world of spirits and isolation.

The Campers' land surrounded a section of what was designated "school land," and in the 1920s the county forced them to put up a school there for their children and those of nearby farmers. After a couple weeks of having their students come home with bloody noses, black eyes, and fear, the farmers sent their children elsewhere. When the State said that students had to attend school until they were sixteen, the Campers' kids came in to Caseyville High School, but the day after their sixteenth birthdays were never seen in the school again.

After America entered World War I "to make the world safe for democracy," the number of volunteers quickly evaporated, so President Wilson and the Congress imposed Selective Service to fill out the ranks of the "democracy-savers." However, no young man from the Encampment ever served: the members of the County Selective Service Board weren't crazy enough to go into the hills to force any registration, much less to draft anyone.

It was different in World War II. Sometime in the twisted history of the Encampment, the residents came to hate Oriental people. One rumor had it that a young Chinese man showed up one winter, was allowed to stay, and ran off with one of the Camper girls the next spring, but that was just hearsay, wrapped in a rumor, and blown on a whisper; no outsider knew the truth.

When any Campers came into Caseyville, the Oriental cooks at the two big hotels made certain they stayed in their kitchens, and if any Campers stopped by the Falls, Kentaru and Misako made themselves scarce.

When the Japanese smashed our fleet at Pearl Harbor, thousands of young men volunteered for service, and those of the Encampment were no different. Unlike their fathers and uncles, draft-age men left the dark hills and signed up in Caseyville.

After the war those who came home went back to their isolated way-of-life, but those who had been in Seattle, Manila, Tokyo, New York, London, and Paris began to spend more time in Caseyville. In the spring of 1946, they were ready for the first Falls' dance.

When my cousin Po-Li (called "Paul" by his family and friends) Cockburn stepped off the *Western Star* onto the platform at the Menninger, North Dakota, station, in May 1946, it was his first visit since before the war. He had finally been mustered out of the U.S. Army and had stopped off on his way home to San Francisco.

When my father Elijah "Lige" Cockburn hitched trains to San Francisco in 1923, he had been surprised that his older brother Joshua had married a Chinese named Mayling Wong and that they had a year-old son. It was an even bigger surprise to my grandparents, Boss and Margaret.

However, when Josh, Mayling, Paul, and a new daughter Suzanne, came for a visit, the newcomers were welcomed into the family, and Josh was scolded in private for being so secret about his marriage and family.

On a subsequent visit Paul made friends with Taro Nakamura, who was his age and the son of the owners of the Menninger Café, so the two hung out together during Paul's latest visit. Even though he was seven years younger, my older brother Boy was allowed to join them.

They went fishing at the res and on the Jacques River, catching a mess of perch and bullheads which we cleaned and had for supper. They treated me to two movies: *The Woman in Green*, starring Basil Rathbone as Sherlock Holmes and Nigel Bruce as Dr. Watson, who fight against a fiendish plot of the evil Professor Moriarty and *They Were Expendable* in which Robert Montgomery and John Wayne lead some PT boats in defense of the Philippines against the Japanese onslaught. We played Hearts and Whist with my younger sisters Barbara and Marjorie, who also made fudge with walnuts for a treat, and one night all of us, except Taro, worked on a thousand-piece jigsaw puzzle until midnight. It was called "Blazing the Trail" and had mountains, covered wagons, and Indians. It took so long because we didn't realize two pieces were missing.

Boy, Paul, and Taro went out to the farm where my uncles John and James Farnsworth lived. John was also a veteran, even though he was only twenty-two. James was almost twenty. All their neighbors were of German descent, but all were loyal during the war and many of their sons served. John and James were known for their shyness, so I was surprised when they accepted an invitation to go to the Falls for the Friday night dance.

I was only four years younger than Boy, who was seventeen, so I tried to argue that I should be allowed to go with the others to the dance, but Mom was adamant: I was not going. Boy stuck up for me, but it was no use.

Friday night came and Boy, who had received his driver's license earlier that year, drove off with Paul, John, and James to pick up Taro. I told Mom I was going to the movies with Bobby Swain and went out the front door.

However, instead of heading for Glen Haven Street, I cut down the hill to Gregory and waited by the park entrance until Boy stopped and I jumped in. Instead of arguing with Mom, we had made our own plans. Of course, I'd get it for disobeying, and so would Boy, but he got it so often, it didn't bother him much, and going to my first Falls dance would be worth the grounding and the extra chores.

Boy could be a terror. Most of the time he was considerate, obedient, and a hard worker, but every once in a while, with no warning, he slipped into a black mood with a short temper and a need to blow off steam.

In good weather, he'd pack up a sleeping bag, tent, and camping supplies, and hike the river until he felt better, even if it took a week. But several times he hitched a freight and rode it to Minot, where he'd gamble up on High Third Street. One time he came home and showed me a hundred dollars wrapped in a handkerchief that he'd won. Another time he came back with a black eye, a split lip, and a limp, but he was happy.

He never seemed to get his "black mood" during the winter. He was like everyone else: slightly depressed due to the lack of sun, and that feeling must have pushed out his more extreme mood. It was lucky for him; he would have frozen to death riding a freight to Minot in January.

Camping was all right with Mom and Dad, but the Minot trips always ended with sanctions. Boy never complained about the extra dishes he had to wash; the extra cleaning he had to do; or the painting, scrubbing, waxing, or laundry that measured out his punishment.

Dad and Boy's mother were married in Detroit, but she abandoned the family, and Dad had moved back to Menninger with Boy. I think he felt guilty about the whole situation and would have handled Boy with kid gloves, but Mom made sure he didn't treat Boy any differently than the rest of us kids. Boy was the big brother to us younger kids, and he developed a strong sense of family. "Families stick together," he would always say.

After I squeezed in the back seat between John and James, I got to thinking about what a good big brother Boy was: most of the time he included me in his social life and watched out for me.

Boy had a definite moral code: he hated injustice. A couple months before, David Starks, a senior, began picking on me. His favorite thing to do was use my stomach as a punching bag. At first I thought I could take it, but after a couple vicious punches to the gut, I came home after school, crying. Boy got the story out of me, rode his bike to the Starks' house, and beat up David. With the injustice smoothed out, the two of them became friends and I was punch-free.

Boy, Paul, and Taro talked up front, but after saying, "Hi, Tommy," John and James looked out their windows and never said a word. I scrunched down and let the dark rule.

Soon the dark outside turned to the light of Caseyville's Main Street. We drove west and turned off Main, went under the big red torii, and finally found a place to park. We got our tickets from Misako (Boy paid for mine) and went into the dance.

It was already a success: you could hardly move around the edges of the floor, which was jammed with a mass of people attempting to dance to the music coming from the five-piece band (they were billed as an "orchestra") and a girl singer on the small stage. There was a soft drink and candy counter on the opposite side, so I split off and stood in line to get some pop.

Caseyville had a bottling plant, so I ordered a cola with the local brand name: "Morovit." I nursed it while I looked over my prospects.

To tell the truth, there weren't that many girls my age in the place, but finally I did see two standing by the stage. Two was not a good number: if I asked one of them to dance, she might say no just because she wouldn't want her friend to feel bad. It would have been better if it had been three or just one. I started toward the stage anyway.

I was about five yards away when a boy asked the brunette to dance and off they went. I tried to move faster, stepped on a woman's foot, said "Pardon me," and kept going.

"Would you like to dance?"

"What?"

"Dance. Would you like to?"

"Sure."

I led the blonde onto the floor. We got into position and began to bump off other couples, but we finally got into a rhythm and completed our dance as the girl singer did her rendition of "It's Been A Long, Long Time," a hit for Kitty Kallen the previous Thanksgiving.

I brought the blonde back to the stage and we both said "thank you" at the same time and started laughing. She had a nice laugh and nice teeth, so I decided I would ask her to dance again later on.

The band got up for a break and her friend came back, so I turned to see if I could find Boy. Suddenly, there was a big movement on the far side of the floor: some people were quickly getting away from something, although a few men moved closer.

I saw that those moving in were Campers. I don't know if they were already there when we arrived or if they came in afterward, but there they were, twenty-five or so, facing off with Paul and Taro.

I saw Boy hustling over from the other side of the stage, and John and James were lumbering their way over from the soft drink counter. I pushed across the floor and stood next to Boy. Six against twenty-five, give or take.

"Are you with them 'slopes'?" a Camper with a scruffy beard snarled. He was a head taller than Boy.

Boy was mad. "Yeah. What of it?"

"We don't like Nips. We especially don't like 'em when they're smellin' around our women."

Paul spoke up. "I told you, I'm part Chinese." I noticed a trickle of blood coming from his nose. Taro didn't say anything.

"Chinks, Nips, it's all the same. You're all 'slants' and you're all leavin', includin' your yellow-lovin' friends."

Boy moved forward with his fists clenched. Paul grabbed him by the arm. "No, Boy, just let it go."

Scruffy Beard laughed, a laugh echoed by the other Campers. Boy pulled forward. Taro said, "He's right, Boy. It's not worth it. Let's just go."

Kentaro had started around the counter, but when he saw it was the Campers, he melted away. The cop on duty was the older of Caseyville's two policemen. He had thin white hair and was so small and skinny, his badge looked more like a shield. He took a step or two onto the floor, then followed Kentaro.

The Campers came in all sizes, but every one of them looked capable of taking care of himself. I noticed they all wore high-heeled, pointy-toed cowboy boots; that must have been their insignias because no one else wore boots. On our side John and James were tall, around six foot four, like many of the men in my mother's family, and well-muscled from farm work. Boy, Paul, and Taro were around five foot ten or eleven. I was the only short one, and small, too.

Paul and Taro kept urging Boy to give it up in quiet voices. The place had gotten so still I could hear them easily. Boy kept clenching and unclenching his fists: I could tell he wanted to test them on Scruffy Beard.

Finally, he turned and took a step toward the door. Scruffy Beard laughed and so did the other Campers. Boy stopped, but Paul and Taro pulled him along, and we walked out the door, laughter mocking our every step.

Boy never said anything as he started the car. Once over the railroad tracks and further down Main, Paul said, "Sometimes it's better to walk away."

Taro agreed. "We wouldn't have had a chance." Then as an after thought, "Maybe some day." No one else spoke.

Boy barely touched the brake pedal as we came to the Gold Star Highway. We just slowed and then he hit the gas as we turned left and headed for the overpass.

As the car reached the top and started down, suddenly Boy yelled, "No, goddamnit! No!" and slammed the heel of his hand against the steering wheel.

I jumped and I knew John and James did, too.

At the junction of the Gold Star and the Mid-State, he spun into a U-turn and gunned the engine up the overpass. As we sped toward the Falls, Paul kept asking, "Where we goin', Boy? Where we goin'?" After the tracks he stopped asking.

The car rolled beneath the red torii and with no parking spaces, Boy slammed on the brakes and boiled out of the car, leaving it in the middle of the sidewalk leading to the front door. Paul and Taro caught on, but were ten seconds behind. John and James never moved fast, so once John was out, I quickly passed them.

It was tough getting in the door because so many girls and women, with some men, were running out, most of the females screaming.

When I did get in, the brawl was on in the middle of the floor.

Boy and Scruffy Beard looked like a two-headed, two-backed monster grappling on the floor with Campers standing around, trying to kick Boy when they got the chance.

Paul and Taro were back-to-back, trying to ward off the circling Campers with judo chops and kicks.

I ran toward the group surrounding Boy and launched a kick into the back of a Camper's knee. He went down with a yell, and a big Camper picked me up and launched me backward into the soft drink bar with a solid punch to my forehead.

I couldn't have been out very long and when I woke up, I noticed that Boy was buried under a pile of Campers, and so were Paul and Taro. In the middle of the tables, John and James were punching Campers with their big fists, but a couple hurled themselves off tables and onto their backs and they went down.

Then two remarkable things happened: the blonde I had danced with came over, sat down, and put my head in her lap; and a big man stepped in and decked a Camper. I learned later he had been one of the kids who had been beaten up at the Camper school.

When he jumped into the fight, a couple of men from Menninger joined him, and then it was a rush of men to grab, sock, punch, and kick a Camper. I tried to get up, but pain and blackness put me back down in the girl's lap. She put her arms around me and told me to stay still.

Fortunes were soon reversed on the floor, and it was the Campers being kicked, stomped, and slugged. Those who surrendered were allowed to stagger outside. John and James were smashing Campers with their big ham-fists. Paul and Taro were chopping, tripping, and kicking their opponents. At the end it was just Boy slamming Scruffy Beard's skull against the floor before some men grabbed and held him until they could drag the unconscious Camper away.

A lot of pent-up emotion against the Campers had been let loose and as Scruffy Beard was hauled through the door, the men surrounded Boy, Paul, Taro, John, and James with their bodies, cheers, and congratulations. As they started to leave, I got to my feet, turned to the girl and asked, "Your name? What's your name?"

"June. June McCurdy. What's yours?"

"Tom Cockburn. I gotta go, but maybe I'll see you around."

"I'd like that . . . Tom."

The Campers were in their vehicles. Some of them were sprawled out on a flatbed truck, and the others were in two beat-up pickups, their pointy-toed boots showing over the sides. They hit the Mid-State and turned left.

Under the lights I could see that every one of us had something wrong with his face. I didn't see mine, of course, but I could feel a big knot on my forehead; I guess the Camper had a ring.

Blood trickled from every nose; Paul, Taro, and John each had a swollen eye; Boy had a mark on his forearm where Scruffy Beard had bitten him; John and James had swollen knuckles, but they didn't think they were broken; everyone was walking gingerly with sore backs, ribs, and legs.

We got into the car and Boy turned east on the Mid-State. As we approached the railroad tracks, two cars marked "Walters County Sheriff" whizzed by with sirens blaring.

As we crested the overpass, Boy said, "You can't let the scum bellies take over. Damn, I feel good!"

Paul said, "Except for my eye, I do, too,"

Taro echoed him. "Me, too."

John and James each grunted, which I guess meant they felt the same way.

"How you doin', Tom?" Boy asked.

"Good."

"How's your head?"

"O.K." I didn't think he had noticed.

Everyone was quiet the rest of the sixteen miles, absorbed in thoughts unique to each of us. I saw the headlights beaming down the highway and then the lights of Menninger, the lights of home.

Boy turned off the Gold Star onto Lamborn, headed downtown, and turned over to Stimson, where we let Taro off. John and James got into their car parked in front of our house; both of them said good night, which was a mouthful for my uncles.

The folks had gone to bed. When we saw each other's faces in the hallway light, we started to laugh and had to shut up. Paul used the bathroom first, said good night, and went up to bed.

After we got into bed, Boy said, "I'm proud of you, Tom."

I didn't know what to say, but what my brother said made me feel good.

"Family and friends stick together; that's what makes us family and friends."

CONRAD FORESTER

When Conrad Forester didn't come back to school in the fall of 1958, none of his classmates at Menninger High could figure out why.

Conrad wasn't an original member of the Class of 1962, like Phil Archer, Art Rolfsrud, or Dotty Zeltinger were. His family moved to Menninger in the fall of 1951 and lived in a one-story stucco house down by the Jacques River. His Dad, Fritz, had once been a section foreman on the Great Northern, but had worked his way down from there.

Fritz Forester had been employed by the Chicago, Burlington & Quincy out of St. Paul when news of the attack on Pearl Harbor came over the radio. Fritz was a little drunk at the time after a Saturday night in a dive in downtown St. Paul and an early Sunday morning lost in the Wabasha Street caves. However, he wasn't so drunk that he didn't feel hatred for the lousy Japs fill up his belly, so the next day he volunteered for the Marines.

Even when he was sober, he hated the Japs for what they'd done, "a stinkin' sucker punch." He could hardly wait to get at 'em.

But at night, staring at the crack in the ceiling that spelled out "wow" in cursive, he had another feeling in his stomach, fear.

When word got around that he had volunteered, half a dozen guys who hadn't and who had no intention of doing so, bought him drinks and told him what a patriot he was. Even the rather homely girl who lived down the hall, and whom he had carefully avoided, tapped him on the shoulder one evening and whispered, "I'm very proud of you."

"What? Oh, yeah, just doin' my duty."

"Well, it's still a brave thing to do."

He never thought much about it until the day he was leaving for boot camp and she saw him in the hall with his bags. He hesitated a moment and then asked her if he could store some things in her apartment until he got back. She agreed and then out of the blue she asked, "Would it be all right if I wrote to you?"

He surprised himself by saying, "Yeah, sure." He gave her an address which she carefully wrote down.

"You don't have to write back if you don't want to. I'll still write. It's something I can do in case you get lonesome."

He liked that and he liked getting her letters, which he answered. They were the only ones he got since his folks were dead and he had no family.

However, he didn't show the picture she sent to any of the guys.

He got shipped out to the Pacific. His buddies said with a name like "Fritz" the Marines sure weren't going to send him to Europe. Her letters kept coming and he tried to answer each of them. It made him feel more like the other men. He was kind of put off, though, because she always signed them "Rose Keller," never just "Rose."

In November 1942 Fritz landed with the other reinforcements on Guadalcanal, just in time for the monsoon season. Guadalcanal was a hell-hole, with the temperature never below eighty, often in the nineties, and everything soaking wet. Even before he fired a shot, Fritz had dysentery, but so did most of the other Leathernecks, so he still went into action. He fired his Springfield .30-06 at trees, leaves, shadows, and things that moved, but he couldn't tell if he had ever actually hit a Jap. One day he and his buddies sneaked off for an ocean swim, to wash off the jungle-stink as much as anything else, and he gashed his arm on some coral. The wound got infected and started turning purplish-black, so he was taken off the line.

Even before his arm returned to normal, a mosquito drilled him and he got dengue fever. His head seemed like it would split open, his muscles and bones felt as though they were being crushed, his fever spiked at 105, and he broke out with red spots on his legs, then his chest, and eventually all over his body.

After a week his fever shot up briefly, then subsided. He began feeling better, but by then he had been bitten by another mosquito that gave him a dose of malaria. The headache, fever, chills, sweats, shakes, muscle and back pains, coughing, nausea, and vomiting almost killed him. It got so bad he told himself he would rather die than go on like that, but the doctors pulled him through, although his "fighting days" were over. He was evacuated, then transferred to the States.

He hallucinated in the hospital in California about Japs coming down the hall to kill him.

Eventually, he got better and enjoyed the attention visitors gave him, especially when they commented on the jagged scar on his arm. They thought it was the result of a battle wound, and he let them think it. Pretty soon he almost believed it himself and embroidered a story to go along with it.

After a medical discharge, he took the *Coast Daylight* to San Francisco, hopped another overcrowded SP string of varnish to Portland, and rode the *Empire Builder* on the GN "High Iron" to the SPUD, the St. Paul Union Depot.

He wore his uniform, although it was pretty baggy on him. He took off the coat and rolled up the sleeves as often as possible so he could describe how he got his "war wound."

Fritz got rip-roaring drunk, what with being a war hero and all, and people wanting to buy him drinks because of his "sacrifice." When the bars closed and his last new set of friends asked him where he lived, all he could remember was the number of his old apartment house.

When they drove off, he was alone. Not knowing what else to do, he walked into the building and up to his old floor. He was holding onto the wall to keep from falling and trying to hum "Praise the Lord and Pass the Ammunition!" when a door opened and Rose Keller stood there, dressed in a wrapper. He hadn't written to her but once since he'd gotten sick, and that was only at the urging of a hospital volunteer. He had dictated the letter to her.

After staring at him, Rose backed into her room, but left the door open. He went in.

When he woke up, Rose wasn't there. She left him a note that there was fresh coffee on the stove. She also said that the clothes he had asked to leave with her back in December of '41 were still in the closet. He had completely forgotten about them. When she got home from work, he was gone.

After leaving the apartment, Fritz passed out three blocks away, hit his head on the curb, and was in a coma. The ambulance took him to the 550-bed Veterans' Administration Hospital across the river near Ft. Snelling. His recovery was slow, but eventually he began to regain his strength. He slept as much as possible despite the noise from the construction of some new medical buildings needed because of the increasing volume of damaged bodies coming back from overseas.

At first it didn't bother Rose; she had been late before. But after another month, she went to a doctor. Looking at the report, she began to make plans. She thought back to the night: it hadn't hurt the way her high school girlfriends had told her it would. It was pretty disgusting, though. Afterwards in bed with him wasn't so bad, especially when he quit snoring. Then it was pleasant to lie there and listen to his breathing. Sometimes it was like the soft breath of a kitten. She could smell the sharp odor of the whiskey and the fermented grain-smell of the beer, but there was also the man-scent, and she liked it.

When he had first gone overseas, she had taken out one of his shirts and a pair of his pants. She hung the shirt from a clothes hanger and clothes-pinned the pants to the hem of the shirt. Then she hung her clothes hanger-man from the front of the closet door and pretended it was real. When her night light was on, it was comforting to see "him" there. But having Fritz in bed with her was better.

Her father had money and he'd help her. He'd help her out of guilt if for no other reason. He was an official with the Great Northern Railway, not high enough to call the president, Frank J. Gavin, "Frank," but still pretty high up in the company. His wife had died twenty-two years before, giving birth to her and her twin sister Iris. Rose knew her mother was a tiny little thing, but pretty with a porcelain doll face, if her pictures didn't lie. She must have had blue eyes because everyone in the family did.

Oh, yes, her father would help her. Iris and she were twins, but fraternal, not identical. Iris inherited the light blonde hair and dainty features of their mother, while Rose had the dark hair, square face, large nose, and strong brows of her father.

Their mother lived just long enough to hold both of them and say each one's name. After she died, their father doted on Iris, who was her mother's miniature, and avoided Rose as much as he could. His maiden aunt came to live with them, but she had much more time for Iris than for Rose, too.

When they were ten, they both contracted scarlet fever, but only Iris died. Their father cried like a lost child at the funeral and even let Rose hug him. Most of the time, however, he was too busy with his job to pay much attention to her.

She had some girlfriends at school, but mainly because she had money and could invite them to her large house for parties and sleep-overs. None of the boys ever paid any attention to her, and she was the only girl who didn't go to the junior prom. A lot of the time she'd go to the movies and pretend that Clark Gable or Errol Flynn or Cary Grant was in love with her, or she'd cut pictures out of the fan magazines and put them in her room, wishing that she looked like Jean Harlow or Miriam Hopkins or Olivia de Havilland.

As soon as she graduated high school, she moved out. Her father didn't seem to mind. She got her own apartment and a job as a waitress. She would go home for a cold Christmas with her father and he would send her a birthday card. Every once in awhile he would call, when he was feeling guilty, which wasn't very often.

Now she'd have to call him.

When Fritz was released from the VA hospital, he made his way down to the Burlington hiring office to see if he could get his old job back, but the "Q" wasn't hiring. He decided to go back to Rose's apartment and get into some civvies.

When she answered his knock, she looked surprised. After she told him how things were, he was shocked. He couldn't even remember the night.

Their wedding was a small affair in the family home on Summit Avenue, but a long way from James J. Hill's mansion. Her father, looking nervous; a few of her relatives, looking bored; and the maiden aunt, who cried into a hanky the entire time, made up the guest list. There were two attendants: a girl from high school that Rose saw occasionally and a "rail" from the "Q," who was the third one Fritz had asked to be his best man, but who would only agree for a fifth of Four Roses. He disappeared with his "present" as soon as the ceremony concluded.

Their wedding gift from her father was a job on the GN. Fritz started out as the foreman of a section gang with guidance from "Bake Head Bill," a twenty-year GN veteran, to teach him the ropes. "Bake Head" got his nickname because when he was younger, he was always talking about being a locomotive fireman.

Fritz and Rose remained in the apartment until Conrad was born, then Rose allowed her father to set them up in a small cottage for the sake of the baby.

When the nurse first placed the baby in her arms, Rose was afraid to look. When she did, she burst out crying. The nurse thought it was because she was so happy, but that wasn't the reason. Looking at Conrad was like looking at a mirror reflecting her own image in red-faced miniature. After she dried her eyes, she vowed to love her son as she had never been loved and hoped she could keep her vow.

If Fritz was disappointed in his son's looks, he didn't show it. Inside, however, he wondered how he had ever gotten into his present situation. Certainly it wasn't anything he had planned. That bothered him. A lot. He found relief by staying out late and drinking with the boys. "Bake Head" tried his best to cover for Fritz at work, but soon even Mr. Keller's influence wasn't enough, and he was transferred to the Willmar Division. Conrad was two and his sister Lise was a babe-in-arms.

When Rose discovered she was pregnant a second time, a feeling of clawing panic ripped through her, and the feeling remained just under the surface of her soul until she saw Lise for the first time. It was almost like Iris had been reborn.

As Lise grew, Rose loved spending time fixing her hair while Conrad sat and watched with the darkest blue eyes Rose had ever seen. Fritz would look at the two children and wonder how two such different beings could come from the same mother. Then he'd go to work as the assistant foreman, drink with the boys after work, and fall into bed.

His work suffered and he was transferred to the Breckenridge Division, but as a regular "gandy dancer." That shook him up; he swore off booze and actually stayed dry for two months. Then the Devil and Demon Rum got him again. Only the fact that he was "Keller's boy" saved him. Finally, he was transferred again—this time to the Minot Division.

One morning while still in Breckenridge, Rose woke up pregnant for the third time. Trudy was delivered at Trinity Hospital in Minot, and once again Rose was transported by her good luck. Trudy was blonde and dainty.

With a growing family, Fritz took the temperance vow again. This time he lasted over a year, but when the Red invasion ignited Korea, recollections of his "sacrifice" overwhelmed his vow. Fritz trudged up the hill to a notorious street, "High Third," and got plastered. The railroad brass put up with him another year and then transferred him to Menninger and a job specially created just for him, one that would keep him out of the hair of the GN and not endanger anyone, except maybe himself.

When Fritz realized his position and the indignity of walking around the Menninger yard, keeping switches clear of snow and ice in the winter and cleaning the depot, he couldn't help himself. He found solace in the Highball, a railroaders' bar on Villard Avenue. Its dark interior and a few whiskeys with beer chasers shielded him from his life and what it had become. When vets wandered in from the American Legion Club, he'd show them his scar and swap war stories with them, stories he actually believed had happened.

Rose doted on her children, especially the girls, although she tried to be kind to Conrad. He had rarely cried as a baby, and even when he was older, he never complained. Whatever the situation, he accepted it.

Rose knew there would be no more children. When she was a junior, her class read *Macbeth*. When one of the boys asked the teacher what it meant in the scene with the porter telling Macduff that drink provoked the desire, but took away the performance, Miss Bachman turned a bright red, started fooling around with the cord attached to the sash weights of the window blinds, and finally stammered, "I-I-I really don't know," amid some smothered laughter from the more enlightened students. In the locker room the more progressive girls opened the eyes of their more innocent classmates.

Years before when Fritz began staying out late, it bothered Rose a great deal: she felt like a failure as a wife. As the years drifted by and Fritz with them, Rose didn't regret the loss of the physical side of marriage; in fact, she started regretting it when he was home. When she would look over at the lump under the bedclothes beside her, she would find herself preferring her old clothes-hanger man. Now she had her three little angels and they were enough.

Gussie Daniels lived next door. She was an elderly widow lady and had outlived three husbands. She told Rose, "Men are just naturally weak and that's a fact." After Gussie started coming over when Fritz was gone, she became the friend Rose had never had. They talked about everything, and Gussie would take care of the children, so Rose could walk downtown and shop.

Gussie had some money, and she would buy little ribbons and inexpensive dresses and shoes for Lise and Trudy, so they could go to church, and cap guns and jack knives for Conrad. Fritz had quit the German Lutheran Church a long time before he hit Menninger, but Rose took the kids almost every Sunday, and the girls had to look nice. It wasn't that important for boys, so Conrad stumped in wearing patched pants and faded shirts.

At first he liked Sunday School in the basement of the church because there was a large sandbox sitting on a table. The sand was contoured to look a little like the Holy Land with a piece of blue paper to represent the Sea of Galilee, a larger one for the Dead Sea, an even larger one for the eastern Mediterranean, and a blue ribbon for the Jordan River. There were cardboard figures with robes drawn and colored on them and faces cut from various religious publications and pasted on the head-part to represent Jesus, the Disciples, the various Marys, Abraham, Moses, and other Biblical figures. There was even a Roman soldier with a spear; he was Conrad's favorite. He liked it when the teacher allowed the students to move the figures around the sand.

When he joined the third grade class, there was a flannel board: the sandbox was just for the first and second grades. It wasn't as much fun to peal the flannel people off the board and replace them with others, except at Christmas time when there were camels and sheep.

Starting with the fifth grade, the flannel board was gone. From then on lessons would be strictly out of books. Even though they had pictures, Conrad rapidly lost interest. He didn't like books. That was an attitude he'd inherited from his father, who hated books, or maybe from his mother who was indifferent to them, although in high school she had started *Gone With The Wind*.

Conrad loved his sisters, although he was somewhat afraid of them. They were almost like dolls, beautiful but breakable. He loved his mother because she fed and clothed him and didn't look breakable. He hardly knew his father, at least not well enough to feel any emotion toward him, good or bad.

It had been difficult for Conrad to move to a new town. Not that he had any friends in Minot, but there was a dog in the yard across the ally and a hole under the fence so he could crawl under and pet and hug the German Shepherd named Blondi, who was so old her coat was getting patchy all over.

In Menninger most of his neighbors didn't have dogs, except for Mr. Bouvette, and that dog acted like it would tear Conrad's throat out if it could. He couldn't have a dog of his own because his father wouldn't abide one in the house.

On his second day in town, he went for a walk west on Gregory Avenue. At Salem Street he turned north and headed toward the river. The Bouvette house stood at the end of the street, and as he approached, a large black and white dog rushed at him, barking the foam off its lips. It was brought up short by a chain attached to its collar, but by that time Conrad was running west on Mill Avenue.

Suddenly, out of the quack-grass infested ditch, a boy and girl appeared. They were about ten and both had dirty hands and greasy, lifeless hair. The boy had faded pants and a torn shirt, while the girl wore a short-sleeved, light yellow dress with enough dirt on it to make parts of it appear grayish-brown. Her bare arms and legs were long and thin. Conrad smelled burned tobacco.

"Jeez, you're ugly!" the girl spat out.

"Ooowee, ugleee!" the boy chimed in.

"Spyin' on us, you little punk?" the girl hissed.

"N-n-n-no."

"Well, I say ya are and I'm gonna cut ya for it!" She pulled out a jack knife.

"Get 'im, Margy!" the boy screamed out through his saliva. He was drooling.

Conrad backed up a couple steps, then turned and ran as fast as his stumpy legs could go, but before he was halfway to Bouvette's, the girl had him by the arm and jerked him around.

Expecting a blade slash, Conrad was relieved when she just slapped his face. "Now, getta goin' and don't never come back on this here road agin."

Conrad ran off, chased by the girl's laughter and the boy's hooting. He dodged to the right to avoid the black and white fury that tore at the air with its teeth and kept going until he reached his yard. He didn't go into the house, however; he headed for the vacant lot next door. Once upon a time there had been a house and barn there, but they had burned so many years before, their existence had been forgotten, except by those who could recall anarchist Leon Czolgosz shooting President McKinley.

The vacant lot was filled with quack grass, pigweed, burdock, sow thistle, Canada thistle, kochia, ragweed, dandelions, goldenrod, foxtail, and, closer to the river, black-eyed Susans, then sedges, cattails, willows, wild rice, and pickerelweed. There were also a few box elders, elms, ashes, one big cottonwood, the boulders from the barn's foundation, and the rusted remains of a Model T hauled in and dumped one night in 1929.

Conrad sat by a large kochia, ripening into a tumbleweed, and thought about what the girl had said. He knew he wasn't pretty the way Lise and Trudy were, but he had never thought of himself as ugly. In fact, he looked like his mother, so how could he be?

In August, like the other mothers, Rose took Conrad up the hill to the school for early registration, but unlike the other mothers she did not then go to a friend's house for coffee.

The second grade teacher was Miss Ankenbauer. She was pleasant enough toward Conrad, but he was far from being a teacher's pet like Janice Dee Mayer or Jackie Nelson.

Most of his new classmates were indifferent, but there was one who really appreciated his presence: Alford Wannamaker was no longer the slowest runner in the class.

While that fact made Alford happy, it was a liability for Conrad. At first it was fun for Alford and Janie Larson and Laura Finch to be able to get away from someone in tag or pom-pom pullaway. To have someone yell, "Pom-pom pull away! Come away or I'll pull you away!" and actually to escape his tag and make it, giggling, to the other goal line was a new and not easily forgotten thrill for the slowest runners.

But after awhile it grew old when Conrad couldn't catch anyone, and out of sheer boredom Phil Archer would allow himself to get tagged and be "it" just to liven up the game.

After winter arrived, tag and pom-pom pullaway changed to fox and geese, with its big wheel, spokes, and hub stomped into the snow. Conrad would always be the first goose caught. If he was the fox, no geese would be caught and what started out as fun became tedious until a goose suddenly developed a limp and waited for Conrad to make him or her a new fox.

One day the indifference of the girls, or at least the girls at the top of the second grade pecking order, turned to dislike, or even worse.

Miss Ankenbauer had her students line up with their workbooks and, while she went to the back of the room to get the filmstrip projector ready, had them go to the front of the room and place their workbooks on her desk, open to the lesson they had completed. Janice Dee Mayer was just ahead of Conrad, and when she glanced down at Ruthie Marie Anderson's lesson, she saw she had a wrong answer.

Quickly, she put her workbook down, grabbed a pencil from Miss Ankerbauer's desk, and began erasing.

When Conrad had attended the first grade at McKinley Elementary in Minot, one lesson that Miss Nedrud drilled into him was that of doing one's own work and not cheating. She taught it to him after she caught him copying another boy's paper, a simple enough worksheet based on their reader with Dick and Jane and Sally, and their pets Spot the dog and Puff the cat. A week of staying in from morning recess and pounding blackboard erasers educated him.

"Watch it," Janice Dee whispered over her shoulder when he bumped into her as she was erasing.

He knew what that erasing meant. "Whatta ya doin'?" he said, too loudly.

Fright filled Janice Dee's eyes. "Be quiet. I'm almost done." Her whisper quivered.

"You shouldn't." Again too loudly.

An arm reached around Conrad and took the workbook from the desk. Miss Ankenbauer, disturbed by the forbidden noise, had silently approached, saw the situation, and acted. "What is going on?"

Janice Dee had a workbook filled with perfect pages, rewarded with 100s and gold stars that adhered to the top right-hand corner of every lesson. The thought of a page with a red check mark and a "95" was too much for her, and she went to her desk, put her head down, and wept bitter tears.

Conrad stood there, waiting for the praise he knew he deserved. Instead, as he looked around the room, he saw glares from Janice Dee's inner circle who were emotionally closing around their hurt friend. The other girls who wished they could be on the inside and instinctively knew it was wrong to squeal on anyone who resided there gave him fierce looks. The boys glowered, not because he had turned her in, but because he had made her cry.

With nothing coming from Miss Ankenbauer, Conrad put down his workbook and returned to his desk. At dismissal time, Miss Ankenbauer had Janice Dee and Conrad stay after, a new experience for the girl, and one which drove her to tears again.

Janice Dee was to remain after school for the next two days and print on the main blackboard "I will not cheat" fifty times. Conrad would also stay after two days and print "I will not break the rule of silence" fifty times on the side board. And, yes, both of them could use the little stools so they could reach high enough.

Conrad thought it unfair that he had to print twice as many words, but he got right to his task and finished it ahead of Janice Dee both afternoons. She took her time and made each letter as perfect as possible, hoping that when Miss Ankenbauer saw her penmanship she would relent and not mark the page with the dreaded "95" or, worse, a zero for cheating.

When she did finish, she sat very properly in her desk, anxiously waiting to smile at Miss Ankenbauer when she was dismissed. During class Conrad sat directly behind her, but for the punishment period he was moved off to the side of the room. Once he looked back at Janice Dee, and she crossed her eyes and stuck out her tongue at him, so he never looked again.

A month later when everyone opened their colorfully decorated Valentine's Day boxes, Conrad had the fewest in the class, thirteen, just behind Alford's fourteen, but one could hardly count. It was a heart cut from a slick-paper college notebook that the wealthier kids had, not the pulpy paper from the "Big Ten" or "Indian Chief" tablets most of the grade students had. The heart was shaded black with a pencil, except for a white rectangle in the middle on which the words "I Hate You" appeared.

In the spring "Shark Attack" was the big game. If it hadn't been for the playground teachers, Conrad would have been shunned, but they made certain he got to play. He was a little faster, but still if it was his turn to be the shark, he couldn't catch any kids unless they weren't trying, and if he was a fish, no sharks tried to catch him.

It didn't bother him much because with the spring the vacant lot was slowly coming to life. In fact, when the Primary grades had their picnic in Orland Finkle Park, Conrad ate his lunch by himself near the west side of the park. When he had finished, he slipped through the hedge and roamed around the vacant lot while the other kids laughed and played, never missing him.

During the summer he became an explorer, finding some char from the long-gone barn; an old Baby Ben clock without any glass over the face, but which still, miraculously, worked; and the bones of a large bird that must have flown directly into a tree during the early blizzard of the previous fall and died. As the dead vegetation in the lot exploded into new life, Conrad explored and enjoyed.

The next fall Alford Wannamaker wasn't so happy: he had reclaimed the title as the slowest kid in the class. Not only could Conrad outrun Alford, he could pass Janie and Laura, too. With his new-found ability, Conrad was grudgingly accepted a little by the boys and tolerated by the girls, except for Janice Dee, Jackie, and their friends.

A few boys like Chris Cockburn, his cousin Rory O'Connell, and their friend Ronnie Kerr even began to talk to him on the playground. After Christmas he was invited over to the Cockburn and Kerr homes to play with their new model trains. Ronnie's was an American Flyer and he bragged that brand up, but Chris had a Lionel and he swore they were the best.

His new friendships ended one afternoon when they were upstairs in the Cockburn house, running the Lionel. Chris and Ronnie were arguing the virtues of their own brand of train. Rory was taking Chris's side, but Conrad was happy just to watch the white puffs of smoke coming out of the smokestack of the black 4-6-4 steam locomotive with "2055" in white on the side of the cab as it raced around the tracks. Ray Johnson, a railroad man and a family friend of the Cockburns, had taught Chris the Whyte System of identifying locomotives by their trucks and the number of wheels, and Chris taught Conrad.

Conrad's leg had gone to sleep. When he tried to stand up to stretch it, he lost his balance and his hand came down on the red plastic caboose, breaking it in two. He was so sorry, he almost started to cry. Ronnie wanted to whip him then and there, even though it wasn't his caboose, but Chris said it was all right.

Apparently it wasn't, though, because he was never invited back to play with the trains again, and the three boys stopped talking to him at school.

Other things happened in the third grade, too.

The teacher, Mrs. Hornblower, had been there since the Hoover Administration. She once had a husband, but he had disappeared so long ago that many people didn't know that she had ever been married and called her "Miss Hornblower." She never corrected them.

She had a wooden ruler on her desk with black letters that read "The Golden Rule: 'Do Unto Others As You Would Have Them Do Unto You.'"

When they had Science, there weren't enough books to go around, so half the class had to slide into the seat of another student. Conrad had to sit with Jake Hogan, who wasn't thrilled.

After a few weeks, two students acted in a completely unexpected way. Chris and Ronnie were generally well-behaved, but for some reason they began holding their book up in front of their faces and when Mrs. Hornblower was reading the lesson to the class, one of them would give out with a raspberry. It helped that they were seated behind Janie and Laura, two best friends who were on the large size. Before Mrs. Hornblower could react, the book was down and cherubic looks had replaced the former grins on their faces. They only had Science two days a week, so the rude sound didn't get boring. Neither did Mrs. Hornblower's reaction.

She would peer over her glasses, her faded blue eyes darting from innocent face to innocent face, looking for any tell-tale hint of guilt. Finally, she would go back to the lesson, but the boys were not dumb enough to make the sound again that day.

After a month of raspberry fun, Conrad saw how Chris and Ronnie had gained the admiration of the class for their audacity. Hardly had the books been opened at the next Science period, when the raspberry resounded in the room, louder and juicier than ever. Mrs. Hornblower slammed her book on the desk and stood up.

"It was Conrad," Jake said, trying to move as far away from his seat partner as possible.

Conrad was still trying to digest the betrayal when he felt a sharp whack on his skull. Mrs. Hornblower had advanced with the sword of righteousness disguised as her twelve-inch ruler.

The class gave out a collective gasp. Several of the boys had been the ruler's target, but they had always received the flat side. Conrad had been hit with an edge and it hurt. He didn't want to show any weakness to his classmates, but he had to rub the growing lump to see if it would feel better. As his hand went up, Mrs. Hornblower grabbed it and pulled him out of the desk, much to the relief of Jake.

From then on, Conrad had the best seat in the house for listening to Science, right at Mrs. Hornblower's elbow.

During the first semester Mrs. Hornblower read Anna Sewell's *Black Beauty* to the class. Conrad hated the check-reins and the whipping that hurt the horses, the poor, lame, overworked, broken-down, and broken-winded horses and ponies, but even the description of the dead chestnut mare Ginger didn't bring tears to his eyes because he had never been near a horse and never expected to be.

The second semester the reading book was *Beautiful Joe* by Marshall Saunders.

Conrad loved most animals. High on the north wall of the third grade room hung a series of framed pictures depicting scenes from the life of Eskimos. They were so old that they had greeted Mrs. Hornblower when she first walked into the room in 1930. One of them showed three male Eskimos holding harpoons and standing over a seal lying on the ice. The seal was dead and its blood crimsoned the ice. Conrad liked the other three pictures of Eskimos with kayaks, dogsleds, and igloos, but he could never look at the one with the dead seal.

With the first line of *Beautiful Joe*, Conrad knew he would like the book because it was about a dog, but as soon as the abusive milkman Jenkins was introduced, Conrad felt both anger and sadness welling up inside. He wondered if the local milkman, Mr. Williamson, was that mean.

The reading sessions only lasted a chapter at a time, or half a chapter if it was long, but Conrad's sadness reached bottom at the end of the second chapter. He had been upset about the milkman spreading typhoid fever (he wasn't certain what it was, but it must have been bad if it killed people), but he was just as troubled by Mrs. Jenkins and how she kept house, allowing it to become filthy, and the terrible way she allowed her children to live. His mother was always cleaning, cooking, sewing, mending, doing laundry, and taking care of the girls. She even had Conrad help with the dishes. He knew what a mother was, and Mrs. Jenkins was no mother.

Conrad couldn't believe the words Mrs. Hornblower was reading at the end of Chapter Two, how Beautiful Joe was mutilated. He thought of Blondi, his old friend from Minot, and wondered how it was possible for anyone to cut off a dog's ears and tail and not be torn apart by guilt.

When the book was put away for that session, the sadness climbed slowly up from his abdomen to his heart to his throat and finally to his eyes where it began leaking out. Conrad quickly turned toward the large windows, but not before Jake exclaimed, "Conrad's crying!"

The entire class turned to see; some of the boys snickered. Knowing all the eyes in the room were on him forced the tears out even faster. There were even some tiny splashes on the wooden floor before Conrad put his head on his desk, his arms wrapped around it.

Despite what some people thought, Mrs. Hornblower was not an uncaring woman; she had two grown sons and a grown daughter. They lived on the West Coast, but she thought of them often. A child was crying in her room; she had to do something about it. Quickly she stepped across to Conrad's desk. She stood beside him and told the other students to get out their spelling words. She remained beside Conrad, protecting him. She almost reached down and touched him.

A few minutes later Conrad raised his tear-tired head, wiped his desk with his shirt sleeve, and got out his spelling book.

The rest of *Beautiful Joe* was mostly happy, and he never had to cry again, although sometimes he had to hide some tears that formed because of something delightful in the book. Jake began to call him "Beautiful" on the playground and out of the hearing of the teachers, and a few other boys took it up. It didn't last very long, however, because most nicknames of three syllables don't have the quick smack of recognition that "Ace" and "Doc" or "Peanuts" and "Skinny" do.

Once again Conrad's Valentine's box had the fewest Valentines in it, although none of them were hateful. Once again he was not invited to any birthday parties, but the worst thing that happened that year was because of his mother.

For a Mother's Day surprise Mrs. Hornblower had purchased with her own money some little kits with which the students could take letters that spelled out their mother's name, string them together, and attach the name to a plastic bracelet. Of course, the cheap bracelet wasn't anything a mother was actually supposed to wear; it was the thought that counted.

To make certain that all the mothers' names were spelled correctly, Mrs. Hornblower began to ask the students the Christian names of their mothers and then she would print each one on the board. The student would gather the correct letters and string each one in order.

When she got to Conrad, he said, "Rose." Immediately Jake gave out a choking laugh. "Rose? She sure doesn't look like a rose!"

Jake's joke fell flat. The ugliness of the words shocked the third graders, but the damage had been done. Conrad's heart died and he put his head on his desk and cried, his sobs the only sound in the room.

Mrs. Hornblower had never faced a situation like that one. First, she stood up and glared at Jake, but he had put his head on his desk, too. Then she sat down and fumbled with her grade book. Then she stood, went to the window, and adjusted the shades. When she saw that Conrad would never stop crying, she walked over to him, whispered in his ear, and gently got him to stand up and walk with her to the principal's office, where he remained for the last hour of school.

Back in the room, she condemned Jake to an hour after school for a week.

For the last few weeks of the school year, the third graders treated Conrad better; at least they didn't tease him or make fun of him. Jake kept to himself, hatred in his heart.

On the last day of school, Mrs. Hornblower left the room to check with the first and second grade teachers because the three grades were having a picnic together on the playgrounds. It was Conrad's turn to be the paper-passer, so she gave him the last pile of work to be given back.

Conrad was anxious for the picnic. His mother had prepared a cotto salami sandwich, which was in the lunchroom refrigerator along with all the other students' sandwiches and soft drinks and the potato salad the teachers had brought.

As he hurried down each aisle handing the papers to the owners, he looked only at the next name and headed down the correct row. The faster he went, the closer he would be to his sandwich. Suddenly, his feet stopped, his arms flew up, and the remaining papers flashed up and then down, scattering all over the floor. Conrad fell. He wasn't really hurt, just embarrassed. He looked around to see Jake chuckling and drawing his foot back. Some of Jake's friends were saying "Good one, Jakey!" and "Way to go, Jake!"

Conrad turned to get the papers before Mrs. Hornblower returned, but something strange happened. Ruthie Marie Anderson and Dotty Zeltinger were down on their knees picking up the papers. The two girls had barely spoken to him in the almost two years he had been their classmate, but they had decided that things had gone too far.

Conrad got up and each girl handed him what she had collected. "Conrad, I'll take mine now; it's right on top." Dotty reached out her hand and he placed the paper in it. "Thank you, Conrad."

He didn't know what to say for sure, but he managed to stammer out, "Y-y-y-you're welcome."

When he resumed his job, but at a much slower pace, some of the other girls thanked him, too.

Mrs. Hornblower was a little upset that he wasn't done when she re-entered the room, but no one told her why.

Conrad thought the picnic was a great success. His sandwich was his favorite and the potato salad was good. Plus he got to drink the Mason's Root Beer his mother had bought for him, a real treat because she usually couldn't afford pop.

He was a little nervous when Dotty and Ruthie Marie came over and asked if they could eat with him. He had sat down beside the caragana hedges along the east side of the schoolyard, so he wouldn't be in anyone's way, but they saw him and walked over.

They sat down and stretched out their skinny little-girl legs, balanced their paper plates of potato salad on their thighs, opened their sacks, pulled out their sandwiches, and began to eat.

They tried to talk to Conrad, but he mostly said "Yeah" or "No" and soon the conversation deteriorated into a dialogue between the girls. Conrad didn't mind. He was busy thinking about the big ant hill he had discovered in the vacant lot and what would be the best way to observe the insects without disturbing their activities.

Summer went by much too fast for him, what with his ants and wild birds and the river at the far end of the vacant lot. Too soon he was back in school, in Miss Daugherty's fourth grade room on the other side of the building from where he had been.

Miss Daugherty was young and relatively new to the system; she had been in Menninger only one year longer than Conrad. Being a young teacher, she still believed she could make a difference in the world, if only she tried hard enough. When she saw Conrad trail the other kids through the door the first day of school, she knew she could make a difference in his life.

Conrad liked the fourth grade and he liked Miss Daugherty. She seemed to pay special attention to him, Ruthie Marie and Dotty didn't avoid him, and he was one of the fastest runners in the class. Now it wasn't just Alford Wannamaker who was mad. Where he got his newfound speed, no one could tell. Whenever anyone saw him during the summer, it was in the vacant lot or down by the river. It wasn't as if he had been practicing his running.

Miss Daugherty wanted to encourage reading, so she made a chart with the names of all her students in a column with little rectangles stretching out to the right from each name. Whenever anyone finished one of her approved books, the student cut out a piece of construction paper the size of one of the rectangles, wrote the title and author of the book on it, and pasted it on the chart.

After two weeks of school, every fourth grader but two had at least one rectangle. Ruthie Marie had the most; Chris, Janice Dee, and Alice Monson were all tied for second, followed by the rest of the class. Alford and Conrad trailed the field; actually they hadn't even gotten out of the gate.

To Conrad sometimes the letters on the page didn't make sense; it was like they were twisted in front of or behind where they should be, and when he tried to sound them out as the teacher said, it didn't come out right. As a result Conrad just didn't like books, except those with lots of pictures. He would rather watch his ants busy themselves in their large hump of dirt or carefully peer into a goldfinch's nest and see the babies long after all the other species of birds had left their nests behind rather than read about ants or goldfinches.

Because of his speed, Conrad was grudgingly accepted by the boys, especially since football and baseball had replaced tag and pom-pom pullaway at recess.

The girls ignored him, except for Ruthie Marie and Dotty, and they usually limited their contact to a greeting, a smile, and a question as to how he was, which he always answered with "Fine."

That all came to a halt near the end of the Third Six Weeks. Miss Daugherty had a prize for the student with the most books read at the end of each Six Weeks' grading period. Ruthie Marie had edged out

Chris by two books for both the First and Second Six Weeks, and she was leading by one on the last day of the Third.

Conrad was feeling low because Alford had finally struggled through his first book, and Miss Daugherty looked so pleased when he marched up and pasted on his little blue rectangle.

For music class the fourth and fifth graders walked over to the sixth grade room, where they all sang together. Conrad was in the last desk in the last row, so he was the last one to leave. As he got up, he noticed that the rectangle Ruthie Marie had just pasted on the chart had fallen on the floor. He waited until everyone had left the room, then he picked it up, daubed some of his paste on the back, and pushed it down beside his name.

Over the years Miss Nedrud's first grade cheating lesson had faded from his mind.

When Miss Daugherty finished counting the rectangles after music class, she announced it was a tie between Ruthie Marie and Chris and she'd be giving both of them a prize. The girls knew better. They kept a daily count and could tell how many books each student had read, which was something Miss Daugherty only checked once a week.

The bell was a few minutes away when Ruthie Marie and Dotty asked if they could look at the reading chart. Their suspicions were confirmed, and they carefully checked all the more recently applied rectangles until they came to Conrad's name. There in glorious pink was the claim that Conrad Forester had read *Little Women* (abridged) by Louisa May Alcott. Miss Daugherty was called, Ruthie Marie was named the winner, Conrad was shamed, and for the rest of the year, no one smiled at him or asked him how he felt.

One thing worked out for him, however: Miss Daugherty absolutely forbade Valentine's boxes.

At the end of the term, each class decided to have a picnic on its own. Miss Daugherty marched the fourth graders down to Orland Finkle Park by the river where they ate to their heart's content, Conrad hit a home run and his side cheered, and whenever he wanted to he could look over and see the vacant lot waiting for him. It was the best picnic ever.

Later that spring he followed some tiny squeaks in the vacant lot and discovered a nest of naked pink things the size of one of his finger joints. The mother mouse scurried off through the grass. Conrad felt sorry because he thought she would never come back, but the next day she ran off again. He liked to sit nearby, watch the clouds, and listen to the babies whenever their mother came back to the nest. Their pink color turned to gray and then brown as their fur came in. He was both sad and glad the morning he looked in the nest and it was empty.

Walking near the river one day, he almost stepped on a nest of grass and down in a small depression, containing ten creamy white eggs. He hid in some brush and waited. Soon a female blue-winged teal came out of the reeds and settled on the eggs. Conrad liked watching her and later was able to see the yellow ducklings with their gray-brown eye stripe leave the nest for the first time and swim.

In April 1953, KXMC-TV began broadcasting out of Minot, but the signal was too far away to reach Menninger. However, the television era arrived in July 1954 with KXJB-TV. It took awhile for people to be convinced that TV was here to stay, but soon antennas that looked like erector set-aliens began cluttering the roof lines of the better homes in town.

Carmichael's Radio Repair Shop became a television store, handling 21" Setchell-Carlson sets for $339. Gussie Daniels went uptown to see what all the fuss was about. She loved her radio with its soap operas and music programs, but one look at the display model in Carmichael's and her loyalty to radio drifted off into the ether.

After the set was delivered and the antenna hooked up, Gussie invited Rose and her family, minus Fritz, to enjoy an evening of viewing.

In 1954 Barney Keller retired after thirty-five years with the Great Northern. The day after his retirement became official, little sparks of electricity shot down the wires along the GN mainline from Minot to Menninger. The telegrapher, Odean Wolfe, listened to the key [.._., .., ._., ., .._., _ _ _, ., ._.,..., _, ., ._.], wrote out the message ["FIRE FOERSTER"], and handed it to the station agent, Miles Thaw. Mr. Thaw was a kind man, and he hated to tell Fritz he was through, but the telegram was signed by an official known to brook no failure to comply with his orders. Still, when Fritz showed up for work, Mr. Thaw let him putter around for his eight hours, and as he punched out, told him the bad news.

Fritz took it as a person kicked in the stomach. His face twisted, his hand went to his abdomen, and tears dribbled from his eyes. Mr. Thaw said his check would be ready at the end of the week, and that he was sorry, but since Fritz was no longer employed by the railroad, he would have to leave the station because no loitering was allowed.

Fritz managed to get up the Dakota Street hill, but then he turned onto Villard and walked to the Highball. Once inside he emptied his feelings while he drained a glass of beer and then another.

The owner, Andrew Juleson, felt sorry for the man crying in his beer. He was a good customer, he was a veteran, he was a railroad man (well, an ex-railroad man), and he had two of the cutest little girls in town. He had a son, too, who must have been born on the south side of the Ugly Barn.

Juleson was a vet. Like Fritz he had been on Guadalcanal, but with the 164th Infantry that came in to relieve the Marines. He served in several major battles in the South Pacific and never got a scratch. Often when he thought back, he wished he had gotten wounded. Oh, nothing too drastic like a blown-off arm or leg, but something that left a scar like the one on Fritz's arm.

Right then and there he offered Fritz a job. Nothing fancy like a bartender; the way he'd seen the alcohol pour down Fritz's throat made Juleson leery of a shrinking profit margin, but he would let him clean up the place and wash the glasses. After all, he was a vet.

It was good enough for Fritz. When he got home, he told Rose he had quit his dead end job with the railroad and had gone to work for Juleson. All Rose said was "Oh, my."

When Fritz got his first paycheck from Juleson, Rose realized she should have said a lot more, but it was too late. Also by that time her father had sent her a letter about his retirement, so she knew the railroad job was as gone as the train whistles you hear fading into the night.

In the summer of 1954, construction began on the new Menninger School to replace the old one built around the turn of the century and which was too small and creaky. The overcrowding meant the fifth graders would all be sent to the grade school on the west side of town during the construction.

Luckily for Conrad, Gussie had given him a bicycle that June. He was the only kid in his class that couldn't ride one, and she thought he needed the exercise, so she wheeled an old one that had belonged to her sons over to the Foerster house and told Conrad he had to learn to ride.

The bicycle was really just a frame with a chain, seat, and handlebars. It had no fenders, which made for a wet and muddy back if he rode it in or just after a rain, and it had no chain guard, so he had to roll his right pants leg up or it would get caught.

Gussie and he took it a little ways up the gentle Fifth Street East hill. She held it steady for him as he got on and then gave him a push. He steered into the curb and crashed.

They tried a dozen times before he got the knack of it; then Gussie smiled at him a quarter block down the hill and walked home. He spent the rest of the day riding down the hill, starting closer and closer to the top. When kids jeered at him as they cut across the large vacant lot used as a baseball and football practice field on their way to the swimming pool, he didn't even hear them.

The next day he used the steeper Fourth Street East hill and only crashed once.

Soon he could ride on the level, which he started to do all over town. Once he got started on a ride, he never got off his bike until he was back home. Some people in the south and west ends of town wondered who that strange boy on the bicycle was.

Kids who lived on the east side of the Northern Pacific tracks had always gone to the Menninger Elementary School in the same building as the high school. In the fall the east side fifth graders would be making new friends from the west side of the tracks like Tim Curtis and Gary Morton at the West Side School. Most of the east siders would walk or ride their bikes on Stimson or Lamborn to get to their new school, but a few of them took Gregory. Since that was his street, that's the one Conrad took, but no one ever invited him to walk or ride with them.

Gussie helped him attach a small wire basket to his handlebars (she taught him a lot about tools because she knew how to use them all), and he was off proudly for his first day of school with Mrs. Bernadette Carroll, his school supplies in the basket.

Mrs. Carroll had three young children of her own, and she knew the intricate and sometimes devious ways the young mind works. She would not tolerate teasing or any hurtful behavior toward a child. If even the hint of such a word or act reached her, she would seek out the suspected perpetrator who was considered guilty until proven otherwise. Hearing of her reputation, Conrad looked forward to a pleasant enough year. It was made even more so when all the fifth graders, east and west siders, lined up against the school during the first recess of the year. "Last one down there's it!" yelled Phil Archer, and away the fifth graders went, running for the other goal, the sidewalk. To the surprise of everyone and to the chagrin of some of the boys, Conrad reached the sidewalk first. He was the official fastest kid in class.

That helped him in touch football and baseball that soon replaced tag for the boys. It didn't help Conrad, at least at first, with a game entirely new to him—hockey. After the rink just north of the school was flooded, the girls brought their figure skates and the boys their hockey skates and skateless Conrad was left out at recess. He sat on the swings until he got too cold and went in. Even Mrs. Carroll couldn't help him.

But Gussie could. The day after she drove by the rink and saw Conrad looking at the skaters, she brought him a pair of skates that had belonged to her boys. Together they walked down to the river through Orland Finkle Park with two scoop shovels and cleaned off a patch of river ice. That's where Conrad learned to skate.

In fact, it came easily to him. The first time he tried it at the rink, he was surprised how much smoother that ice was than the cracked and rippled river ice.

Gussie also gave him a hockey stick, which she helped him re-tape, and a puck. Soon he was a hockey player, one of the three fastest, along with Phil Archer and Art Rolfsrud.

The rule was no lifting the puck, but, for some reason, Conrad's legs got more than their fair share of puck bruises, although the shots didn't appear intentional.

In the spring Conrad began to hear of a new club the inner circle of popular kids had formed, the ABC Club. He heard it was a secret club, with a secret membership, password, and meetings. He knew he'd never be able to join, but then another rumor floated around that anyone who could discover where a meeting of the Club was being held would automatically be allowed membership.

For the next two months Conrad was able to find out about ABC meeting places. Sometimes suspected ABC members were whispering just loud enough for him to hear, sometimes he would find a "lost" note near his desk, sometimes a kid who was obviously not a member would tell Conrad what he had heard.

Conrad would ride his bike to the abandoned house on South Avenue, to the west side of the reservoir, under the old bridge on Glen Haven, to Janice Dee Mayer's garage, but no matter where he went, he found nothing.

The second to the last day of school the inner circle kids approached Conrad as a group. He thought maybe they would let him join because of his persistence. Instead, Janice Dee revealed the truth: it had all been a hoax. There had never been an ABC Club, but everyone wanted to thank Conrad for falling for the trick so easily. Amid the laughs, Conrad got on his bike and rode home with an empty feeling.

The next day he felt better and the feeling disappeared. The school picnic was held on the grass where the rink had been, and Mrs. Carroll had made barbeques and beans for everyone. Conrad just had to bring a small bag of potato chips and a root beer. He ate by himself where the north hockey goal had been and enjoyed watching the other kids talking and eating.

That summer he didn't spend as much time in the vacant lot as he used to. He had his bike and he had television.

Sunday nights were the best. Lise, Trudy, and he would run over to Gussie's and get their usual places. Conrad had the couch, Lise got a rocker, and Trudy sat on Gussie's lap. Usually she would have a snack for them. Sometimes it was popcorn, sometimes a bowl of ice cream she made herself, or it could be as simple as some roasted sunflower seeds from the flowers she grew in her garden. When it was popcorn, Conrad was careful to eat just one kernel at a time to make the melted sweet cream butter and tangy salt flavor last as long as possible.

Conrad would lie there in the dark and watch Ann Sothern as *Private Secretary* and marvel that she could have been born in North Dakota, which is what Gussie said. He would laugh at Jack Benny and Rochester, a Negro with a strange raspy voice, and ride the range with Gene Autry and his horse Champion. The show would begin with a song: "I'm back in the saddle again; Out where a friend is a friend . . . ." When it ended, a man in a cowboy suit and hat would walk out in front of a chuck wagon and talk about Holsum Bread, so great for growing cowboys and cowgirls. One evening Gussie invited Conrad over for supper, after which they watched TV. The man who did the sports was the same man who plugged Holsum Bread, but without his cowboy clothes. That evening the TV camera was left on after the commercial and Conrad saw the man throw a loaf of Holsum Bread into the chuck wagon and laugh. The next week he was no longer the Holsum pitchman.

Ed Sullivan on *Toast of the Town* showed Conrad a world inhabited by singers, dancers, comedians, celebrities in the audience, Broadway stars, movie stars and film clips (he'd never been to a movie), All-American football teams, performing bears, trained chimps, circus acts (he'd never been to one), the pantomime artist Marcel Marceau, magicians, unicyclists, balancing acts, jugglers, and his favorites, the ventriloquists and their puppets: Ricky Layne and Velvel with their funny way of talking, and Senor Wences with Johnny's face drawn on his hand and Pedro, who was a head in a box and said "s'awright." Johnny was the girls' favorite because when Senor Wences moved his thumb, it was like Johnny's mouth was moving and a little voice came out.

Lise and Trudy had to go home after Ed Sullivan said good night, but Conrad got to stay for *Rocky King, Detective*, with Rocky opening the show by walking down a narrow hallway and lighting a cigarette. It was a different kind of show because sometimes "dead" people would get up and once in awhile props would get knocked over. Gussie said it was a live performance like a play. It was also different than most of the other shows because it was produced on something called the DuMont Network, not CBS. Conrad liked the way Rocky always ended each show by talking to his wife Mabel on the telephone and saying something nice. Clorets Gum was the sponsor. Around Christmas time the program disappeared.

Next came *China Smith* with an actor Conrad thought had a funny name, Dan Duryea, playing an adventurer in the Orient. When that show ended, a man came on playing a violin while the words "Florian Zabach" were written across the screen and Conrad knew it was time to go. He would thank Gussie and hustle home.

Other programs he enjoyed were *The Halls of Ivy* with a British couple as the president of a Midwest college and his wife and *Meet Millie* about a Manhattan secretary and her meddling mother. *The Millionaire*, sponsored by Colgate-Palmolive, featured a strange-looking, dark-haired man named Michael Anthony, whose looks somehow reminded Conrad of himself. He was a secretary to billionaire John Beresford Tipton (you never saw his face), who handed a cashier's check to Mr. Anthony every week to give away to some person to see how it would change his or her life. Conrad wondered how such a gift would affect his life. Other than helping his mother, sisters, and Gussie, he could come up with nothing.

I've Got a Secret with host Garry Moore was a special favorite of Gussie's, so Conrad liked it, too. She also enjoyed the plays on *Climax!* hosted by William Lundigan, a program which was first done live, and *Schlitz Playhouse of Stars*, which was also done live at first and which Conrad didn't like so much because it started with someone pouring beer into a glass which reminded him of his father.

Topper was a show about two ghosts and a ghost St. Bernard named Neil. All three tried to liven up the life of a banker, but the show didn't last past July. Conrad didn't like it much anyway because he didn't think ghosts would smoke cigarettes the way the ghosts on *Topper* did. He didn't realize that since the sponsor was Camel Cigarettes, the smoking was a product plug.

He did like Jackie Gleason, who made them laugh, and when the comedian said, "And awaa-ay we go!" all four of them joined in.

If Conrad could convince his mother he had no homework or that it was done, sometimes he and the girls were allowed to watch TV before supper if they promised not to bother Gussie, who usually didn't watch at that time. Then *Captain Jim, Superman, Kit Carson,* and *Beat the Clock* kept them entertained. One evening Conrad went to Gussie's early, and when he saw the local weather program, the weatherman looked very much like Captain Jim, except without his space helmet. The Captain would rocket down from outer space and interview some kids, show cartoons, fire up the rocket, and blast off into space until the next afternoon. Once Conrad saw Phil Archer on *Captain Jim*, and another time there were Janice Dee and Jackie Nelson talking to the Captain. He remembered that they hadn't been in school those days.

During the summer the school building was completed, and the "new" smell greeted the sixth graders as they entered Mrs. Caroline Goddard's room. Mrs. Goddard was an older woman and was "no nonsense." Her nickname among the more language-daring members of the school was "Mrs. God-awful."

Conrad tried his best to get his work done and keep on her good side. His speed kept him on the recess football and baseball teams, although the boys ignored him the rest of the time.

The girls also left him alone, except for one major event. Mrs. Goddard had obtained a recording machine that could make records. If a record was sent to Fargo, it could be used as a master to make others. Mrs. Goddard's idea was for the sixth graders to sing, have it recorded and copies made, then give the records to their parents as Christmas presents. Enthusiasm reigned.

After several practice sessions Mrs. Goddard put a "Recording—Do Not Disturb" sign on her door, lined up the "choir," and put the blank record on the turn table. She set it spinning, put the stylus down, and gave the downbeat. Thirty-one young voices trilled and warbled to the best of their ability on three traditional Christmas carols. When the last note died away, most of the kids looked at each other and smiled, proud of their accomplishment.

As Mrs. Goddard played the record after it came back from Fargo, the kids, especially the girls, stopped smiling and looked at each other with open mouths and squinty eyes. Something was terribly wrong. What was it? They asked to hear the record again. It was . . . it was . . . it was somebody's voice off-key and grating. It was Conrad's.

Now, to tell the truth, Mrs. Goddard was tone deaf, so she thought everything was fine and smiled to think that her singers wanted to hear themselves again.

She wasn't smiling, however, when a delegation of young ladies approached her after school and told her they wanted to record the songs again . . . without Conrad. She called in Mrs. Carroll from the classroom next door and asked her to listen to the recording. When asked for her opinion, Mrs. Carroll looked out the windows, then at the imploring faces of the girls, and then at Mrs. Goddard. She whispered, "I think the girls are right," and left the room.

The next day the singers were lined up again, Mrs. Goddard put another blank record on the recording machine, told Conrad to turn the machine on and then guided him over to the window, where she told him to look outside until the singing was over, then he could turn the machine off.

That time everyone was satisfied; in fact, some of the girls thought they were better than the high school choir.

At Christmas there were thirty records given as gifts in the homes of the sixth graders, but not in the Foerster house. Since he hadn't been on the record, Conrad decided he had no right to give it to his mother. Instead, he walked down to the river and sailed the record as far as he could. It cut into the snow and disappeared. The next spring the ice broke up and the disc sank into the mud.

Actually, Conrad had bigger things to worry about than a record. His father had been fired again. One night a Korean War vet walked into the Highball with some friends. He had grown up in Menninger and was passing through. One of his sleeves was pinned to his shirt because he'd lost an arm at Pork Chop Hill.

Juleson gave him a drink on the house, and both he and Fritz talked to the young man as vets often do, being careful not to pry, but just to listen to anything he had to say. After the young man left, Fritz had a few drinks himself.

The door was locked and Fritz had a few more drinks, then he started talking to Juleson about the young man and eventually worked in his own service. At first it was the same old line, but soon he was crying and blubbering out the fraud he had perpetuated for years about his scar. Juleson was shocked and then disgusted. He fired Fritz on the spot. However, he did drive the stunned man home.

With Fritz home, things got tense because when he wanted a drink in the worst way, Rose refused to give him the money, so he'd sit and mumble to himself. Sometimes he scared the kids because it appeared he was having terrible dreams and howled like a dog or screamed like a big cat.

As Christmas approached, Rose knew she couldn't afford both presents and a tree, so she began to get on Fritz to find some part-time work, any kind, just to bring in a little money. He tried hiring out to shovel snow from driveways and sidewalks, and people hired him because they felt sorry for the family. Fritz did bring some money home, but a lot of it got drunk up at one of the bars on Chicago or Villard or at Helgo's, a seedier bar on St. Paul Street.

In mid-December Rose asked him why he wasn't shoveling somewhere because there had been a light snow. When he didn't answer, she continued to ask him until he blew up. To help settle him down, Rose said it wasn't so much for her, but that the kids wouldn't have a

Christmas unless he could earn some money. They wouldn't even have a Christmas tree.

Fritz stared as that information sank in. Finally, he put on his coat and cap, pulled his gloves out of his pockets, and headed outdoors. Rose couldn't see where he was going because the windows were so frosted over; besides, she had to comfort the kids who were upset by the fighting.

It was late afternoon when Fritz grabbed an ax from the garage and cut across the vacant lot and the ditch into Orland Finkle Park. His boots filled with snow so he tried to hurry. If it had been even an hour later, the darkness would have hidden him from the curious eyes of the police chief, Nate Coulson, who had seen movement against some trees in the park where no one should have been on a cold December day. He pulled his car over, got out, and edged through some bare caraganas. He saw the movement again and heard a metal-against-wood sound. Someone was chopping down an evergreen.

When he got closer, he saw a five-foot tree go over. Immediately the chopper grabbed the lower trunk and began to pull the tree through the snow. Coulson was about to yell, but decided to see where the tree would end up.

Fritz was pleased with himself, even though it cost him freezing-cold feet. He was glad he'd passed up the larger trees; the one he was dragging was heavy enough.

When he reached the house, he tossed the ax into a snow drift, opened the door, and backed in. When he turned around, Rose's eyes were enormous and her mouth gaped. The children were hesitant. Just as they started to smile and come toward him, a voice said, "O.K., Fritz, come along with me."

Unfortunately for him, court was in session that evening. "Fifty dollars or ten days." He had to take the ten days.

Rose only came to see him once. She told him they let her keep the tree, so the kids were happy.

Judge Neasmith let Fritz out two days early because it was Christmas Eve. Chief Coulson gave him a ride home to make certain he didn't try to cadge any drinks in one of the bars.

The day before, Gussie had come over and forced a twenty-dollar bill on Rose, telling her to buy a present for each of the kids. Rose tried to give the money back, but Gussie was already out the door and into her son's car. He was taking her to his home in Fargo for the holidays.

Lise had a bad cold so she couldn't walk uptown with the rest of the family, and there was no one to look after the kids if Rose went by herself. Then a savior walked unexpectedly through the door.

Rose told Fritz if he hurried he could make it back uptown before the stores closed, handed him the twenty, and told him what to get each of the kids at the Silver Dime Store. When he looked perplexed, Rose scribbled the name of each present on a scrap of paper, gave it to him, and told him to hurry.

Fritz labored up the hill onto Lamborn and headed downtown. It was cold that late afternoon and gray, as December usually was. When he passed the Norwegian Lutheran Church, he looked up to see if what he heard was angels, but it was only Christmas carols coming out of a loudspeaker in the steeple. Heading down the slight hill was easier. A couple cars slowed down, but when the drivers saw who it was, they sped up again. As he crossed the tracks, he thought he should warm up, so he passed the Dime Store and went into Gimpy's Holiday Spot instead.

He stood by the door, telling himself he should leave, that he would leave . . . just another minute or two. The sounds of the bar glasses, the muffled noise of the men and a few women enjoying themselves over drinks, the occasional burst of laughter proved too much. He bellied up to the bar, displaying his twenty.

After a couple of long-desired beers, he tried a shot or two, then he bought a round for his old pals, Hoyt Walkup and "Highball Harry," a couple of barflies. Hoyt, who had just been paid for bootlegging some booze at Helgo's for some dry teenagers, showed off by buying a round for Highball and Fritz. Finally, Fritz stumbled toward the door. The blast of cold air awakened him to the fact that he had a job to do. He hesitated and walked, hesitated and walked, until he reached the Silver Dime. The door wouldn't open. He pushed again. It was solid. He noticed the lights were off. What would Rose say? What would the kids say?

Down the sidewalk he could see people; at least he thought they were people. He lurched toward them. Hogan's Harmony House of Food was still open. He went in. Wandering around, he found the one shelf devoted to small toys. He couldn't read Rose's note; it looked blurry. He picked up a couple of little dolls and a cap gun and went to the check stand. When he put down all the money he had left, the girl told him it wasn't enough. He said he'd be back and began to navigate the aisles again.

Rose was worried. Fritz should have been back an hour ago. Maybe someone ran over him as he was crossing a street. Worse, maybe he was drinking up the Christmas money.

Suddenly there he was, stomping his feet and trying to get his overcoat off. First he had to put a paper bag down. That couldn't be for the presents she had written down; it was much too small. Where was the larger bag?

He smiled crookedly at her as he walked into the living room where the kids were listening to carols on the radio. He dropped onto the couch and called them over. Slowly, they moved, the girls first and Conrad in back of them.

"Da-Daddy didn't forget." He opened the bag, reached in, and pulled out two pink pieces of card stock with twenty bobby pins on each one. He handed them to the girls. "Me-Merry Chrissmass." They stared at the presents.

Fritz reached in again and handed something to Conrad. His big hand covered the object until he withdrew it. Conrad looked down; it was a small jar of Skippy Peanut Butter.

Fritz fell back against the couch. The girls ran to their room. Little wailing cries sounded in the darkness as Rose opened and shut their door, trying to think of a way to comfort them.

Conrad went to his room and shut the door. He put the Skippy on his chest of drawers. He remembered what his mother had said he would probably get and that wasn't it. He had daydreamed about Mr. Potato Head ever since he saw one on TV. He put the pillow over his head and tears warmed his nose and cheeks. After a few minutes he fell asleep thinking that he wouldn't even eat the Skippy: it was creamy and he only liked the chunky.

When he went back to school, and the kids were asking each other what presents they got, Conrad decided he would lie and tell them he got a Mr. Potato Head, just what he wanted, only no one ever asked him.

Without a paycheck coming in and Fritz's railroad pension barely covering the house payment and groceries, things looked pretty bleak until Rose got a job as a custodian's helper, housekeeper, and second cook at the hospital. A "Jill-of-all-trades." There were only two problems.

Since the Foersters didn't own a car (Fritz had sold their last one before they left Minot), Rose had to walk to work seven blocks, much of it uphill, which was tough in the winter time. On the way home it was easier because it was mostly downhill, and Rose made good time because she could hardly wait to see her kids, especially Lise and Trudy.

The other problem was that Fritz wasn't reliable enough to baby sit. Mostly he just sat on the couch, staring at a calendar. It wasn't one of the better calendars with a new picture every month. It had one big picture and then the months on twelve smaller sheets were torn off after each month was done. The big picture was of a tropical beach with palm trees.

That problem was solved when Gussie volunteered to stay with the kids any time Rose had to do night work. People in the neighborhood knew when that was because if the front porch light at the Foersters' house was on, Rose was working.

For a time it seemed that Fritz would clean up his act. Whether it was over the Christmas fiasco or not, Rose didn't care, but it did mean something when he told her he was through drinking. Sometimes she even let him stay with the kids without Gussie, although she worried the whole time she was working the night shift.

Toward the end of March, Barney Keller parked his port-holed 1955 Buick Roadmaster in front of the Foerster house and went in to see his daughter for the first time in almost five years. He was shocked by how care-worn she appeared; she was shocked by how thin he had gotten. He told her it was his "ticker."

He had brought some clothes for the kids; everything was too small.

He told her he was moving to Phoenix. St. Paul was too blamed cold. He'd like it if she would take over the Summit Avenue house. She said no. He said he was leaving her everything in his will. She didn't say anything. Fritz had been on the couch the entire visit and hadn't said a word. The kids came in from school and didn't know who the thin man was, although Conrad liked the car out front. When Barney tried to hug the girls, they shied away. He did shake hands with Conrad, but the boy's hand was limp.

As he was leaving, he held out an envelope. "Rose, I want you to take this."

"What is it? Money?"

"Yes."

"I don't want it."

"Take it for the kids, then."

"No."

He tossed the envelope on the floor and left.

When Fritz heard the word "money," he immediately got off the couch, just in time to see several hundred dollars in bills spill onto the floor before Rose gathered them up. She held onto the envelope the rest of the night, and in the morning Fritz didn't know where it was.

While she was in the bathroom, he went through her purse—not there. She was starting on the day shift, so he patted down the dress she had put on the bed—nothing. After the kids had gone to school and Rose was heading up to the hospital, Fritz began a systematic search of the house. Sometimes he was on his knees; sometimes he was moving furniture; sometimes he was on a chair looking in the light fixtures. He tried to find a loose floorboard. He pulled off the mattresses. The only thing he found was frustration.

When Rose was around or the kids were home from school, he had to sit quietly and pretend everything was fine, so his searches were confined to two or three days a week.

By mid-April he was getting desperate. Rose was hinting very firmly that he should get a job, and if that happened, he could say goodbye to the easy money.

He had gone over the main floor a half dozen times and the crawl space once, although he couldn't believe that Rose had gotten up there. He pried, poked, and pounded; he searched and swore. He checked the shed and the garage, then he checked them again. He had done the basement once. Maybe he should try it again.

The musty smell followed him around the low-ceilinged space. The lighting was so bad he had to carry a flashlight. He checked every shelf; he looked over, in, and under the washing machine; he felt all over the water heater and furnace. When he was reaching around the chimney, his hand knocked something onto the floor—a white envelope. His heart raced. He opened it. Beautiful green met his gaze.

Upstairs he counted it—five hundred dollars! He was out the door.

He started his tour at the Captain's Quarters on the corner of Villard & Dakota; its neon steamboat sign was on although it was early afternoon. He felt great: money in his pocket and booze on the bar.

Next stop—the Highball. He had just gone through the door when the bar maid called out, "Fritz, Andrew doesn't want you in here!" Upon hearing his name, Juleson appeared out of the backroom, advanced on Fritz, who held up his hands in defense, spun him around, and propelled him onto the sidewalk.

Fritz picked himself up, shot a single finger at the Highball, and crossed the street to Guthrie's. He didn't like to drink there because the animal heads on the walls—bison, deer, elk, moose, and pronghorn—and a huge Kodiak bear rearing up by the door, all shot by Guthrie, gave him nightmares. He had a few drinks, bought a round for the house, and left.

Around the corner on Chicago, he located the entry to the Royal Flush. By that time there were more people in the bars, and Fritz felt like a big shot, flashing his wad and buying drinks for everyone.

Gimpy's Holiday Spot was next. By that time Highball and Hoyt had joined him like pilot fish with a shark. Finally, Gimpy had to tell Fritz the bar was closed to him, that he should go home. His bleary brain signaled that Gimpy was right. Fritz lurched out the door and started to turn left. That was when the pilot fish took over. With Fritz in between, the three stumbled across the tracks to Helgo's.

Pete Helgo would serve anyone, any time, any race, religion, or color, as long as the color of their money was green. When the "Three Musketeers" walked in, he was skeptical and tapped his yellow teeth with his corncob pipe, wondering if he could throw all three of them out, but when what was left of the wad came out of Fritz's pocket, Pete hustled behind the bar.

Hoyt and Highball were long gone when Fritz came to; so was his money. He tried to get up off the floor while Pete sat in his rocking chair smiling at him. Finally, he was up and noticed it was dark out. Either that or Pete's windows were grimier than they used to be.

Pete motioned to the door and Fritz staggered out. It took him a couple of minutes to figure out his directions, then he turned to the north, took a couple of steps, and passed out.

He heard voices and when he woke up, Chief Coulson was looking down at him. "I think he's come around, Mrs. Foerster."

Rose's face appeared. "Yes."

"I think he'll be O.K."

"Yes."

Coulson left. Rose walked to the girls' room and then to Conrad's room, saying goodnight and shutting the doors behind her. When she went to her bedroom, she left the door open.

Fritz felt his forehead. There was a big knot there and it hurt, but then his whole head felt like little demons were inside using jackhammers to pound their way out. He was so thirsty. He wanted water, but found he couldn't speak. He decided he'd just lie there. Rose would come back soon and then he could ask for water. He fell asleep and dreamed of wild animal heads chasing him.

Rose woke up a couple of times during the night. It had taken quite awhile for her to get to sleep. What right did Fritz have spending her money? Not that she would have spent it. Never. She should have burned it in the furnace when she had the chance. What made her change her mind and put it behind the chimney? Did she secretly want the money after all? No, now her mind was playing tricks on her. She had to sleep.

Through the mists of restless sleep, she heard a noise—a gasp? a moan? She fought to listen, but it didn't come again. She could hear a slow, rhythmical, almost humming sound. It must be Fritz's breathing. Each time she woke up, she heard the sound.

The alarm clock went off at six, as usual, but she was already awake, and two seconds later she silenced it.

Coming out of the bathroom, she noticed how quiet the house was, then the refrigerator clicked on—it was the same humming sound she had heard during the night. She moved into the living room and stared down at Fritz.

His skin was a sickening purple-gray wax, but his lips were pale. His left arm was hidden by his body, but his right hand was bluish. His closed eyes seemed to be sinking into his skull. She felt his forehead; it was cold. She tried to lift his arm, but it was stiff and tight. She saw some purple-black on the underside.

She went to the bedroom, got a blanket, and covered his entire body. She made coffee and sat at the table until her cup was empty.

She got the kids up, fed them, and got them on their way to school. None of them asked about their father, or even seemed to notice him.

The funeral was a dry one. The only tears were shed by Highball and Hoyt, but they had been shunted off to the back of the church by the usher, away from the pews, so no one saw them.

Some people (and there weren't that many who attended) said the little family was in shock, but that wasn't it. Fritz had ceased to be an active part of Rose's life years before; he was more like an unpleasant and treacherous presence. Lise and Trudy rarely thought of him, even when he was eating at the table right across from them. At the church they didn't see their mother cry so why should they? To Conrad his father was like a faint smell of smoke on a summer's night, a shadow of a ghost that wafted off into nothing.

Rose couldn't afford to bury Fritz so the county put him in the "Stoneless Graves" section. When Gussie drove the family through the gates of the Eternal Peace Cemetery and back home, none of them ever visited the grave again. The cemetery's name had been changed from Eternal Rest; the women discussed it on their way back to town and agreed they liked the old name better.

The school year came to a close. The sixth grade picnic was held in the baseball park south of town. Mrs. Goddard drove and brought some of the girls with her, but the rest of the girls and all the boys rode their bikes. Conrad played baseball on a real diamond for the first time and legged out a couple of hits. He ate his sandwich and potato chips and drank his root beer in the visitors' dugout and watched the other kids enjoying their food and pop in the grandstand or stretched out on the outfield grass.

After everyone else had gone, he tramped around the trees, bushes, tall grass, and weeds that surrounded the ball field. He saw a furry white tail rustle through the underbrush and carefully searched until he discovered a nest of baby cottontails. He didn't touch any of them for fear the mother would abandon her babies.

The summer went by quickly, what with the vacant lot, his bike, and television. Then he was in seventh grade.

Of course, the upper class boys saw him as a new target. His was the first head to get a "swirly" in the boys' lavatory. One of the junior boys had an autumn cold. As he walked down the hall, he sneezed juicily into his hand and rubbed it in Conrad's hair. The next week Conrad was sneezing and coughing.

All seventh graders had to endure an initiation administered by the seniors in order to become loyal Menninger High School Muskrats. Some of it was mild, such as being blindfolded and told to eat a human eyeball (a green olive), but some of it was more physical, like being swatted with a ping pong paddle. The seniors had something special for Conrad, however.

With all the other seventh-grade "worms" (as they were "affectionately" known), he was led blindfolded into the basement of the gymnasium. When it was his turn to be initiated into becoming a loyal Muskrat, he was brought in front of a table of seniors. One of them told him that the school board wanted to meet him. Did he want to meet them?

He didn't know what to say, but when the question was yelled at him, he said, "Yes."

"Here comes the board."

Five senior boys walked heavily into the room. Conrad could tell where they were and was told to face them. "Now bow to the board." He did. "No, no, bow and hold it." He bowed and stayed bent over. "Conrad Foerster, do you want to meet the board?"

"Yes."

"Louder."

"Yes!"

At which point another senior boy came up behind Conrad carrying a long wooden paddle with the words "Board of Education" painted on it and spanked him with it, hard. When the shock forced him upright, he was told to bow again and the "board" met him again to even more laughter.

He was now initiated and allowed to leave. As he took off the blindfold, he used it to wipe his eyes. As soon as the initiation was over and the dance began, he sneaked up the stairs and out a back door.

Maria Elena Mendoza was sad. Her father had run away with that Garza woman and had left Maria Elena, her little sister Malinal, and their mother alone in the Valley, while he and his *puta* went to Michigan to pick apples.

Her mother didn't have enough money to get back to Crystal City, Texas, or at least she said so. Perhaps she just didn't want to carry her shame around among her relatives and friends. Ramon was so handsome, why would he go off with a *zorra* like Carmelita Garza?

Mrs. Mendoza worked until the hoeing of sugar beets was done, then got a job in a grocery store bakery in Cooperville, where the girls went to school. That made Maria Elena even sadder because she knew for certain she wouldn't be going back to Crystal City to cheer on the Fighting Javelinas football team; see the Popeye statue; or be with her friends Isabel, Solana, Mariposa, and Clara Soledad. She even began to miss the big Del Monte canning plant.

After working in the grocery store three months, Mrs. Mendoza heard of a bakery in central North Dakota that was looking for an assistant baker, so she packed up the girls and headed to Menninger.

She was an immediate hit. Not only could she make the traditional American breads, cakes, cookies, and pies, she also added Mexican breads and pastries: the chewy sweet bread called pan dulce; the egg bread, pan de huevo; cuernos de azucar ("sweet horns"); empanadas (turnovers) with a variety of fillings; and cinnamon, chocolate, sugar, and peanut butter galletas (cookies).

Mrs. Mendoza had to get right to work, so Maria Elena enrolled Malinal in the fourth grade. She liked Miss Daugherty. She seemed so friendly and was a lot younger than the other fourth grade teacher, Miss Prentice. They were late getting to school, and by the time she got to the high school side and registered, it was too late to go to her fourth period class.

Following the principal, Mr. McHale, around the school made Maria Elena even sadder. When she was in the office, at her locker, or looking into the classrooms, no one smiled at her. It wasn't that they appeared unfriendly, just curious. She missed her friends more than ever.

Mr. McHale showed her to the lunchroom and left her. She was at the end of the line and no one paid any attention to her. She looked at the hamburger hot dish, green beans, and dinner roll; the meal looked the same as what she had eaten at Cooperville High.

She glanced around the lunchroom and saw it was pretty crowded, although some students had finished and left. Then at a far-corner table she saw a boy all by himself. He had black hair and was a little darker than the other kids in the room. As she got closer, she saw he had the start of a faint black mustache.

She stood looking down at him. "¿Puedo sentarme con usted, amigo?"

Conrad stared up and choked on his roll. He had to take a big slug of milk to get it down. "Wha-wha-what did you say? I don't understand."

Maria Elena realized her mistake. "Excuse me, I thought perhaps you were . . . you understood Spanish."

"No." He looked away.

Marie Elena sat down. "Do you mind?"

Conrad shook his head. He realized he liked having her beside him. She introduced herself and then asked him who he was. As she ate, she continued to talk to him and he gave some short answers. When they were both finished, she asked him to walk with her to their fifth period class and continued to ask questions.

She was rounder than most of the girls in his class, and Conrad was beginning to notice girls like that, not the straight-line, skinny-legged sticks he was used to. He also liked the way she talked, the accent, the rolling r's, the warmth.

He remembered one day when he was in the vacant lot. He had been there since the early morning. It was cloudy and he was chilly, but he wanted to see if the robin fledglings were going to leave the nest, so he endured. The clouds disappeared in the late morning and the sunlight draped itself over everything. He closed his eyes and let the sunlight splash his face with warmth. If sunlight could have a sound, it would contain the musical, mystical warmth of a southern land revealed in Maria Elena's voice, a warmth missing from the northern European sounds of brittle harshness in the speech of his classmates.

Maria Elena and Conrad stood off by themselves as the other kids gathered outside the door to the English room. He dared to look in her eyes and saw they were the same rich brown of the little animal he had scared up while he was walking the river east of town. Back at home he got out the animal book Gussie had given him and found a picture. The little animal was a mink.

Conrad didn't realize it, but some of the other seventh grade boys were actually jealous of him. His speed had allowed him to be picked very quickly by the older boys in Phy. Ed. when they were choosing touch football teams, plus he had a mustache, well, a shadow of one. When Maria Elena began a friendship with him, that only increased their jealousy.

Her presence also made a difference for Conrad in another way: the upperclassmen began to leave him alone. No more "swirlies," no more stacked lockers, no more tripping in the hallway.

Maria Elena invited him to her house on the west side, and he surprised himself by going. When he didn't ask her to his house in return, she invited herself. His mother seemed pleased and his sisters loved it. She invited him to her birthday party and he went. He even brought a present, a light green chiffon scarf which she wore to school the next day. His mother had picked it out.

She had made a few friends among the girls—Dotty, Ruthie Marie, Alice Munson, and Marla Meusel—but whenever she could, she'd rather be with Conrad.

They exchanged Christmas presents, and she got him to go to a sock hop in the gym. He even danced with her. She helped him with his school work, especially his reading, and his grades improved. Not an "honor roll" improvement, but they were better.

He created a little scandal when he stopped attending the German Lutheran Church and started going to St. Andrew's Catholic Church with Maria Elena and her family. They would always arrive a half hour early so Mrs. Mendoza could say a rosary in honor of Our Lady of Guadalupe. She prayed to the Virgin for her help in returning Ramon to her. "Our Lady will not fail me," she would tell her daughter.

"Yes, my mother," her daughter would reply.

For the first time in his earthly existence, Conrad was enjoying life with another human being. Also for the first time, the school year whizzed by. The winter months seemed as short to him as summer vacation.

Christmas came; he blinked, and Maria Elena had bought him a Valentine.

He blinked, and he was holding her awkwardly at a seventh and eighth grade St. Patrick's Day Dance, which had to be held on the sixteenth since the seventeenth was a Sunday.

He blinked again and it was spring. Lise and Trudy had gone out after school to give away their May baskets. There was a knock at the back door, but when he answered, there was no one there. He looked around and then down; there was a May basket. He picked it up, expecting it to have "Lise" or "Trudy" on it, but the little card said "Conrad." He had never received or given a May basket before, so he didn't know the rules. As he stood there, he heard a light laugh from the corner of the garage. Just as he started toward the sound, Lise and Trudy saw him from the driveway as they returned home.

"Oh, Conrad got a May basket!"

"Now he has to kiss her!"

Maria Elena stepped from her hiding place behind the garage and stood there expectantly.

"Well, go on," teased Lise.

He brushed his lips on Maria Elena's cheek.

"Conrad kissed a girl!" Trudy laughed. The sisters heard voices, followed by a knock at the front door. They took off to intercept the basket givers.

Maria Elena took the basket from Conrad and put it on the ground, placed his arms around her waist, wrapped her arms around his neck, and kissed him. It felt good. He moved forward to kiss her, but she put a finger on his lips. "Only one kiss per basket, mi coriño."

Malinal stepped up to them. "C'mon." She had a small box with May baskets in it.

"We're delivering May baskets to her friends. Would you like to come along?"

While Malinal ran from her friends, but not too fast, Conrad and Maria Elena held hands and enjoyed the little chases, but there were no more kisses.

One Saturday she invited him to meet her uptown. He put his bike in the rack in the Railroad Park, and they walked around the main block talking. He was comfortable enough by that time to let his guard down and tell her about things he liked and didn't like. She did the same.

At the Silver Dime Store she pulled him inside and took him up and down the aisles. She bought a small red and white woven bamboo cylinder. When they were outside, he asked her what it was.

"It's a Chinese finger trap."

"How does it work?"

"Here, I'll show you." She put it on the first finger of her right hand and held it up.

"So, that's no big deal."

"Give me your hand." She slipped the trap on the first finger of his left hand. "Now, get it out." He pulled, but the bamboo only tightened. "Wow, that's pretty good." She began to walk and he had to follow her, the trap tugging his finger. "Wow," was all he could say.

At first he was a little self-conscious, especially when some adults smiled or snickered as they passed, but after awhile it seemed all right.

Maria Elena bought two peanut butter galletas at the Golden Crust Bakery, paying awkwardly because of the trap, and they ate them as they walked around the block again.

They crossed Chicago to where his bike was.

"I have to go home now."

"O.K., but how do I get loose?"

She pushed her end of the trap inward and squeezed the bamboo with her free hand. Her finger came right out. "Push on the end."

He did and was able to pull the trap off. "Wow."

Maria Elena gave a soft laugh. "Sometimes you can be very funny." He stood there, not knowing how she meant it. She moved over and gave him a hug. "You want it?"

"Sure."

"Goodbye, Conrad. I had a nice time."

"Me, too." He put the trap in his pocket, got on his bike, and watched her cross the street. Before she disappeared around the corner, she waved. He gave an answering wave and peddled home.

A couple weeks later she helped him study for his finals, and his report card was the best one he'd ever had. On the last day of school, Maria Elena and Conrad brought some sandwiches, chips, and pop and had a little picnic themselves over on the elementary playground by the teeter-totters. They made plans to spend as much time together as they could over the summer.

The next day Conrad was in the vacant lot trying to tempt a squirrel out of the big cottonwood with a small pile of peanuts. The squirrel was hesitant, but had made a tentative move when he let out a chatter and scurried to the far side of the tree and onto a limb, making sounds like little pieces of metal skittering across the bark.

Maria Elena came running across the lot. Conrad could see tears. "What's the matter?"

"Tenemos que ir."

"What?"

"We have to go."

Earlier that morning Mrs. Mendoza had gone to the post office for the mail. It was always unsettling for her to walk into the lobby with its large WPA mural of a bunch of war-painted Indians chasing a herd of buffalo. Why they would have a herd of buffalo and wild Indians in a post office was beyond her.

There were the usual bills and ads and one letter with an address in a masculine hand that looked vaguely familiar. She tore open the envelope, read the short letter, and dropped to her knees. She took the rosary from her purse and began with tears flowing. First, she made the Sign of the Cross ("En el nombre del Padre, y del Hijo, y del Espíritu Santo. Amen."), followed by the Apostles Creed ("Creo en Dios . . ."), then the Our Father ("Padre nuestro, que estás en el cielo . . ."), followed by "Dios te salve, Maria, llena eres de gracia . . ."

Sam Dickson and his wife always went to the post office together in case the mail contained a check or a refund, and neither trusted the other with extra money. When they saw Mrs. Mendoza on her knees, Sam said, "I think she's ill." His wife dragged him by the sleeve. "Don't touch her; she might be contagious." They got their mail, looked for any checks, and quickly left, disappointed, and giving Mrs. Mendoza a wide berth.

When Catholics came into the lobby, they knew what she was doing because of the rosary she held, but the Protestants wondered if they should buy any more bread or cookies baked by a crazy woman.

After she had concluded a decade, she struggled to her feet (she had bad knees), went to the car, and showed her daughters the letter. When they looked at her, she said they were packing immediately and leaving for Cooperville. Both of them protested, but she wouldn't listen. Ramon was back and wanted her. That was all there was to it.

When Conrad asked Maria Elena why she had to leave, she told him her father would be hoeing sugar beets on a farm outside Cooperville, that he was sorry for what he had done, and that he wanted his wife and girls to join him.

A car horn sounded from in front of the house.

"Quickly, what is your box number for the mail?"

"It's 123."

"Good, that's easy. I will write. Write to me."

"I-I-I will."

The car horn was insistent.

"I have to go." She embraced him, kissed him on the lips, and took off running.

Conrad stood still for a few seconds, then started to run also. The car was moving when he got to the sidewalk. He saw the sad brown eyes of Maria Elena passing him in a car crammed so full of stuff, he didn't think there could be room for anything else. He couldn't even see Malinal.

He raised his hand to wave and saw tears fall from Maria Elena's dark eyes.

After she had navigated her way onto the Gold Star Highway, Mrs. Mendoza said, "See, my daughter, Our Lady never fails."

"Si, mi madre."

Conrad stayed in bed for the next two days. Rose didn't know what was wrong and was going to call a doctor. Instead she had Gussie come over. After Gussie talked to Conrad a few minutes, she knew what the trouble was. She had three sons. She told Rose not to worry and left.

The next day when Conrad went outside, he did something he had never done before. When he heard shouting, he walked over to Fifth Street and saw a baseball game in progress on Slant Field. It had that name because it was built on a hill. Home plate was at the top and the bases stretched out on the flat, as did right field, but left field was down the hill. Slowly, he worked his way up the street and finally sat on the curb protected by the chicken wire fence that served as a backstop behind home plate.

No one said anything to him so he sat in the sun, missing Maria Elena. Someone calling his name broke through her image. Rory O'Connell had to go to the dentist, and rather than play one short, the boys wanted Conrad to fill in.

He didn't have a glove so they loaned him one. With his speed he played left field, and after he got used to looking at the plate and having his eyes level with the catcher's mitt, he did all right.

He struck out the first time at bat, but the next time he legged a single into a double, and on Ronnie Kerr's hit, he scored the winning run. A couple boys even slapped him on the back.

When he told Gussie about it, she went into her house and emerged with a baseball glove. "It's yours." He thanked her and used it during that summer when he was accepted somewhat into young male society. Baseball kept him busy when he wasn't in the vacant lot or walking the river to the east of town.

While baseball was good, letters from Maria Elena were better. He'd ride his bike to the post office and if one was there, he'd put it inside his shirt and ride home with it nesting next to his heart. The paper felt warm when he read it. He liked it when she said she missed him.

He'd get out some paper and scratch out a letter filled with misspellings, put it in an envelope with the address she had sent him, and mail it. He was too embarrassed to ask his mother or sisters to proof his spelling. He knew he was a lousy speller; his teachers had told him often enough.

On the corner east of Slant Field, there was a large glacial erratic. The granite boulder was mostly hidden by saplings, volunteer lilac bushes, and weeds. Conrad began to ride his bike over to "Little Gib," so named because before the vegetation took over, it looked like a smaller version of the Rock of Gibraltar. He'd hide his bike in the weeds and push through the bushes until he got to the base of the huge stone. He'd put his hands on the low side and climb up, then he'd lie down and let the world drift by. On sunny days he let the warmth from Little Gib enter his body. He'd imagine Maria Elena there with him, and the warmth on his back and the warmth in his heart made him feel stronger.

School began. Eighth grade was a frustration and he nearly failed.

Maria Elena and her family had gone back to Crystal City and her letters were full of words that continued to light up his eyes, but he also realized how many miles away she was. An emptiness rushed into his stomach every time he passed the locker she'd had the previous year.

He tried out for the junior high football team, as Maria Elena wanted him to, but he flunked off. Without her there to help him study, he didn't care.

That is, until he read a letter she had written after she had received the letter in which he told her. The combination of disappointment and encouragement urged him to do better, which he did. Because of Maria Elena he was eligible for the junior high basketball team for which he had played as a seventh grader. He wasn't a great shot, but with his quickness he got a lot of lay-ups after stealing the ball.

Dances didn't interest him, but he was actually invited to a couple of birthday parties.

There was no junior high baseball team, so the seventh and eighth graders had to compete with the upperclassmen. Everyone who went out made the team, but almost all the younger ones rode the pines the entire season.

Maria Elena's last letter in May urged him to study his best for his final tests. She also said that she and her family would be heading to Cooperville for a season of beet hoeing.

Conrad worked hard at reviewing for the finals. He even had Lise quiz him the way Maria Elena had. When he got his report card, it looked like a stuttering man trying to say, "D-D-D-D-D-Dumb," but at least he passed every subject, even English 8, which had cost him a spot on the football team.

The prospect of going into senior high gave some of his classmates the urge to pull one more stunt. Their spokesman, Jake Hogan, greeted Conrad and asked him, "Goin' to the class picnic?"

"No, we didn't have one last year."

"Yeah, but this is our final year in junior high, so we want to go out in style. It'll be in the park this afternoon. See you there."

Conrad went home and told his mother. She made his favorite sandwich and sent him uptown to get chips and a root beer. In Hogan's he saw a large can of root beer with a twist top. It was the biggest container of pop he'd ever seen and it was on sale.

At home his mother put his food and root beer in a paper bag and he left on his bike. The last class picnic had been in the baseball park, so off he peddled, pumped up the Salem Street hill, kept going south to Dunnell, went right, crossed the NP tracks, and swung onto Chicago. He surprised himself about how excited he was as he bumped over the GN tracks and headed into the trees surrounding the ballpark.

When he came out by the grandstand, there didn't seem to be anyone around. He peddled a circuit on the road around the ball diamond and football field. He saw no one. Maybe the picnic was at the West Side School; some people called it the Park School.

He pushed back on Chicago, more slowly. He went left on Stimson and continued to the school. He saw some little kids playing on the swings, but no one else. He straddled his bike and thought. The only other place for a picnic was Orland Finkle Park. Wouldn't that be a good joke—the picnic was almost in his backyard!

With renewed energy he headed east on Stimson until he turned and sped down the Fourth Street hill, forgetting about the dip at the entrance of the park. He hit it at a good clip, and, while he was able to maintain control of his bike, the sack containing his lunch and the root beer bounced out of the basket.

He put the bike down and walked back. The cap had come off the can and the bag was soaked. His mother had wrapped the sandwich in wax paper, so it was all right. He took a drink; the soda was half gone. He searched the park; none of his classmates were there. He sat on a picnic table and ate his sandwich and chips, washing them down with the remaining root beer. He took the ping-pong picture Maria Elena had given him from his billfold and fixed his eyes on her face. Her voice filled his mind. He put the wax paper and the chip bag in the soaked sack and threw it into a trash barrel. He put the can in his basket and peddled home.

Conrad parked his bike in the garage and walked over to a workbench. He punched a hole in the side of the can and widened it a little, then he worked a tin snips into the hole and began to cut out a round piece of metal. Then he drove a nail through the neck of the can and pulled the nail out. He inserted a long piece of wire into the hole. When he had finished, he washed the can out and put the cap back on firmly.

He took a ladder off the hooks that held it on the wall and carried it to the backyard, where he put it against an elm tree. He climbed up and wired the can to a limb. He was hoping a wren would build its nest there.

A few days later a wren did go inside the can, but she saw that the hole was too big and offered no protection if a larger bird wanted to get inside, so she left.

Conrad never saw the little bird because the night before, he had gotten up, dressed, packed some things, including Maria Elena's letters and the Chinese finger trap, pushed his bike out to the street, and rode away to the east. When his mother went to the kitchen for her morning coffee, she found a note: "Went to find Maria Elena."

She called Nate Coulson, and he put out an All-Points Bulletin, but searching for Conrad proved unsuccessful. Rose had seen a Crystal City return address on an envelope, so most of the search was concentrated to the south. Gussie told Rose not to worry too much; when he got cold and hungry, Conrad would come back. Lise and Trudy were more upset than Rose, who went about her daily routine while they cried in their room until time dried their tears.

A block west of the Foersters' home, the corner lot had been sold for a new house. A backhoe came in and began knocking down some old box elders. When the backhoe appeared, a sparrow was sitting in a nest, preparing for her second brood. The sparrow flew to a tree across the street and watched her tree fall.

Instinct drove her to find someplace else to lay her eggs. She flew east and saw the "root beer" bird house hanging empty, as it had for over a month. She poked her head in, then flew off to gather nest-building material—stems, roots, dead grass and leaves, feathers, paper, and anything soft. Females didn't usually take the lead in building nests, but she had no choice: her mate had been killed when the tree fell.

After she had settled into her new nest, the heat of summer turned on. The metal can absorbed it, and the little bird realized that it was too hot for any babies to survive. She left the nest and flew to the east, searching for some new place.

When school began, the new freshmen gathered in their Home Room. There were a number of new class members, most of them coming from the various one-room schools in the District. A few comments were made about the absence of Linda Gullickson, whose widowed mother had found a man who ran a bar and had moved to Calvin City. A few kids also mentioned Conrad and his disappearance. No one could figure out why Conrad would run away just when he would be a freshman.

Two weeks later Rose received a phone call. Barney Keller had suffered a massive heart attack in Phoenix and passed away. The lawyer was calling from St. Paul, where the body would be shipped and buried beside his wife and favorite daughter. Rose wouldn't have gone just for that, but the lawyer told her that he had drawn up her father's will and he had left everything to her: his money, his stocks, and the Summit Avenue house she had grown up in.

Rose looked at her two sun-blessed daughters and thought of the advantages St. Paul offered over Menninger. She began to pack immediately.

Gussie drove the three to the station to catch the *Western Star*.

"Don't worry about Conrad. I'll keep the police on the lookout."

"Oh, I know it's probably wrong to leave, but I have my girls to think about."

The big diesel sounded its horn.

"When he comes home, I'll take care of him until you come back."

"I'm not certain I will come back."

Gussie hugged each of the girls, then the women embraced. The conductor yelled, "'board!" and Gussie was alone.

Two freshmen, Jake Hogan and Pete Lindsay, had been in Orland Finkle Park with their b-b guns, trying to kill a big gray squirrel that lived high up in a basswood tree. They thought they'd hit it a couple of times, but he was so far up the tree that the b-b's apparently had no effect. Each time he was hit, the squirrel shrugged, looked down at them, and chir-r-r-r-ed. Finally, they gave up.

As they walked the gravel road near the west side of the park, they saw the root beer can swinging on its wire. Ping! Jake's b-b hit. Ping! So did Pete's. "Good shootin', Jake."

"Yeah, but a little too easy."

They walked around the curve and then paralleled the Foerster house.

"Wanna pop a window?" Pete asked.

"Nah, but maybe someday," Jake answered. They walked with their guns pointed back over their shoulders with the vacant lot on their right, the weeds taller and thicker than ever.

At Gregory they turned right. "I wonder where Conrad is."

"I don't know, Pete. Probably haunting some poor girl's nightmares," Jake responded. They laughed. "See that sign?" He pointed to where "For Sale" was nailed to a wooden stake on the front lawn.

"Yeah."

"Let's shoot it."

"All right."

They moved to the far side of the street in the shadow of some trees, checked both ways for cops and traffic, raised their guns, and aimed. "One, two, three." Two light "pops" and two small holes in the sign.

Suddenly, Old Lady Daniels was striding out her door. "Get outta here, you damned scallywags, before I take a horsewhip to yuh."

The street echoed with pounding feet and laughter.

MISS HUTCHINSON

Until I was eighteen, Miss Hutchinson was the most beautiful woman in the world. Of course, I thought my mother was beautiful, and, later on, movie stars, too, but in a different sort of way.

When Miss Hutchinson moved her chair beside you to help with drawing or coloring or making the letters of the alphabet, she always smelled nice, like lilacs, and her breath was always minty, although I never saw her chewing gum.

I liked it when she was beside me and praised the way I had made "K" or "X" or the easiest one, "I." For me the ones with two feet, "walking letters" such as "A," "H," and "N," were the ones I liked the best, then came the "pogo stick letters," the ones that would have to hop, like "F," "P," and "T." The "sliding letters" with the long base such as "B," "D," and "E" took up too much space, and the "rolling letters" like "C," "G," and "J" were hard for me because I could never seem to get the curve just right, even after Miss Hutchinson helped me a dozen times. For me "M" and "W" weren't as difficult as "O" and "Q." Handwriting was my worst subject, or maybe it was just that I liked the smell of lilac and mint next to me.

When Miss Hutchinson smiled at you, it made you feel like you could do anything. Our reading class was divided into three groups based on ability: Owls, Robins, and Crows. I wasn't bad enough to be with the Crows, but I made enough mistakes to keep me out of the Owls. While one section was reading aloud, the other two sections were to be working silently on another subject. Then the next group would rotate into the little red reading chairs, followed by the final group. After the Crows would finish, Miss Hutchinson would take them into the cloakroom and work with them for awhile; then we

Robins would file in as the Crows left, and we would go over sounds and "sounding out." She didn't have to do that much with the Owls, so I was torn between my need to be an Owl and my desire to be with Miss Hutchinson as much as possible. After the Second Six Weeks, Miss Hutchinson announced the names of those who had been promoted to Owl (I was one), and those who would now by Robins. She said that no one would remain as a Crow, and for that reason she was especially grateful for all the time her "little scholars" had put into their reading lessons. Then she smiled her glorious smile and we smiled back at her and at each other. I was proud that I and we had pleased her.

Grades one, two, and three were on the west side of the building, and we always had our fifteen minute recess first. One day just before the bell, the kickball went flat. The bell rang and the kids began lining up to go in. As I went by, the third grade teacher said, "Jimmy, please take this ball to Miss Daugherty and tell her what happened so she doesn't start lining up for a game of kickball." I ran around the addition that housed the coal bin, mower, and other equipment and tried to fight my way through the crowd of fourth, fifth, and sixth graders, yelling their way to fifteen minutes of freedom. When I finally found Miss Daugherty and delivered the ball and the message, I knew all my classmates were inside, so I ran into the building by the Intermediate door, took the stairs into the basement, and turned to go through the boys' lavatory. If I could make it through there, the Primary stairs were just on the other side. I could take them and be in my room without being too late.

However, there were two seniors wearing red and gray letterman's jackets and smoking cigarettes in the stalls. When they heard me running, one of them grabbed me, held me upside down over the toilet, and said, "If you tell on us, we'll catch you and drown you in this can like a rat." The other one reached around and flushed it, some of the water splashing onto my hair. They threw their butts in the other toilet, flushed, and left, but not before one of them turned and said, "Remember!"

I was terrified and hid in a dark corner where the janitor kept his scrub buckets and mops, which were dry, but which had a stale odor. I sat down on the concrete and felt the tears on my face. Soon I heard a sound and lay flat on the floor. I knew someone had come into the room, but I was too scared to look. Then I heard a woman's voice, "Jimmy, Jimmy?"

I ran out, nearly tripping over a bucket, and flung myself into Miss Hutchinson's arms. "I was worried about you so I came looking."

She led me over to the sink, took out her handkerchief, wet it, and wiped my tears. Just then a boy came into the room, said "Oops!" and disappeared the way he had come.

Miss Hutchinson and I walked hand-in-hand up the stairs and into my room. For some reason the kids began to clap.

One late fall day after school when all the other kids had gone home, I was trying to walk all the way around the big incinerator, which sat on a concrete support, leaving about a four-inch wide ledge around the circumference. I was edging along when suddenly my foot slipped and I went into the ash pile. A couple of live coals got inside my sneaker, but instead of taking my shoe off and dumping the coals out, I ran the one block home and got two good-sized burns on my left foot. That night Miss Hutchinson came over with a bottle of Mentholatum, but by that time my mother had already doctored the raw flesh. Miss Hutchinson also brought a red plastic cowboy for me, although I don't know why she had one. "I know you like cowboys," she said.

That winter a soap company began a program called the "Cleanliness Inspection Patrol." The idea was to get kids to wash with the company's bar soap and pass a peer inspection for six weeks. Any student who did it perfectly would get a ticket to the Saturday matinee and a free bag of popcorn.

A wall chart was tacked up in all the grade rooms and the principal came to each class, explaining the procedure. Every day there would be two student monitors, a boy and a girl, who would walk around the classroom and inspect each student's hands, fingernails, face, neck, and ears. If everything was clean, a sticker featuring the company's bar soap was given. If you had dirt on one of the five areas, you got a yellow sticker, and if two or more places were dirty, you got a red ticket.

At the conclusion of the inspection, each student with a bar soap ticket proudly went up and placed it on the line with the thirty small rectangles extending from his or her name. When they were done, the yellow stickers went up as it was announced what part of their body was dirty. After that, the red stickers slunk up to the front and put their scarlet symbols of shame in line, while listening to two or three or four of their failures.

When the program started, Miss Hutchinson refused to allow it in her room, but when we first graders protested as loudly as we dared, she relented, but she would not allow the mention of anyone's dirty places.

As time went by, more and more of the boys dropped out of the running, but only one girl had. On the very first day, Winona Warren, an Ojibwa Indian whose folks had moved from the hilly reservation near the Canadian border, was discovered to have neglected to clean two spots; she got a red sticker and kept her head down as she trudged up to put it on the chart. No one else got a red that day, or even a yellow. Of course, we should have been expecting it because the Warren family lived down in the river bottom where only the poor whites and the Indians lived, and none of them had city water.

As the weeks went by, I washed two or three times in the morning before coming to school. My line of soap bar stickers grew and grew. A week before the contest was to end, the *Menninger Messenger* came out with the coming movie attractions. I asked Mom what the Saturday matinee was, and when she said it was a Tim Holt Western, I let out a yell that woke up my Dad on the couch. Tim Holt and his sidekick Chito Jose Gonzales Bustamonte Rafferty were my favorites, ever since I started going to movies at age four.

On Thursday of the final week, there were only two boys left in the competition and all but three girls. Allen Newman and I were the two cleanest boys in the first grade, and it was his turn to be the boys' monitor. As he approached my desk, I was already in the saddle with Tim and Chito, ridding the border country of bad guys. Suddenly, I looked down in stunned amazement—I had a yellow sticker! I inspected my hands and fingernails; they were pinkishly clean. Was it my neck? That was always tough for me. Or was there wax in my ears? Or did Allen cheat me? When I looked at him across the room, he was smiling, and when my name was called, I couldn't face the humiliation. I ran into the cloakroom, put my face in my coat, and bawled.

When Miss Hutchinson knelt beside me, I put my arms around her and got her blouse a little damp with my tears. When I had dried up, she said, "Now you know why I didn't want any part of this. The hurt is not worth the prize." For the second time in my life, she wiped away my tears. She looked at my five areas and said, "Jimmy, I think you are just as clean as can be."

For a wild moment I thought I'd get to see Tim and Chito until she continued, "But a rule is a rule, and maybe Allen saw something I didn't . . . Are you ready to go back to your desk?"

I was, but if I had seen Allen smiling, I would have slugged him.

Every morning the Menninger Dairy would send milk up for the primary grades in pint bottles. We were allowed to bring something from home, usually cookies, to go with the milk. Winona sat right across from me and she rarely had anything. Once in a while she had some kind of flat, fried brownish thing, but most of the time she just opened her milk, put in a straw, and watched the other kids.

Shortly after the Inspection Patrol ended, Miss Hutchinson called me aside as the other kids were going for recess and said, "Jimmy, how would you like to share your cookie with Winona? I hear your mother makes some of the best chocolate chip cookies in town." That was true; they were the best, but I didn't want to share them. We could only bring one and I wanted it all.

"With who?"

"Winona."

"Why can't she bring her own? Or buy some uptown?"

"Some people just don't have the money for things. Since her mother was killed in that car accident, her father is lucky just to be able to keep the family together."

Miss Hutchinson had grown up in Menninger. When she was thirteen, she was in a car crash that killed her parents and put her in the hospital for weeks. After she got out, her aunt and uncle raised her. She graduated from Menninger High, went to the closest teachers' college, and after graduating, got a job as the first grade teacher in the same building in which she had attended first grade. I knew that she would feel bad about Winona losing her mother that way, so I decided I'd share.

The next day after recess the milk was passed out. I opened mine, took out the wax paper with Mom's chocolate chip cookie in it, and stared at it. I wanted the whole thing, but I remembered Miss Hutchinson and broke it in two. One part was a little bigger than the other, and I almost kept it, but I finally wrapped it and put it on Winona's desk, whispering, "Here."

Her dark eyes stared at me and then at the wax paper. When she opened it and saw the cookie, she smiled and whispered, "Thank you, Jimmy."

That was the first time we had ever spoken to each other.

Suddenly, I was afraid. The rule was that during milk time there was absolutely no talking. Finally, I dared to look at Miss Hutchinson. She had been watching me and my heart jumped, but then she smiled and very slowly nodded her head.

About a week later I asked Miss Hutchinson if I could bring two cookies. She said she thought it would be "a splendid idea." I thought it was a splendid idea, too, because I could have a whole cookie to myself.

In the fall and spring one of the playground games for the first grade was kissy-kissy. The boys would chase one or more of the girls up the big slide and when the girls slid down, the boys would be waiting and kiss them. We didn't play it in the winter because sometimes snot would get in the way. Kissy-kissy was a game reserved for the first graders because the second and third graders didn't play since they were at the stage where they were too busy trying to avoid "boy-germs" and "girl-germs."

In the fall Winona was one of the two girls that hadn't played kissy-kissy. After the slide had warmed up enough in the spring, Mavis Arnold had been chased to the top with three other girls, so she was kissed at the bottom, too. Winona would join in with tag and pom-pom pull away, or fox and geese in the winter, but she would just stand by the incinerator and watch when kissy-kissy was in progress.

One recess I saw her looking at me; suddenly, I was running toward her, yelling and waving my arms just the way I did when I was chasing Carol Ann White or Beverly Huston. For just an instant Winona hesitated and then with a smile took off for the slide. When she came down, I was waiting for her with a kiss, and two or three other boys took their turns. I don't know if Miss Hitchinson saw us or not (it wasn't a game to be encouraged, and we had to do it when the outside teacher was on the other side of the playground by the swings), but on the way in after the bell, I felt a hand on my shoulder. It was Miss Hutchinson, who had been on duty. She smiled at me, but didn't say a word.

On the last day of school when I opened my desk, I found something wrapped in a piece of pink and white checkered cloth. I unwrapped it; it was a corncob doll. Its face was painted on and it had brown eyes like mine. It had some brown yarn for hair; my hair was brown. I was kind of put-off by the fact that it looked like it had a blouse and skirt, but then I thought they could be a shirt and coat, so that was all right. The clincher was a pair of eyeglasses made out of twisted pieces of wire. I was the only boy in first grade with glasses; I think I inherited my Dad's weak eyes.

I looked over at Winona, but she was intent on coloring a picture of a rainbow and clouds she had drawn in art class. (I had done a tree, but Miss Hutchinson had to show me that the trunk of a tree shouldn't meet the ground with a straight line across; it should show some slight up and down variation because most of the time the earth isn't completely level.) I quickly put the doll back in the desk; if the boys saw it, I would be a target all summer.

Later that afternoon the Primary grades had their school picnic in Orland Finkle Park down by the river. The day was filled with games, swinging, food, and the excitement that can come only from the anticipation of a long, sunny, school-less summer.

When the picnic was over and I was walking out of the park with my friend Chris, his cousin Rory, and my first grade pals Billy and Jerry, I noticed Winona trailing us. When the others crossed Gregory and headed up the Fourth Street hill, I hung back, pretending to tie my shoe.

Winona came up and whispered, "I hope you liked my present."

I whispered back, "I did. Thank you." Then, "See you next year."

She smiled and said, "I hope so," and went skipping down Gregory toward her home.

That was the last time I saw Winona, or Miss Hutchinson, for that matter, except once.

In April 1951 the Clarence Iverson #1 oil well had come in and western North Dakota was a "black gold" mine. My mother's parents had a farm near Prairie Rose, right in the middle of oil country, and they made more money on oil leases in one year than they had by farming in five.

In June 1952, a month after I had passed first grade, Grandma died. Grandpa wasn't doing too well, and being a bookkeeper didn't exactly help Dad's eyes, so it was decided we would sell the house and move to Grandpa's farm.

Miss Hutchinson and another female teacher had left for a vacation on the West Coast, so she was gone when we moved out. I did leave her a goodbye note inside the storm door of her apartment, which was on the same block as our house on Lamborn.

She answered it two weeks later with a note of regret about not seeing me off, but she said she knew I would do well in my new school. After that we exchanged Christmas cards for a few years, but that faded out, and then, so did she.

I spent the rest of my school years in the Prairie Rose School. When I was a sophomore, I told my Dad I wanted to be a farmer; after all, I was doing as much work as either of the two hired men (Grandpa had died in a Big Muddy nursing home). Dad said he wanted me prepared for modern farming, so I could anticipate change and thus be prepared for it. That meant going to college. Also, I think he was afraid that someday soon the oil was going to run out, and I would have to rely only on the farm for a living.

I decided I would go to North Dakota State University, which had only a couple years before been North Dakota Agricultural College, and which many people still called "Moo U."

When I was writing out my high school graduation announcements, my mother suggested it might be a nice idea to send one to Miss Hutchinson. Suddenly, I was ashamed I had lost contact with her, and I debated whether or not to send her one. I finally decided to because of all the teachers I had ever had, she was still my favorite. Within a few days I received a small check and a long letter filled with reminiscences and good wishes. She also wrote that Winona had become one of the first Native Americans to graduate from Menninger High School and was going to college to be a teacher.

I had arranged to visit the NDSU campus four days after graduating from PRHS, so Monday I was on my way early. I would stay that night in Fargo with my cousin and be on campus on Tuesday.

Out of Minot I caught the Northwest Highway, slowing down for Templeton, but generally keeping it wide open. When I was on the outskirts of Fishtown, I saw a sign, "Menninger." At Fishtown the Northwest headed south to the Mid-State, then swung east to the Gold Star at Caseyville, and went south again. I could turn east, go to Menninger, and hook up with the Gold Star there, so I cranked the wheel over, floored it, and Fishtown disappeared in the rear view mirror.

When I drove down Lamborn, I was surprised to see our old house was gone, and that there was a new school whose playground extended over the location of the school I had attended. I wasn't surprised to see "Miss Hutchinson—First Grade" on one of the doors after I entered the building and told the janitor why I was there. "Yes, Miss Hutchinson," he said. "Fine teacher, fine teacher" and something about her being in her room tidying up for the summer.

The door was open, but I knocked anyway. I knew the way she looked at me over some boxes she was taping shut, she had no idea who I was. And I was shocked at her appearance. I introduced myself and after a minute of awkwardness, we mentioned a few things that brought laughter, then with little else to say, I turned to go. She walked me to the door, wished me well, and held out her hand. I took it, but my handshake had no warmth in it.

It had been a mistake to stop, and I didn't even try to look up Winona, as I had intended.

All the way to Fargo, at my cousin's house, and all the way home, I was bothered by a vision. All I could see was Miss Hutchinson, beautiful, kind Miss Hutchinson, with her face disfigured. From her hairline down the right side of her face and stopping at the side of her mouth in a jagged "C" ran a scar, a pinkish-gray, waxy welt, stark in its ugliness. I didn't want to think about it . . . see it . . . remember it, but I couldn't help myself.

I endured the drive home. Finally, I turned into our yard. Even before Mom could say anything, I was blurting out, "Mom, I stopped in to see Miss Hutchinson!"

"You did? That was nice. How was . . ."

"Mom, listen. Do you know how she got that terrible scar on her face. It's so ugly! When did it happen?"

"Why, Jimmy, Miss Hutchinson got that scar in the accident when she was thirteen. You just never noticed."

THE HORSE

I grew up in a town that was lily-white. Except in the movies and magazines, I didn't see but one black man, or Negro as they were called back then, before I was twelve, and that's when one came to our door to tell us that the car in front of his had run over our dog and hadn't stopped.

There were three or four Indian families who lived down the hill and on the north side of the Jacques River and one that lived on the south side, but as long as they stayed in the valley, they didn't count.

The Ft. Sully Indian Reservation was ten miles north of our town, but some of the families had moved off the "res," which looked like our town dump, except with log cabins. Some were living in Sacred Water, some in the little village of Divide, and some in Menninger.

The Moon family was one of these, but they were only half Indian. Basil Moon was a Cut Head Sioux from the res who had worked for my grandfather Boss on his farm out by Chokecherry Lake, until Boss had to fire him for wrecking a Farmall tractor.

Ronalda Haugland Moon was a full-blooded Norwegian from the Divide River Valley, south of Ft. Sully. She'd converted to Catholic when she got married, over the objections of her family; that was the reason her parents rarely came to visit.

All of the children had been baptized Catholic, which was another reason the Haugland grandparents didn't visit. The family would all sit in the back pew of the church, near the confessional, every Sunday. At least that's what I was told: I wasn't Catholic. The kids attended the public school because the Moons couldn't afford St. Ignatius of Loyola, the Catholic one which was three-and-half blocks up the hill from where I lived.

The older boy, Ole, was not a Haugland. In fact, his Indian name was Small Wind. Basil had been married before, but his wife was killed in a car accident when the white man she was with went off the highway and into Sacred Water Lake. They were both drunk.

The two younger boys, Erik and Thor, were twins. The two girls, Kelda and Nona, I didn't have much to do with. I would sometimes go hunting, fishing, and trapping with Erik and Thor, but outside of that I didn't hang around with them much. There was another girl, Ole's older sister, but she had stayed on the res.

The Sioux grandmother still lived on the res. They said she had started out as a good Indian, but went wild when she was about fifty. She would say she was Ida Two Elk (she refused to call herself "Moon" anymore), the daughter of the warrior He Who Stands, who fought with Teddy Roosevelt and the Rough Riders, and his wife Jab, who bore thirteen children and outlived five of them, and she wasn't going to live in any white town or do white things anymore. She put up and lived in a tipi, summer or winter, and went back to the old ways.

Basil Moon didn't have much in this world besides a rusty '47 International pickup, a woebegone house, a wife who worked at the Gustavus Turkey Processing Plant in town and raised a huge garden, and his kids, but somehow he found enough money to buy plenty of guns and knives, so Erik and Thor had shotguns anytime they wanted them.

Once when I was a junior, I arranged a hunting date with Erik and Thor. I got up early and walked west on Stimson, across the tracks, down the hill on Chicago to Park Avenue and through the ditch to their place. The dogs barked until they caught my scent. Ronalda was up, making breakfast, and one of the girls was with her. She let me in and scurried away.

"The boys will be down right away. Would you like a flapjack?"

"Sure."

She had just dropped some more batter on the griddle when I heard a crashing noise. The Moon kids slept upstairs in two small rooms, but there were no stairs. Instead, there was a hole in the ceiling and an old coal chute which was used like a stairway. Erik, then Thor, came sliding down the chute, Thor smashing into Erik's back and getting a punch. After they got off the chute, Ole followed. I hadn't expected him.

I was afraid at first because during the summer after eighth grade, I had gone to the Moons' house, and in the backyard I saw Ole entering a sweat lodge he'd made, naked. Just before going inside, he stared at me with hard eyes. The twins told me he was preparing to go on a vision quest, but it was already two years later, and he still hadn't done it. I thought maybe my seeing him naked had spoiled it for him, and he'd have it in for me. Also, because of a stunt my friend Ronnie Kerr, my cousin Rory, and I had pulled down at the river earlier that fall, Ole had been arrested and spent a night in jail. I had kind of apologized, but you never know.

After our junior class forced our English teacher, Miss Ashton, to resign, we got a new teacher, Miss Eva Waters. After Ole's night in jail, she heard about him and within a week he was in our classes. He had dropped out of school when he was a junior, so he was a junior again.

At first some thought Ole was retarded because he never spoke and didn't seem to be able to read when Miss Waters called on him to do so in English class. A couple more times that fall he came along with Erik and Thor when they went hunting with me after school, and I found out he wasn't retarded, just quiet and thinking his own thoughts. I guess after you're put out on the front step at night when your mother needs the bed for herself and her latest man, you have a lot of time for your own thoughts. As to reading, he was just too shy to do it in front of strangers.

That morning Erik and Thor said they didn't have time to sit down, and all of us grabbed a couple of flapjacks and stuck them in our pockets. The Moons grabbed their gear and off we went down the riverbank, the flapjacks warming us in the chill air.

It wasn't like being with a bunch of white boys, who were always talking and boasting about this and that. We walked quietly, climbing up and down the NP railroad embankment and then over Glen Haven, which crossed the river at the Steel Bridge. We could never be quiet enough to get past the Bouvette place, where Styke always sent up a howl, the light would come on, and a boot and a curse would be hurled out the door, followed by a yelp.

Through Orland Finkle Park, onto the Gold Star Highway, across the bridge to the north and down to the river again. Walking a mile brought us to our hunting grounds. When it was just Erik, Thor, and

I, we would hunt together, but four people seemed to be too many, so Ole and I paired off.

To my relief, he didn't seem to be mad at me. He didn't seem happy with me, either, but we got along. During the morning and afternoon lulls, we'd do a little talking. It was then I found out about his mother, the fact that he had a sister living on the res, about his shyness in reading ("I know the words, but they just don't come out right."), and his attitude toward white people. He wasn't so upset about the Indians losing their land as a lot of them were; he figured if they weren't strong enough to fight for it, they didn't deserve to have it. He was angry with the way the whites had tried to destroy Indian culture and were trying to keep Indians dependent. Also, he hated the white men who came to the res looking for women.

I was glad he didn't hate me for the loss of land: I figured I didn't take it, and if I had been an Indian, I'd have felt the same way Ole did and fought for it. And I didn't respect any of the men who went up to the res on Saturday night and still found time to go to church on Sunday, so we were able to talk quite a bit.

I also discovered he was a better hunter than anyone I'd ever been with. He could sit in the same position when ducks were overhead and never move except for an occasional blink. He could also imitate ducks with his voice; he didn't need a call. And he could belly crawl through buck brush or snake berries from Long Pond to Cliff Pond and never make a sound.

After that we only hunted a couple more times together; mostly I hunted with my cousin Rory or Ronnie or both of them. The last time Ole and I were out that fall, we walked down the river further than we usually did, all the way past the railroad bridge. He wanted to keep going, "C'mon, Chris, we don't have our limit."

"No, we have to get back to Erik and Thor. They're way back there."

"Let 'em be. I've never been this far down river before. C'mon."

"No, you go." I started back along the rock-strewn bank, half expecting to hear him behind me, but that wasn't Ole. When I reached the road, I looked back and I couldn't even see him.

The twins didn't seem too concerned. They said he'd come home eventually.

He did, but not until Monday, missing all our morning classes.

"Where you been?" I asked.

"Out in the Viking Hills."

The Viking Hills were the series of glacial hills way out on the east end of the county where Grandpa Boss's farm was. There was a large hill running off to the west and towering above the prairie. The Norwegian settlers called it the Viking because it looked like a man lying on his side, metis buffalo hunters called it Cut-Thumb Butte because one of them had lost his thumb nearby, but the Sioux called it Buffalo Hump.

The hills themselves had short grass on top, but the ravines between them ran to trees, buck brush, prairie rose bushes, and a little higher up, snake berries. Nesting between some of the hills were small lakes and sloughs, and four big lakes: Chokecherry, South Finger, North Finger, and Big Sam, which was the largest and two miles northwest of Buffalo Hump. Nobody lived in the hills. It was wild and the soil was too gravelly and hilly to grow crops. Even Boss's farm was a farm in name only. It had some pastureland, but no plow had ever turned a furrow on it. Boss and his hired men had raised some horses and cattle on the farm and some sheep way on the south end.

"What'd you do there?"

He didn't speak for awhile as we walked down the hall. Before he turned into the Study Hall for detention, he said, "There's spirits out there."

I found that a little strange. He had been out to Boss's farm plenty of times, and when Boss died, his will said Ole could use the land any way he wanted—for hunting, trapping, raising horses, or just being on it. Ole started raising Appaloosas, and he hired a couple men from Ft. Sully to herd the sheep, most of which they'd sell off in the fall. The Vikings were just a little to the east of the farm, so he must have gone there before.

I didn't see him much that fall; he spent every weekend in the hills. After the cold weather came, he stopped going, and it was a good thing because it gave him a chance to make up for the lousy grades he'd received so far.

Back when he was a junior for the first time, Ole was approached by the track coach to try out for the team. He was a natural distance man. When he ran his very first race at the Indoor in the University Fieldhouse, he set a school record for the mile and would have for the

880, but caught an elbow from the winner as they rounded the final curve.

During the outdoor season he was just as good in the Regional Meet: he set a couple of meet records and two school records, but at the State Meet he faded to eighth behind the blistering pace of a couple of runners from a reservation from the southern part of the state and some distance men from the southwest counties, where they traditionally had more outdoor practice because of better spring weather. Everyone expected big things from him the next year, but he didn't come back to school that fall. In fact, he hadn't taken any of his final tests and flunked every class except Physical Education.

Right after the last day of school our junior year, he went up to Ft. Sully to spend some time with his grandmother and sister. When I talked with his brothers, they said he was living in the tipi and listening to his grandmother's stories for hours on end. He also wandered around the hills south of Sacred Water Lake and walked down the Divide River Valley to the Viking Hills, where he spent a lot of time. One time when they were visiting, he came back from the Vikings with blood on his face. He had killed a deer with a bow and arrow and badged himself with the warm blood.

He also built a sweat lodge near the tipi and continued the ceremonies he'd learned from his grandmother. I guess he was finally working up to his vision quest.

Later I was told by Joe Eagle, a holy man at Ft. Sully, that he kept trying to perfect his spirit such as only the most dedicated men would attempt, warriors like Crazy Horse or Sitting Bull. He could have gone on his vision quest almost any time and no one would have doubted he was ready, but he didn't think he was, not until the summer after our junior year.

One early morning in the Moon of Cherries Blackening (as Ole called it), he showed up at home. He had been fasting two days and wanted the twins to accompany him on a vision quest. Their mother looked upset, but let them go. I found out most of what went on from Erik and Thor, from the grandmother, and from Joe Eagle. Joe would tell me things for awhile and then get silent. He explained that he shouldn't be telling things about a warrior, but that his tongue liked to move and his ears liked to hear the tongue, so he talked, but then was ashamed. His shame never lasted long enough, however, to keep him quiet the next time.

Erik and Thor were surprised Ole asked them. They had usually made fun of Ole's vision quest ideas, and they let him know they would never do anything like it. I guess he asked them because they were his brothers and he could trust them.

They walked the river several miles and then turned east, taking country roads whenever possible. By late afternoon Buffalo Hump was bulging out of the prairie, and Ole had them drift south so they would be hidden from any highway traffic, even though the East Highway was over a mile away.

At the base of Buffalo Hump, he told them that some holy men from Ft. Sully had come down the day before and cleared a spot for the vision quest. They had put up a pole in the center and hung tobacco from it; then they drove smaller poles into the ground at the four cardinal points. They attached a colored cloth on each pole: white on the north, yellow on the east, green on the south, and black on the west. They covered the cleared area with sage and pine boughs and placed a buffalo robe to the east of the center pole.

He told them that he had already purified himself in the sweat lodge and kept his spirit strong. They were to make a camp below Buffalo Hump, make certain he wasn't disturbed, and be ready for him when he came down with food and water he had brought. He had them gather some rocks for a fire ring and collect some wood and sticks in a little ravine. While they were gone, he stripped down to his breechclout, rolled his shoes up in his pants and shirt, and packed them away. When he tried to strike a match, his hand was shaking so much he couldn't do it, and Eric lit the fire. In addition to having no food for two days, he hadn't drunk any water since that morning. All the walking had pretty much worn him down.

When the fire got going, he reached into his knapsack and brought out some sweet grass, put it in a small baked-clay container, held it in the flames, and when it caught, offered it to the four cardinal directions. Then he wafted the grass around so his body was centered in a ghost of smoke, threw the remaining grass into the fire, and started up Buffalo Hump.

The twins never went up to see what he was doing. They gathered some more wood, opened a can of beans, and put it near the fire to heat up. They poured the beans onto plates and ate them, sopping up the juice with slices of homemade bread. They washed the plates, checked their .22's, rolled out their sleeping bags, and went to sleep.

They thought he would come down the next morning, but he didn't. After breakfast they picked up their rifles and walked off to the south until they could see him sitting motionless on top of Buffalo Hump. He never moved in all the time they watched. They scared up a meadowlark and its song followed them back to camp.

That night Thor woke up with a start. He poked Erik. "Did you hear that?"

"W-w-wh-what?"

"That sound, like somebody yelling . . . up there." He pointed to the top of Buffalo Hump. Erik sat up, but it was quiet. "Maybe we should go up and see."

"No!"

"He might be in trouble. You can't go without water in this heat."

"He can come down if he wants to." Erik lay back.

"But what if he can't."

"And what if he can? Then he'll be mad because we wrecked his quest. You have to do one by yourself."

Soon he was lightly snoring and then Thor dropped off.

The next day was another hot one. They felt the heat the moment the sun crested the hills behind Buffalo Hump. After breakfast, once again they walked to the south, but this time they didn't see Ole. They walked back to camp, arguing about what they should do. The meadowlark was still there.

Around noon they heard something, and, looking up, saw Ole rolling down and then stopping in some buck brush. They ran up and carried him down to camp. His breathing was shallow and they were scared.

"He's gonna die."

Erik knelt down and listened at Ole's mouth. A minute later he said, "I don't know; I think it's better. Get some water."

Thor brought the big canteen. The water was warm, but it was still water. They splashed some on his face. Nothing. Some more. Nothing, but they heard the meadowlark off to the south, and then Ole moved and tried to say something. Erik lifted his head, put the canteen to his lips, and tilted it. Ole coughed. When Erik tried to take the canteen away, Ole's hand pulled it back, and he took a few sips, then he lay in the shade and his breathing was stronger. When he sat up, took a drink on his own, and asked them to make him something to eat, they knew he'd be all right.

When Thor opened the can of beans, he heard the meadowlark fly off to the south, its song fading.

After eating beans and bread and drinking a lot of water, Ole told them that he'd had his vision the night before.

"But I must have fainted. I don't know. I remember the vision and then nothing until I was hot and tried to walk and then nothing until I was choking on water."

"We heard you yell," Erik said.

"Yeah, I wanted to go get you, Ole," Thor added.

"It's good that you didn't. You did just what was required. Thank you. But now I ask you something more."

"What?" Erik asked.

"In my vision I was a long way off in the olden days. Out on the prairies there was a fire that drove me to a hilltop where there were some mares. I was going to catch one and escape when a spotted stallion came up the hill bringing a storm that put out the fire. He knocked me down and reared over me; his face was flames and lightning came from his eyes. I thought his hooves would crush me; I hid my face, but nothing happened. When I looked, I was alone."

No one spoke for awhile.

Finally, Thor asked, "What does it mean?"

"It means I am no longer 'Ole'; that name is dead. That person is dead. I am The Horse, and that is what you must call me. Now, let me sleep."

Later Erik and Thor told me they thought their brother was "touched," so they let him alone. The next morning he thanked them again and told them to go home. He took a canteen and some jerky and headed for Ft. Sully.

I didn't see Horse that summer. I was busy working at Hank's Super Saver, and that was the summer my four-year old cousin Theresa was molested, so I had other things on my mind.

In the fall when he came to school, Horse had grown his hair out, wearing it in short braids (which got longer as the school year passed) or Apache style. There was a big stink about it, especially the day that we went to the Activities Room for our senior pictures. A photographer from Fargo came and set up his camera. Each of us sat on a seat, which was really part of the suitcase in which he carried his equipment, he said, "Smile," and that was it. When Horse sat down, Principal McHale came in and ordered him to his office, where he told him that if he didn't cut his hair, there would be no senior picture.

We had been taken out of English IV class, and when Miss Waters found out why Horse wasn't back, she went stern-faced and marched down to McHale's office. Within a minute, Horse was on his way for the picture, even though the photographer had already started taking down his lights.

I didn't think Horse would want his picture taken because I'd read that a lot of the wild Indians in the olden days thought that a picture of them captured their spirit. Horse was getting wild, but not that wild, I guess.

He did stop attending Mass, however. After a couple of weeks, the priest went down to the Moons' place, something he usually did just once a year when he brought them a Parish Poor Basket at Christmastime, but he had to make an exception. After he told Ronalda it was her responsibility to get "Ole" to Mass, she politely whispered that she no longer could control him or his ways, but that she would most earnestly pray for him and light many candles. The priest went away. Thor, who had been upstairs listening, told me he felt embarrassed for his mother and mad at his brother.

That fall we only went hunting together twice. The second time they let me drive the '47. It was the first day of deer season, and the school said it was all right if you had a written excuse. Thor didn't come: he never went deer hunting because he couldn't stand the sight of one being gutted.

Erik, Horse, and I went out to the Vikings, where the hills were lousy with deer. We'd make a little stand out of brush on top of one of the hills and wait. When a deer came through one of the draws, we'd shoot. If none came for awhile, one of us would walk a wide circle and stir the deer up. Pretty soon one of them would come sniffing the air, and that would be the last sniff he ever sniffed. After being out for only two hours, all of us had knocked ours down. It was a warm day, so we had to gut each deer as quickly as we could.

The other two would hold a deer carcass on its back while I pushed the knife in and ripped the belly open from throat to crotch, but being careful not to slice into the guts. I cut the membranes and pulled out some guts. I cut the diaphragm and dark blood spilled out. Erik looked away, but the blood didn't seem to bother Horse. It didn't bother me, either.

I cut and pulled more guts, then stabbed my knife through the pelvic bone, cut around the anus, tied off the intestines, and removed the colon, anus, lungs, heart, trachea, and liver. We threw the guts, lungs, trachea, and liver into a pile which we left for the coyotes and other critters.

We put rubber ponchos on and back-packed the deer to the Moons' pickup. It was a good day.

The other time was in the Moon of Leaves Falling and it was just Horse and I. We drove north of Big Sam and decided to do some pass shooting. There's a big peninsula sticking into Big Sam from the north and three smaller ones that extend from the big one to the west, the south, and the southeast. In high water two of them go under, but the southeast one is higher. In fact, it has a good-size hill right in the middle of it.

We walked onto the southeast peninsula and built a blind on a point. Horse brought the Moons' black Lab, Licorice, along, and he'd swim out for the geese we shot as they flew by from one part of the lake to another. At first there were several other hunters that kept them flying in from other lakes, but after we each had two honkers, everything went quiet. Sitting there for an hour was too much, so we walked into the trees and undergrowth on the hill. It was like no one had ever been there before, and it took fifteen minutes to get through to the other side. One of my hands was bleeding from a thorn. We had to tie up Licorice at the blind, or he would have been full of stickers, thorns, burrs, and ticks.

I decided to walk back to the blind along the beach, but Horse tramped back over the hill. I talked to "Likker" and waited for Horse, but he was gone a half hour. To anyone else I would have lipped off about wasting time or screwing around, but for Horse that seemed normal.

Other than that I didn't have much to do with Horse, except when I'd talk with him in school or at the Super Saver when he came in with Ronalda, so he could carry her groceries home.

I remember one Saturday night they came in. I had eaten supper at home and had slapped a big slice of onion on my hamburger. I was watching *Perry Mason* on TV and when I noticed the clock, it was three minutes to seven. I didn't have time to brush my teeth; I just took off running the two-and-a-half blocks to the store. If you forgot to put on deodorant or comb your hair or wear a clean shirt, the boss, Hank Simonson, would call you up to his office for a reprimand. I didn't want that, so I was standing by the Ford (not the car, the brand of gum) penny gumball machine, putting in pennies, pushing the lever, grabbing gumballs, and cramming them into my mouth. They had the word "FORD" stamped across them in black, and they came in almost all colors, but the rarest of them all was gold.

Just as Ronalda went past me, out came a gold gumball. I picked it up and just on a whim handed it to Horse.

"Hey, Horse, look, a gold one. You can have it if you want." My mouth was pretty full anyway, and after I had chewed all the flavor out, I'd be spitting the wad in the garbage can.

He looked at me. "Sure, Chris . . . Thanks." And that was all there was to that.

Another reason I didn't see Horse much that spring was that I was spending a lot of time in Caseyville, where my girlfriend BethAnn lived.

Horse didn't go out for track that spring. He spent any spare time in a new willow sweat lodge he had made behind the Moons' house or out in the Vikings or up on the res talking to the Old Ones. Some of the track guys tried to talk him into coming out, and when he just walked away, they took him down and gave him a "red belly," but that didn't work. He just lay there and let them slap all they wanted to. Even when they gave him two "purple nurples," it didn't seem to bother him. When they finished, he just got up, tucked in his shirt, and went home like he didn't even feel it.

Before we knew it, the night of our graduation had come. In Horse's way of talking, it was the Moon of First Eggs. We gathered in the Activities Room to put on our caps and gowns and pretend we weren't nervous. With Miss Waters' help Horse had earned his diploma, and when the yearbook photographer wanted a shot of our class, we gathered around one of the tables on which many of us had eaten hot lunch. Some of us boys got on the table, the camera flashed, and there we were, most of us smiling, preserved for posterity. The picture made it into the yearbook; Horse is almost laughing off my right shoulder. That was the only picture of him that made the yearbook.

When we lined up to walk to the gym, our superintendent, "Olger the Ogre"; Principal McHale; and BeeZee, the cop, approached and asked Horse to come with them. They went into the Office, and a few minutes later the administrators came out and told us we could go to the gym.

BeeZee's sister Dotty asked, "Where's Horse?"

Olger replied, "That doesn't concern you."

"He's our classmate, so it does."

"Miss Zeltinger, if you wish to participate in graduation, I suggest you refrain from interfering in school business."

"But . . ."

"Miss Zeltinger!"

Dotty was my friend and she looked over at me for support. I felt I had to say something. "But, Mr. Wax, Horse has earned the right to be with us."

"Cockburn, I am carrying out a school board directive and if Mr. Moon . . ." Suddenly, he realized he was arguing when he didn't have to be. Also, he could hear some of the others whispering and that could be a sign of revolt. "You and Miss Zeltinger can consider yourselves on notice: one more word and I shall take you out of this line and into my office."

I had worked too hard to become the valedictorian to blow it then, so I shut up, not liking myself for not supporting Horse, but unwilling to lose what I had. Dotty looked around, saw that I was done, ran to the Office, and tried to get in the locked door. She pounded on it, but no one answered. When she turned around, tears were coming down her cheeks, and she ran into the girls' lavatory.

If Miss Waters had only been there, but her sister had taken ill and she was with her.

McHale, who was acting as our advisor in the absence of Miss Waters, got us going, and Dotty and Olger joined us in the lobby of the gym. When the band started "Pomp and Circumstance," we walked down the center aisle two-by-two and onto the stage. I saw my family; my mother looked at me with such pride, I knew I could never have given up my right to make the valedictory address.

I didn't look at where I knew the Moons were seated. Even when I was speaking, I never looked over there. I found out later they had left almost right away to find Horse, and when they learned that his diploma would be mailed, they went home.

As far as I know, he never went into the school again. When the yearbook came out, where he should have been among the seniors, there was a blank space with "Picture Unavailable" and "Ole Moon" under it. I guess he shouldn't have grown his hair so long. Or quit the Church. Or been an Indian.

That fall I went to the State Teachers' College in Minot, and at the end of the spring quarter, I got a job in a warehouse, working the graveyard shift. In June (or the Moon of Fattening Horses) I received a letter from Erik, saying Horse wanted me to come up to Ft. Sully on the summer solstice for a ceremony. Even though I had to beg for a day off, I went, leaving as soon as I punched out at 7 A.M. on the time clock.

I drove the Red Highway to Ft. Sully and, following the directions in the letter, I wound my way through the hills on back roads that turned into trails that turned into tracks. Cresting a small hill, I saw a lot of battered pickups and cars and some picketed horses. There were also many tipis.

As I got out of my car, I felt a hand take my arm. Turning, I saw it was a teenage boy with a rifle. Two more teens stood behind him, but off to the side. They appeared to be guards, but I had passed them on the trail and hadn't even seen them.

The boy didn't say anything, but by the pressure on my arm, guided me up a larger hill.

The hill was dominated by a thirty-foot forked tree which had been stripped of bark and which appeared to have been shot with many bullets and arrows. I could tell it hadn't grown there because I saw where it had been placed in a hole and raised, standing like a naked barber's pole without the striping. A buffalo skull had been bound into the crotch by rawhide, and grass was sticking out of the eye and mouth holes. Red clay had been rubbed on the skull, which was facing west, the direction from which I had come. A broad strip of back hide and the tail had been left attached and were hanging down. Something long, black, and sun-dried dangled lower down the pole. Streaming off the pole from the crotch were three rawhide ropes, reaching the circumference of a circle of Indian people, old and young; men, women, and children; all seated on grass that had been tall and green a few days before, but which had become flattened. Generally in Ft. Sully you'd see the men and boys in cowboy shirts, jeans, and boots; the women and girls would be wearing cotton dresses, or more rarely, the girls might be in shirts and jeans. Now they were dressed in buckskin or doeskin, some with beadwork and some plain, and moccasins. Many of the young men wore nothing but a breechclout. All were strangely quiet.

Eventually, I learned that this was the first Sun Dance Ceremony at Ft. Sully for over seventy years, and normally there would have been drums and bone whistles, chanting and singing, cries and yells, but that day no one wanted to give away the location to the Indian Police or the BIA since the Sun Dance had been outlawed in 1904. Later on, as I thought about it, I came to believe that the authorities probably knew all about the dance, but chose not to do anything, either because they just didn't care or because they didn't want to confront so many people. There appeared to be over five hundred of them, plus over a hundred horses and ponies, with painted symbols on their sides and feathers braided into their manes and tails.

I saw a buckskin which looked familiar; it should have been: it belonged to Dotty Zeltinger, and I had seen it in the Fourth of July Parade in our town for at least eight years. Looking around, I spotted her almost directly across the circle from me. I tried to move to my left to get over there when someone took my arm and said, "Come." It was Horse's grandmother Ida.

She led me off to a tipi and held the flap for me to enter. As my eyes got used to the dim light, she explained that Horse had chosen me to help him with the Sun Dance because I had stuck up for him at graduation and because he knew I could do what was required.

I wanted to tell her I had chickened out on graduation night, but by then she was bringing over some sweet grass that she had burning in a clay bowl and began wafting the smoke over me, purifying me, so I shut up. She had me remove my shoes and socks and then took me out into the sunlight.

A muffled drum beat began and then a deep, low chanting. Ida took me over to the end of one of the rawhide ropes, and I noticed that a young man stood near each of the other ropes. They were in nothing but breechclouts and I felt out of place in my t-shirt and jeans.

Suddenly the drumming and chanting stopped, and Joe Eagle and some other old men entered the circle with burning sweet grass and tobacco. They walked around the pole and then gathered in three small groups near the rawhide ropes, looking to the west.

The circle parted and three young Sioux walked in. I knew each of them: Stephen Red-Tailed Hawk, tall and lithe; John Black Bear, a chubby kid who couldn't have been over seventeen; and Horse, not as tall as Stephen, but more muscular. All of them were barefoot and wore only breechclouts.

Each of them walked over to the end of a rope, and it was only then I noticed that each of them carried a long, thin blade.

Ida turned me so that I looked directly into Horse's eyes. A white man might have winked or smiled, but he stared directly ahead and was silent.

The drum and chanting started low, but began building in volume and tempo. Horse held out his hand. I didn't catch on so Ida took my right hand and held it palm up. I felt the knife in it.

Off to my right there was a brief cry of pain which made me look over. Stephen was bleeding from the chest where the young man in front of him had pushed a knife through. To my left there was a gasp: John was bleeding and I could see tears on his cheeks.

I just stood there, not knowing what to do, until Ida said, "Take a fold of skin above his breast, pinch it, and insert the knife so it comes out the other side."

"What?"

"Pierce him as the others have done."

I looked over and saw that both of the others now had two slits in their chests.

My hands were shaking so much I almost dropped the knife. I really just wanted to run away, but I had failed Horse once; I couldn't do it again.

The drums and the chants seemed to shake the ground. No one cared about the police or the BIA. The sound was piercing me; I couldn't even think clearly. I just acted.

Reaching out, I took some skin between the forefinger and thumb of my left hand and pinched it into a fold. I lined up the blade and told myself it was just like a deer with no hair.

I pushed on the knife. Getting through the skin was difficult; it didn't want to give, and I had to put more pressure on to cut into it. Once inside, the tip of the blade slid more easily to the other side, where I had to shove it out. The blood didn't gush; it just ran out in two streams, down Horse's belly and onto the earth, turning part of the breechclout dark red.

He didn't cry out or gasp. All I heard was a release of his breath when the knife first went in and again when it came out.

Before I pulled it out, Ida stood beside me and pushed a flat piece of bone about ten inches in length along the knife and through the holes.

I tried not to think what I was cutting when I felt the resistance in his muscles as I withdrew the knife.

When I pinched up a second fold of skin, Ida whispered, "Too much."

With all the noise, I couldn't hear. "What?"

"Not so much; you took too much; too much muscle."

By this time the other two dancers were already pierced, and I could see that the trick was to take just a small amount of skin and muscle. I looked at what I had done. While the other dancers had bones with about a half inch of flesh above them, Horse had a good two inches.

I pinched a smaller piece, stabbed the knife through the skin, shoved it to the other side, and forced it out. Ida secured another bone and I withdrew the knife.

When I looked at my hand, it was wet with blood, and blood was flowing down the front of Horse's body. I know people say that I fainted then, that the white boy couldn't take it, but, really, I didn't pass out. With the heat and the stress and the fact that I hadn't eaten anything for breakfast, I got lightheaded, and things got dark. Ida grabbed me, and two men helped her before I went down, but I never fainted.

They took me into Ida's tipi and let me rest. When I felt better, I walked out and saw that rawhide thongs had been formed into figure-eight loops around the protruding bones, and the ends had been braided and knotted to the rawhide ropes attached to the center pole. Horse and the other two were dancing while keeping the ropes taut, trying to pull the bones through their flesh. Sometimes they would dance away from the pole and lean back, the flesh stretching out in two grotesque triangles. Occasionally, one of the dancers would even bounce himself forward and backward against the stretch, but that must have been too painful because after awhile they rarely did it.

The drumming and chanting kept up through the day, and when one of the young men exerted himself more than normal, cries of encouragement rose above everything else. The families of the other two tried to stay close to their boys, but, of course, there were only a few of us on Horse's side: his grandmother, Dotty, a couple of his friends from Ft. Sully, and me.

Finally, after three hours both of Stephen's bones pulled free, and he fell in a pile of dust, his family screaming and yelling and carrying him away to a tipi.

By that time both John and Horse had pulled one bone through, and John redoubled his efforts on the other one. When I looked at Horse, I could see that he was in trouble: my first cut had gone in much too deeply.

About an hour later John went down, the second bone falling away in a flash of blood. He was carried away in a dead faint.

Still Horse's right breast refused to give, even though he was pulling at it with every ounce of strength he had. When he leaned away from the pole, the skin would arch out, and he would strain to pull the bone through, but couldn't do it.

Late in the afternoon I had to sit in the tipi. I was hungry; I was tired; and I was angry at myself for the thick cut.

After I ate some food Ida brought and drank some warm water from a bucket, I went outside and stood beside Dotty, who hadn't moved since she had crossed to Horse's side of the circle that morning. She was crying.

How he kept moving, I'll never know. He was dancing and chanting very low, so you had to strain to hear it.

Time passed and the dark came slowly. Still that piece of flesh refused to tear. Finally, some of the people began to leave. Those who came from a distance took down their tipis, loaded them into pickups, took a final look at the hanging warrior, shook their heads, and drove off. Others just got on their ponies or into their vehicles and went down the hill.

I figure about midnight I went inside the tipi and lay down. I needed to close my eyes for a few minutes.

When I woke up, the first thing I noticed was Ida's breathing somewhere in the tent. The next thing was that the drums and chants were gone. When I walked into the chill air, the stars were out, but most everyone had left. I saw a couple of figures sprawled out in sleep in back of Horse—his friends. Three or four Old Ones sleeping around what had been the circle. And Dotty. I walked up to her and she was sleeping sitting up. Her face was dirty where the tears had been.

I went over to Horse. He was sitting on the ground, leaning back, and the stubborn flesh was stretching the rope as taut as it would go. He looked asleep or passed out. His body was covered with dried blood and dirt which had stuck to him when it got caught in his sweat. He wasn't sweating anymore; either it was too cold or he had no more fluid in him to sweat out.

I kneeled beside him and listened. His breathing was so light, I thought maybe he was dead, but with my ear right next to his mouth, I could hear it.

I walked into the shadows and took out my jackknife. After finding a granite boulder, I used it to sharpen the edge as best I could and walked back to Horse. I got behind him, put my arms around his body, inserted the knife into the wound, and cut almost through it. He jerked at the first cut, and I thought he woke up, but he didn't say anything and didn't move again. I wiped and clasped the knife, stuck it in my pocket, and grabbed him around the shoulders. I put all my weight into pulling and the skin ripped free. We fell back, his cold dead weight on top of me.

Quickly, I pushed him off and moved over to the tipi. Ducking inside, I said, "Grandmother, come quick. The Horse is free!"

For an old woman just roused from sleep, she moved so fast, she was outside and lifting Horse's head before I even had time to get out of the tent.

She was chanting something in Lakota, and everyone was waking up, then rushing over with shouts and war cries. Dotty ran over, then went back to the tipi, emerging with a bucket and cloth. She began to clean the dirt and blood off.

Horse tried to get up, but he was too weak. When he tried to speak, his voice was so raspy and faint, no words made any sense. By the time we got him into my car, his body had gone from chilly to hot, and the fever kept getting worse. We decided on the way down that we would take him to his sister's cabin, which was much closer than Ida's tipi.

Ida pounded on the door to wake up the sister, while one of Horse's friends and I got him out of the car and carried him onto the porch. The lights went on, and the sister stood there in some kind of wrapper, her black hair all wild looking. She probably didn't want to let us in, but she did.

She brought out an Army surplus cot that the Indians got after World War II and set it up. We put Horse on it and covered him up. He was shaking so much I thought he'd vibrate the cot right across the floor. Ida got a rag and some cool water and began to smooth it on his forehead.

With nothing more to do, Horse's friends left, making sure the door didn't slam. A few minutes later Dotty came in. She'd had to go down to a little slough and get the buckskin, which had wandered off during the day.

"How is he?"

"I don't know . . . Hot . . . Not good."

She knelt by his side and took the rag from Ida, who went over to an old chair. The sister had gone back to bed. I walked over and lifted the blanket. Blood had seeped through the gauze and poultice Ida had fixed to his chest up on the hill. Our moving him must have broken some clots loose.

When I went out the door, I could see first light. I walked back inside. "Dotty, I have to get back. I work tonight."

"I know." She dipped the rag in the basin, squeezed it out, placed it on Horse's forehead, and got up. She walked me to the door. "Thank you for coming. You did a great thing."

"I cut too . . ."

She stopped my mouth with her hand. "Sh-sh-sh. It meant a lot to Horse that you would come. You're a good friend to him." She placed her hands on my shoulders, stood tippy-toed, and kissed my cheek. She walked back to Horse.

I started my car, flipped on the lights, and drove off. My eyes were burning; I knew it was my fault Horse was hurt so bad. I gassed up in Sacred Water and drove to Minot. When I had asked for a night off, Sarge, our foreman, said I could have it, but that I'd have to make up for it by working Saturday to midnight because we were doing the inventory in addition to all the loading and unloading. That night at work I fell asleep on the sugar sacks up on the third floor and when Sarge found me, I almost got fired.

Horse had a rough time of it for a couple of weeks. I never got down to see him, but Dotty was there a lot, and Grandmother Ida every day. After Ida took sick, he was alone at night, unless you count his sister and her male friends, who were in the bedroom.

One night Tom Gravos, a rail from Menninger, came home with the sister, but made a fuss about having Horse, who was asleep, being in the house. The cot's wooden side bars extended into handles, so they grabbed them and carried Horse outside.

After awhile he woke up in the dark on the porch. He got off the cot and went into the front room, where he heard noises in the bedroom. He could hear his sister giggling, and then the deeper voice of a man. Silence . . . and then noises from behind the door which must have reminded him of his childhood.

He walked over to the lever-action Winchester hanging on the wall, got it down, and chambered two rounds. His right side was still so sore he couldn't heft the rifle with that arm, so he wedged it between his left arm and side, staggered over to the bedroom door, kicked it open, and when a naked man jumped out of bed, fired.

The bullet smacked into the wall, the sister screamed, the man cursed. He grabbed his clothes and went right out the window, glass, screen, and all. Horse fumbled his way to the opening, trying to lever in the other bullet. As he stood there, the sister jumped on his back, driving him into the floor, the rifle discharging, the bullet kicking up dirt in the general direction of the fleeing man.

Horse was out cold. When he woke up, he was on something lumpy. It was Tom Gravos' billfold. Horse got it open and saw the name on a driver's license before the sister came back in and snatched it away from him.

After awhile he went back to the cot, rolling onto it. The sister had disappeared and he was too tired to care. In the morning he walked down the hill, through town and to Ida's tipi. She was in the hospital in Sacred Water so he stayed there until he was better.

That winter Grandmother Ida died of cancer in the Moon of Seven Cold Nights.

I drove down for her funeral which, surprisingly, was in the Catholic Church. Before I went back to Minot, Horse and I talked about the night of the Sun Dance and afterward.

Soon after the funeral, white men who came to Ft. Sully looking for some action found their tires had been slashed or their engines were fouled with sugar or their brake lines had been cut. Once in awhile when one of them would come back for a second time, he would be clipped from behind by a blunt object and would come to stripped naked.

It wasn't too long and such men started to avoid Ft. Sully.

I was working my second summer at the warehouse in Minot, and I hadn't seen Horse since Ida's funeral. I hadn't even written. When I was home one weekend, my Dad came in with the news that Tom Gravos had been attacked and was in the hospital with a broken jaw and a concussion. Gravos claimed he'd been blindsided by Horse.

The police went to Ft. Sully and had the BIA send out men to look for Horse or anyone who knew where he was, but Horse had disappeared.

After Gravos got out of the hospital and felt better, he and some of his railroad gang, along with some of the barflies, organized a sort-of posse and went out to the Vikings because everyone knew that was Horse's stomping grounds.

They looked all over and found nothing. The next weekend they brought dogs. Again nothing.

Angry at being made fools of, they drove into town, hitched up a bunch of horse trailers, went back, and loaded up the Appaloosa stallion, the six mares, and two colts and brought them back to Menninger. I heard it was tough catching the stallion, but the animals had been in a corral and eventually they roped them all. If they had been free-ranging, they'd still be looking for them.

They unloaded them in a pasture near the reservoir where a dozen or so other horses were, and some of the men stayed in the barn that night, laying for Horse. He never showed and the next night there were fewer men. After a week the only one in the barn was Gravos, and what with no Horse, and Ted Jones, the land owner, worrying him with a bill for keeping the Appaloosas, he started bringing a bottle of whiskey in with him at night for company.

About ten days after the Appaloosas were taken, it clouded up in the southwest and rain came gushing down, punctuated by lightning and thunder. It kept it up all night, and in the morning when Gravos staggered outside, the Appaloosas were gone.

Gravos got his posse together, but what with the rain there were no tracks visible anywhere. Cars and pickups scattered around the county, hitting every highway and county road. Some of them even ventured off onto the township roads and farm trails and got stuck, angering the men even more.

They checked everywhere they could think of and then gave up. When my Dad and I talked about it later, he said they should have checked the Divide River Valley. He figured Horse was smart enough to move the herd at night down the valley and keep the horses in the trees during the day.

Three days later the rural mail carrier came in and said the Appaloosas were back in their pasture.

The posse tore out the East Highway and sure enough there they were, feeding on grain and hay that had recently been scattered for them.

From what I was told, the cursing was fierce, and if Horse had been there, they would have lynched him sure, but he wasn't, so in aggravation they walked over to Boss's old pasture and shot every one of the horses. Shot them and just left them there. The colts, too.

Gravos kept up the search into the fall, even though fewer and fewer men went with him, but they couldn't have found Horse with a small army in that country. He knew every draw, hill, slough, patch of brush, and strand of forest from Aldrichville to Sacred Water, plus, he had been digging caves in the hillsides and disguising the entrances, so unless you stepped into one, you wouldn't know it was there, although it might be three feet in front of you behind a prairie rose bush or a glacial boulder.

During the winter Gravos hired Oscar Sigurdson, a farmer who owned a Piper Cub and who supplemented his income by shooting foxes and coyotes from it, to fly over the hills, looking for tracks, but they never found any.

The next spring Gravos retired from the railroad and disappeared Down South for a few months. When he came back, he had a hound dog that he said could trail a skunk through a polecat factory and never lose the scent. He demonstrated the dog down in the trees surrounding Pepple Field, our baseball park, and no matter who went out into the trees and no matter how they jumped ditches, climbed trees, or walked through water puddles, the dog found them every time. The most remarkable thing, though, was that it never barked or bayed.

One morning that fall Gravos went out to the Vikings with the hound, vowing to get Horse. He brought a rifle with him, so none of his posse dared to go along.

When a locked car parked on an approach to the East Highway was identified as his, Jack Hall, the sheriff, went to look for him. He found Gravos, all right—behind a boulder, shot right through the forehead. The hound had gotten hungry so parts of his face and thighs were missing.

The sheriff found something else—blood spoor. Gravos had shot whoever killed him, but the trail disappeared after a couple dozen yards.

One thing about a small town: it's hard to keep anything a secret. Soon everyone knew what the sheriff had found, including me. The sheriff organized a posse and even got the governor to send up some men. Once again they scoured the Vikings and the Ft. Sully Reservation on foot, on horseback, with dogs, from airplanes, and came up empty.

I drove back to Minot because I couldn't do anything with all those eyes looking around. As I sat in class or in the apartment, I tried to "see" where Horse would hole up. I was in Philosophy class when suddenly I knew. For the rest of the week, I tried to figure out another place, and there were probably dozens, but if he had gone to a hidey-hole I didn't know about, I'd never find him anyway, so I had to try my hunch.

I bought a bunch of stuff like bandages, antiseptic, aspirin, soap, washcloths, and towels, anything I thought a wounded man might need and drove to Menninger.

Erik was working at a gas station as a mechanic and Thor had gotten a job at an elevator. I stopped at both places and eased the conversation around to Horse, but I could tell they had no idea where he was.

At home I dug out the biggest knapsack I had, loaded the stuff in it, and drove out the East Highway. I turned south of Big Sam and followed the gravel, winding through the hills around Chokecherry Lake and into the farmyard that had belonged to Boss. I parked the car in the barn, hefted the backpack and my gear, and set off. When I crested a ridge, I could see the white bones of the horses the posse had shot. Horse hadn't done a thing with them.

I went west for about four miles and then cut north, keeping a low range of hills on my right and a series of sloughs on my left. The tough part would be crossing the East Highway without being seen. Waterfowl season hadn't started yet, so there wasn't much traffic, and the ditches were high with wild growth.

I came to the south ditch and hid there for a long time. A couple vehicles passed. I could see all the way to the east where the highway crested the Vikings about four miles away. To the west, however, the road curved, and I figured I would just have to chance it. I checked the east, then the west, took a couple of breaths, and sprinted across, keeping low and sliding down the side of the ditch.

I lay there listening, but all I heard were some red-winged blackbirds in the cattails fifty yards to the north. I eased my way up, checked both directions, and started off, walking in the reeds and sedges of a slough that was fall-drying. Two miles and I was in a gravel pit, where I made a cold camp, ate and drank and went to sleep under the stars in a sleeping bag.

The next morning was Sunday. At dawn I said my prayers, did my latrine duty, ate some jerky and bread, washed them down with water, and cleaned up any tell-tale signs that might give me away. I moved east, keeping watchful and freezing stock-still with every odd sound or movement.

Off to the north stood an old one-room school. I got behind a large clump of grass and studied it for a long time. It would be just like the cops to sit in there with binoculars and radios and nail me for being dumb.

I stared at it, but saw no movement. Finally, I got up and headed east again. If the cops were there, I wanted them to get me before I gave anything away about Horse. I walked and the day brightened, but no cops came.

When I got below South Finger Lake, I went to my right and started walking down what looked like an ancient drainage channel with a spongy bottom and steep, rough hills on either side. Suddenly, there was Big Sam, the sunlight glinting and some pelicans bobbing on the surface.

I sat down, drank some water, and waited, looking for movement, looking for an odd color, looking for anything that shouldn't be there. But everything was as it should be.

I got up and moved to the shoreline. I walked it as it curved around to the southwest, then the south, and then to the southeast—I was on the peninsula where Horse and I had hunted geese our senior year.

Stripping off my gear, I hid behind a growth of prairie rose bushes, looked around once again, and pushed my way into the mass of trees, thickets, thorns, and tormenting things that tried to keep me out.

I thought I could find an entrance, but the undergrowth was so thick I couldn't get down on my hands and knees, and that was what it would have taken. Finally, I started to call softly, "Horse, Horse."

I moved around calling for about ten minutes before I heard my name coming from near the base of the hill on the south side of the peninsula. I followed it to a cluster of prairie rose bushes, then worked my way up the hill and came down behind them, and there was a little entry hole. I crawled in. Horse had burrowed out a cave. I was surprised that the sand and gravel soil hadn't caved in, but he'd shored it up in places. Hanging down from the ceiling were things that looked like snakes or worms, but I guess they were roots and must have been helping hold things together. He had some shelves packed with food and clothes, some guns and ammo, a few traps, and some utensils.

Horse had rigged up a stove, complete with a stovepipe that went up through the roof and ended in a hollow stump. He burned small willow and alder branches in it, so it was virtually smoke-free. The alder was sent to Ft. Sully from tribes way out west and found its way to the "Ghost Horse," a nickname that his growing legend had developed.

He was lying on a bunch of pine boughs with a blanket drawn up around him. Two large candles were burning next to him on an upturned box.

"Horse."

"Hey, Chris. How'd I know it would be you?"

I walked over to him. "How're you doin'?"

He didn't say anything, just pulled back the blanket, and I could see a small doeskin bag hanging from his neck and a blood-stained cloth over his left side about ten inches below his Sun Dance scar. "I think he got my kidney. At least I'm peein' red."

"What happened?"

"I was leanin' over a big rock, sighting in a deer below, when he shot me. He sneaked up behind, got in back of a boulder, and shot me. I just whirled around, saw a head, and fired. It was just instinct, I guess, but if I had known it was Gravos right then, I wouldn't have hesitated anyway. He had that dog. Boy, was he good. Brought Gravos right up to me and didn't make a sound. I tied him up near Gravos."

I had to get close to hear him and I could see he didn't look too good. His cheeks were sunken in a little and his eyes looked yellowish. His breath had a kind of ammonia smell to it.

"I stopped up the bullet hole and got out of there. After I made a couple miles, I let myself pass out, and I passed out again about a hundred yards from here, but no one saw me, and I don't think anyone's been close to here. I haven't heard anyone and it rained so my scent is gone."

"I don't think they have any idea where you are. I didn't see anybody out looking, but you know they won't give up on a murder charge."

"Gravos shot me first."

"Yeah, but they'll still charge you. I'm pretty sure they think you're up on the Divide or on Ft. Sully. They aren't looking around here."

He closed his eyes and was quiet for awhile. I could see he was sweating. I told him I'd be right back and went to get my gear. I checked the countryside, but I didn't see any movement.

Back in the cave, I poured some water on a rag and mopped his forehead. "It don't do no good. I've tried that."

"I'll go get a doctor. You've got to have a doctor."

"No, he'll have to turn me in . . . and I'm not goin' in."

I unpacked what I had brought. I tried to show him what it was, but most of the time his eyes were closed. Finally, I said I had to go; I had to get back to Minot.

He opened his eyes. "Chris, there's something else. I think Gravos got me in the guts, too; I think I'm gut shot. At least it feels like it."

"Horse, I have to get a doctor or take you to one."

"No. It's too late anyway. You'd better go." He reached out and patted my knee. "Thanks. Thanks for everything you've done for me. I haven't said it before, but I appreciate it."

"I didn't do anything."

'Well, I think you did. Tell Dotty 'Hello' for me and tell my family about me when you see 'em."

"You'll be all right, you'll see."

"Maybe."

I started to leave.

"Chris."

"Yeah."

"Next time you look for me, look in the sky."

"What?"

"Look up."

I had no idea what he meant. Maybe he was delirious. "I'll see you next week. O.K.?"

"Maybe. Goodbye, Chris, and thanks."

"Goodbye. See you soon."

I beat it back to my car as fast as I could go, but still I was careful not to walk in the open and get spotted. I gunned that car out onto the East Highway, didn't stop at the junction, turned onto the Aldrichville Highway, and sped off to Ft. Sully. It took me awhile to locate Joe Eagle, but when I told him I'd seen Horse, he didn't ask any questions; he just got in and away we went.

We drove to the gravel pit and down into it. We had to wait for a pickup to pass out of sight before we headed for the cave. Joe Eagle was an old man, but he was wiry and tough and easily kept up with me, so we made good time.

It didn't make any difference. When I crawled into the cave and got used to the dark, I could see Horse wasn't there. Joe Eagle came in. He pulled out a Zippo and lit a candle.

"He's not here," I said.

He grunted and walked over to the pine boughs. He bent down and smelled. "The Horse is dead."

"What? How do you know?"

He turned and headed for the entry. "We go."

"We've got to look for him."

"He's dead. Let him be."

Walking back to the car, I kept looking around, trying to think where Horse would go, but I couldn't figure anything out. I tried to clear my mind and let something pop in, but nothing did.

Joe Eagle never said a word on the way back. While we were coming from Ft. Sully, he told me a lot about Horse, his vision quest, the Sun Dance, his shooting at Gravos in his sister's cabin, and, when I asked him, about the doeskin bag, but going back to Sully, it was as if he were suddenly ashamed of revealing so much and just sat there, looking out the window. He did say goodbye, though.

Over the next few years I'd go out to the Vikings, sometimes to hunt, sometimes to look for Horse, and sometimes just to think.

During those years Horse became even more of a ghost-legend. Hunters would swear that they'd seen him on top of a hill, on the other side of a lake, or crossing a road at dusk. Up on the res they said he wasn't dead at all, that he was living as their ancestors had, and that no white man would ever take him. They even started to say that Gravos hadn't wounded Horse, that Horse killed him for violating his sister, and that he would live wild the rest of his life.

Joe Eagle knew Horse was dead, but then Joe died. I knew Horse was dead, but I couldn't locate his body no matter how many times I looked at the sky.

One June day just before the summer solstice, I started thinking about Horse, and the next day I drove out the East Highway. I parked in Boss's old farmyard, crossed the highway, and worked my way around Big Sam until I came to Horse's cave. Some of the roof had fallen in around the old stump, and water had dampened the interior. Everything he'd left there was wet and dirty and rotting away.

I felt bad coming out of the cave, but the day had blossomed into a sun-filled delight. Water birds of all kinds were on the lake, making all kinds of noise. The lake reflected blue because there wasn't a cloud in the sky. The whole valley had greened up, so all I could see was bright blue and green, and that made me feel like walking. Away from the lake I heard a meadowlark off to the east, so I headed in that direction, climbing up into some of the highest hills, sweating and panting, but enjoying it.

I went northeast into an area where I'd never been before, it was so rugged. There were no roads, or even trails. The hilltops were probably twenty or thirty feet lower than Buffalo Hump, but there were a lot of them, stretching out to the northwest and southeast for miles.

I hadn't expected to be out so long and I'd left my canteen in the car. I figured just a little more and then I'd head back. I was walking by a steep hill, and I heard that meadowlark or a different one singing over the top. I started to climb up, I don't know why, and when I reached the top, I saw a cut that started a few yards from the west side of the hill and went east, splitting the hill in two. There must have been a spring there a long time before, and the water from it tore the gully through the soil. The gully had filled in with Russian olives and chokecherries, and it would have been easier just to walk beside it to the end, but I decided to explore it and got down and inched my way into it.

The tops of the trees were thick enough to make it dark, but I could see enough to pick out rocks and gravel. I moved forward, but it was basically crawling, with very little standing. The gully turned north, then south and then went east again for a long stretch until it ended above a lake I had no idea was there.

Also, as I approached the end, the wind would catch itself in the trees and the sides of the gully and make a moaning sound that made me wish I'd brought a gun.

I sat where the gully ended and looked down a fairly sharp drop-off to the lake below. Seeing the blue water made me even thirstier, but I decided to sit where Horse had probably sat and try to figure out where he might be.

When you're off by yourself for awhile, your senses get the better of you. They start telling you things that aren't true. One morning I was alone in a blind on the Jacques River east of Menninger. It was cloudy and the gray-dark of the dawn was slow in lightening up. Out of the dark I could see a rock across the river. I had stood on that rock before; it was covered with orange and light green lichens, but after awhile my eyes told me it was a Hereford cow lying in the grass. My brain said it couldn't be, but my eyes kept saying it was. That morning as I listened to the water rippling through the rocks of the ford, I slowly began to hear a voice. It was female and it was calling my name. Once again I knew it wasn't true: it was just the water, but it was so real that I almost stood up and said, "Ma?" because maybe something had happened to Dad, and she had come to get me.

Sitting above that drop-off, I heard the wind in the gully do the same thing. Voices were trying to speak to me. Logically, hearing voices didn't make sense, but something in me wasn't so sure. Was that what Horse had heard? Spirit voices? Maybe they had spoken to him. I didn't know. I did know I was thirsty, I was tired, and I had my jackknife out in case something came out of the darkness behind me. I was just about to climb up the hill and go back the easy way when I heard a sound from back in the gully.

It wasn't a voice and I didn't think it was the wind, but I couldn't place it. It came again, and it sounded like the muffled rattle and chunk of something hitting tree branches and then the ground.

After a few minutes of daring myself, I went back in, got down on my hands and knees, and started moving into the gloom. About halfway to the bend, I saw something long and gray-white. As I reached it, I picked it up. It was a bone. There was another one beside it. Both in high school and college Biology classes I had to memorize the size and shape of the major bones of the human body. The bones were femurs and I knew they hadn't been there before.

I looked up, trying to see where they had come from. There was an especially dark area about three-fourths of the way up some Russian olives. I wedged myself over to the base of one of the trees that had a crotch and worked my way into it, trying to avoid the thorny stickers, but getting stuck a couple times anyway.

I took my jackknife and when I found a thorn, I'd cut it off, then move a little higher. About ten feet off the ground, I found some rawhide lashings binding a wooden scaffold to four trees. I eased my way onto it and it held. In the middle was a blanket, or what had once been a blanket. It was rotted pretty good.

I reached out and tore it away from a lump on the west side and put my face close to something white. It was a skull. I had found Horse.

When I jumped back, I nearly fell off the scaffold. I don't know if it was fear of falling or the fact that Horse was there, but tears blurred my vision.

I stayed up there a few minutes with the skull seeming to smile at me, and the wind moaning at the drop-off. Then I got down and made it back to my car, being very careful no one saw me.

I took the East Highway back to town. On the way in I tried to imagine Horse struggling up to that scaffold which he had made, probably years earlier. He had been weak from shock and loss of blood when he made his climb, but had enough left to get up onto the scaffold, wrap himself in the blanket, and lie down to die. I was healthy and the climb up the hill itself darn near killed me.

At home I got a tarp, some rope, a pick and shovel, and a large lantern with a shield that directed the light. I ate supper and lay down to rest. The night was going to be a long one.

Back out near Big Sam, I parked as close as I could get to where Horse was, but that was three miles away. I had waited until dark, so I had to be careful walking, not to step in a badger hole or turn my ankle on a rock. Every once in awhile something would scurry off in the grass, but I tried not to think what it was.

At the scaffold I used the lantern to see what an extraordinary job Horse had done. Not only had he put up the scaffold, but he had interlaced small branches to make a sort of shield above and below, so that even in the winter it would appear to be just a heavy growth of trees.

The only way I could get the bones out was to crawl with a few in one hand to the drop-off, place them in the tarp, go back, and do it again. I had to take each femur separately. The bones of the torso, the ribs, spine, neck, arms, hands, and such like I tried to keep wrapped in the shirt, but it started to tear, so I had to take the arm bones out. The tibias and fibulas stayed in the pants and the foot bones remained in the boots. Still it took quite awhile and I left the skull until last.

After I got it onto the tarp, I put the light on it, but the skull wasn't Horse, not Horse the Warrior, and I put the light out. Just then I remembered the doeskin bag. Joe Eagle had said it was a medicine bundle, and it contained things which gave the warrior power or which represented his spirit animal or which just meant something special to him.

At first I didn't think I should open it: it was like peeking into a person's diary, but finally my curiosity won out, and I tugged on the drawstrings and dumped the contents onto the tarp.

There were two Knife River Flint arrow points, the kind you find every once in awhile in the Vikings and on the prairie east of Menninger; a little tied-up bundle of what looked like horse hair (probably from the stallion, I guessed); the beak, dried head, and breast of a meadowlark with its yellow and black V'd feathers; a couple of small, black, water-smoothed stones; and a folded piece of wax paper tied with rubber bands.

When I tried to stretch the rubber bands, they broke. I unfolded the wax paper and something small rolled into my hand—a gold gumball. I'll bet I sat there for a full minute, just staring at the stuff, but mostly at the gumball. Then I quickly scooped it all into the pouch and put it back inside the shirt. I felt what I'd done was dishonorable and I wanted to get it out of my sight.

I tied all the bones in the tarp and carried it back to the car. It's surprising how light a human being is when he's nothing but bones.

I drove the car up to Boss's place and parked. It was two miles to Buffalo Hump.

On top of the butte, I stayed a little to the south of the crest, so anyone on the East Highway wouldn't see the lantern. Since it wasn't a real grave, I didn't have to go six feet down; still it took me a couple hours to get the depth and size I wanted.

I placed the tarp in so Horse was facing east. That's the way Christians did it, and although he didn't go to church anymore, I figured it couldn't hurt. I filled in the grave and smoothed the dirt out. I didn't want anyone digging him up, so I went over to a gully, cut off a tree branch, and worked it over the grave, trying to make it more natural. When I had it the way I wanted it, the sky over the Vikings was getting lighter and the stars were gone.

I sat down on the south side of Buffalo Hump, below the skyline, and rested. I thought about Horse, how he just wanted to be left alone, and I guess if it hadn't been for his sister, he'd have done it, too.

She had died in the Sacred Water hospital and Horse's Dad, Basil, was buried up on the res. I figured someday I would tell his mother, brothers and sisters where he was, but I'd put that off as long as I could. They were more white than Indian anyway.

There were yellows and pinks and purples off to the east when I stood up and walked over to the grave. Trying to figure out what to say, or what an Indian would say, left me blank, so I just said The Lord's Prayer and what I could remember of the Twenty-third Psalm, patted the dirt above the skull with my hand, picked up my tools, and walked down the hill.

The morning was losing its chill as soon as the sun cleared the hilltops behind me. After I put my stuff in the car and got a drink from my thermos, I walked over to Boss's pasture. The bones of the nine horses were scattered where the coyotes had left them, and I searched around until I found the skull of the stallion.

I picked it up and the jaw fell off, so I had to carry both pieces to the base of Buffalo Hump, one in each hand. I built a little cairn of rocks and placed the jaw down first and then the skull part on top of it. If there was a hunting ground in the sky, at least Horse would have a stallion to ride.

I didn't pray over the horse's skull; I just walked away.

About halfway to the car, I heard a meadowlark.